DARK STAR'S CAPTIVE

AVERY STERN

Published by Blushing Books
An Imprint of
ABCD Graphics and Design, Inc.
A Virginia Corporation
977 Seminole Trail #233
Charlottesville, VA 22901

Avery Stern
Dark Star's Captive

Print ISBN: 978-1-63954-198-0
v1

Part I

TRANSITS

Chapter 1

The reactor core needed thirty-six hours to be functional again, so he ordered an engine overhaul.

"It's old," warned the tech. "No one here knows exactly how it's put together."

"We'll all learn something," said Rhys. He called everyone in over the comm, Sydell included. God knows where she'd been the last twenty-four hours since he'd taken his paddle to her, after she'd nearly gotten herself killed crawling around in one of the ship's vents. She hadn't been pleased about it at all, but it was time for her to suck it up.

Except for Sydell, who had not shown up yet, he led the team to the engine room. With the ionic generator running, the ship had grown uncomfortably hot, and this room was the worst. It would be a tough job. All the same, he put everyone to work, cleaning parts, cataloging the serial numbers of each piece, figuring out what would need to be replaced and when.

Then the doors hissed open, and at last she wandered

3

in. She wore a fitted tank top with thin straps that bared most of her shoulders, and shorts rolled up snugly to the tops of her thighs. She'd not even bothered to tie up her mass of dark, wild hair.

He'd wanted to ignore her today, but this, on top of her lateness, would not allow for it. He stopped her as she walked in the door.

When she saw him, she blushed deeply but did not avert her face. Instead, she looked up at him directly, her brown-eyed gaze broken only by a series of her anxious blinks.

"You need to be in your jumpsuit," he said sternly, then clarified, "for safety. A lot of parts in here get hot, as I'm sure you're aware."

She started to turn, but he put a hand on her elbow. She jumped as he did, like he'd touched her with a spark. "Don't worry about it now. You're late already and you need to get to work. Just be careful. And the next time you're called over the comm, you show up immediately. Understood?"

She nodded, and he stared at her another moment until she said, "Yes."

He put her to work wiping down all the parts, before they ran them through the nanoscrubbers. She kept her distance from him. Afraid of him, probably. More afraid than when he'd punished her the first time. He intended it that way when he'd told her about his time working for Parsons in human traffic. Better she be afraid than dead, cooked to a crisp in a vent or some other stupidity.

And it wasn't a lie. Yes, he'd worked for the most notorious crime-lord in the system, just omitted the fact that he'd been only fifteen at the time, shipped out to his father on Mars after his mother had died. He'd never met his father before that, never known that he'd been working with Parsons as a slaver.

What a rude awakening *that* had been. He'd left them at eighteen and joined the army, just before the Mutiny, damnable luck. He hadn't left Parsons because he hated it, though. Playing master to people had come terribly naturally to him, and he'd left because he'd been getting a taste for it.

He threw himself now into the work of getting the engine apart. Being adrift in the belts like this annoyed him. He needed to be back on Europa, needed to get back to work. The Io City government breathed too close to his company for comfort, and Parsons' people were everywhere. Even on the ship, it seemed.

But that wasn't something anyone needed to know, not yet. So, he could only divert himself, occupy his mind with pieces, and try to lose himself in the tedium of it in order to pass the time.

"Should we take apart the cooling system?" asked the tech.

"We have the time to do it. I'll do it," said Rhys, because if he wanted a thing done right, he usually had to do it himself.

As he started in on the tubing connecting the cooling hub to the reactor, he glanced at Sydell, where she sat near a corner. Her eyes were on him, but she jerked her head away. Something about her crouching over a bundle of parts kept his attention on her for a moment. The sulky turn of her arched pink mouth. The cleft of her breasts peeping out of the top of her tight little shirt. Without willing it, his mind returned to an image of her bent over his desk as he spanked her, her ample bottom quivering, her downed panties stretched tight around her hips, just barely covering her pussy.

Nope. He turned back to the cooling hub. He'd already decided how it would be with Sydell, from the beginning. *Not like that.* He'd been busy of late, and it had been some months since he'd spent any time with a woman. He'd fix that when he got to Io City. But Sydell was his recruit, even if she had been compelled to it, and he wasn't about to lose his head over her.

He caught her two or three more times, gazing at him, and looking away when caught. He couldn't keep away; he stepped over to where she sat, towering over her. She jumped and stared up at him, startled. The piece she'd been holding clattered into the tub beneath her.

"What are you doing with that connector?" he demanded. "You can't clean it like that, it needs to be opened. Look, I'll show you."

She rearranged herself, slamming into the tub of parts with one knee, which overturned. He sighed. She stammered something incomprehensible. What was wrong now? "Go take an hour," he ordered. "Have something to eat." He tried to voice it in his lightest tone, while still sounding as though he was not to be argued with. She slinked off.

He became immersed again in the cooling system; he'd no clue how much time had passed when the pilot approached him.

"I think everyone called it a day," Walt said. "I need to go check the Nav specs. We good?"

Rhys rubbed at his aching temples. "Uh, yes. I didn't realize it was so late."

"Yep." Walt stood there, awkwardly, rocking a bit on his heels with his hands behind his back, as though he wanted to say something.

"What is it?" Rhys asked, trying to hide his impatience.

"Oh. Well. I never did get to thank you. For helping Sydell."

Rhys could only nod. Walt's eyes were bright, too large behind his glasses, and his words ran slow and somber. It had meant a lot to him, it seemed.

"I still can't believe she stole that jammer," Walt said in a breath, shaking his head.

"Really?" Here, Rhys' surprise was genuine. "I'd have thought you'd come to expect that kind of thing from her."

"She's usually smarter than that. I don't know what the hell she was thinking."

"Yeah, it was pretty damned stupid." He turned back to the cooling hub, went on with what he'd been dismantling. "But I think she had a mind to get caught."

Walt considered this, his head cocked to one side, in a small, almost robotic motion. "I guess it's possible. Sometimes she does seem a bit… self-sabotaging." This came out as reluctant as a pulled tooth, along with a grieved sigh. "But she's always been terrified of field prisons."

"She needed to be caught," said Rhys simply. "And it was quite the gamble on her part, but here she is. Things could be a great deal worse for her."

"Oh, I know. But are you saying she wanted to end up here? She could have just stayed on when you offered her a job."

"She would never have boarded this ship willingly. She had to have her arm twisted." Rhys paused, pulled out a long section of tubing. "Anyway, when she stole that jammer, it was her instinct running her."

"It usually does." Walt gave a small smile, accepting and affectionate at the thought. From the corner of his eye, Rhys spotted much in the smile, devotion, possibly even love. *Hopeless,* he thought. Sydell had been a handful for Walt as a friend. Anything more than that, and she'd wreck him. Any mate of hers would have to be strong, know how to keep a handle on her.

"I didn't plan to recruit her, to be honest. Not until…" And Rhys stopped there. When had it been? When she'd sobbed into his shoulder, after he'd punished her the first time, and told him all those things? He'd seen it then, seen exactly what she needed and knew that he could give it to her. Then those cops had carried her off, and he wasn't letting them have her. "Well, it was a last minute decision," he finished with a shrug.

"Your instinct running you, too?" asked Walt with a sheepish grin. Or was it a sly grin? Rhys frowned. What the hell did he mean by that? Walt went on quickly, "But, seriously, thanks for helping her. It's good for her, working on the ship like this. You're good for her."

Rhys shrugged. What did Walt want here? After a moment, Rhys said, "She thanked me for helping you out, too."

"Really?" And here, Walt sounded sincerely shocked. "That doesn't sound like her at all." He frowned to himself, pensive. "You really have been good for her," he said finally.

"Maybe someday she'll think that, too," said Rhys. Then he launched into something about the Pilot Academy, because he didn't want to talk about Sydell anymore, not like this and not with Walt.

When he entered the mess later to get something to eat, he found her sitting at the bar. He thought she'd gone skulking off to her room. Why was she still here? "I told you to take an hour. Do you know how long an hour is?" he asked.

She shrugged and fidgeted with her cup, peeling back the lid. "I thought we were all done for the day."

"That's not what break means. Head back and clean

up everything that's laid out on the floor. I'll be over in a bit to start putting things back together, and you're going to help me."

She nodded and then moved toward the door, where he stood. He remained in place for a moment, watching her closely, making her wait to pass. She twitched under his gaze, tucking her face beneath her messy hair, the silly green streak in it swinging across her forehead.

He stepped back and let her pass, lowering his head with a smile. He watched her leave, his eyes on her bare, shapely legs. He'd had no intention of going back to it tonight, until he had seen her. He would have forgotten her if she'd not still been in the mess. Why hadn't she just gone to her room?

He made some noodles in the agitation module and ate quickly, hungrily, not noticing the taste. Impatience to get back to the engine room distracted him. Something about her had changed, since he'd taken her to task in his loft, he was sure of it. Or rather, had to be sure of it. He thought briefly about his earlier rule, as to Sydell. *Off limits.* And then he'd had that talk with Walt, and come to find her here, alone, in her little shorts, like she'd been waiting for him.

Perhaps Walter was right, and he was running on instinct after all.

When Rhys came back into the engine room, his presence greeted her like heat, like a pressure on the back of her head. She did not turn but remained hunched over the tubs of pieces she'd collected, utterly still and pretending to be enthralled with them. He came to settle near her without a word, taking up some of the parts she'd cleaned and getting them put back into place. He'd taken down the top of his jumpsuit and tied it at his waist, wearing beneath it a sleeveless undershirt. After telling her she had to wear her thermal. Hypocrite. But she wasn't about to say it aloud.

Yet, she kept staring at his rounded shoulders, at the muscles curving into his dark-downed forearms, and at his hands, square and strong, capably putting the engine back together as if they had their own intelligence. This was Rhys, who'd taken her ship away, who'd bought her like chattel on a whim and who thought nothing of whipping her ass red when he felt like it. Rhys, who'd clipped her wings, whom she'd hated since almost the moment they met. But she could not stop staring at him, despite her panic that he would notice, that he would call her out on it.

He had become the most attractive man she'd ever known. *You're still crazy*, she told herself. Stricken with whatever it was that had descended on her the other night after suffering such awful humiliation at his hands... no, it was like a flu, or a fever; it can go on for a bit, but it goes away eventually. It had to.

She leaned in to grab another piece from the tub and dropped the two she was holding; they clattered to the grated floor, and one rolled down into a small trench by the cooling hub. He caught her eyes in his, in a way that made her hold her breath, then his dark brows lowered disapprovingly, and he said, "You're distracted. Pay attention to what you're doing." He reached down into the little gutter and got the part.

An angry heat came up into her chest, and her breaths came faster. "How the hell am I supposed to do that, with you lurking around like an enforcer bot?" she snapped. The words escaped hot from her mouth, like they'd been trapped there.

He shot her a sharp look, eyes narrowing, and every-thing heightened; the colors in the room brightened and her ears roared, and she thought her nerves would shatter.

"*Excuse me*?" he asked, stepping in and crouching next to her. His eyes scoured her face, as though he were testing her.

She glowered at him for a moment, then bowed her head back over her work. She moved the pieces about pointlessly; he was so close, she could feel the heat coming off his large body.

"You're just fooling around now," he accused, and she could not speak. The pieces in her hands lost all meaning; she might have been holding two fish, and if she were, she would have known just as much what to do with them.

In a low voice, he asked, "Are you going to help me get some work done, or should I take your little shorts down and spank you again?"

His words liquefied her, and her head went light. The deliberate way he spoke, as though he knew exactly what effect he was having on her, made her unsure of what to say, even if she could have spoken. Did he mean it? Would he? The room sort of spun a little and she dropped one of the pieces, yet again, and then tried to pick it back up.

"Would that help you?" he pressed. "Or would it just make things worse?"

A pause. The silence roared. Her stomach contracted.

"Sydell, you're so horny, I can smell it," he said cruelly. She gasped, a jagged breath torn from her, outraged, and before she could think, she flung her hand out to slap him.

He caught it, and his eyes locked on hers with an aggressive gleam. He reached out with his other hand and touched her waist, and it was like he'd applied an electric charge; her whole body hummed with it like a live wire.

Her jaw dropped. He smiled, triumphant. "That's why you're so distracted," he said, softer now.

Her mouth stayed open, in a kind of dumb gratitude that he'd said it, that he'd made the awful thing too tangible to deny. But why had he? Did he mean to spank her, like he said? Or… and for a brief, insane second, she thought he might lean in and kiss her, right where she knelt.

He did not. Instead, as he held her there, steadying her, he ran his other hand along her waist, in a long, luscious stroke, not yet releasing the hand he had caught. He stopped just beneath her arm, his thumb only just brushing the side of her breast. Then he slid his hand back down and stopped at the button of her shorts.

"What were you trying to tell me, prancing around in these, hmm?" he asked with a soft laugh, tugging at the waistband.

She could only stare at him, knowing her face had to be bright red from the heat tingling beneath her skin.

"What do you want, Sydell? Do you want me to do this?"

His tone demanded an answer. It was too much, she couldn't… but what if he stopped? She would die if he stopped. So, she nodded, quickly.

In a dexterous motion, he undid the top button of her shorts, zipped down the fly and tugged at the loose flap. The next thing she knew, he had slipped his hand down into her shorts, over her panties, so that he held her tender mound, with nothing between his hand and her body but a thin layer of cotton.

A pulse surged up from where he touched, and her body rocked forward; he held her by her wrist still, keeping her in place. He pressed the end of his palm against her most sensitive spot, while his long, firm fingers rested farther back, right on the crease of where she opened.

"Oh my god," she said under her breath; it sounded distant, like someone else had said it.

He ran his fingers along the split of her and she gasped as her whole body sang and that intimate place contracted, a quick spasm of pleasure. He laughed, delighted, clearly having felt for himself her reaction. He stroked her insistently, making her squirm at the sensation of it, while all her own motions only increased the friction. Bolts of pleasure swam up through her core, and she half-closed her eyes, in his thrall completely.

He kept up his strokes, his hand firm and knowing. He stretched his fingers and rubbed farther back, embarrassingly close to her asshole. She whined and tried to shimmy away, but she was trapped in her own shorts. Her breaths grew short, tight, as arousal tugged at her like a wave; yes, it was like feeling a wave dragging the sand out from under her body, tugging her out to the ocean irresistibly. The irresistible urge to…

"You want to come, don't you?" he asked, already sensing it, and her face burned. Heat rushed pulsing down to her groin, so that for a second, she thought she would come in that instant. He stilled his hand, however.

That was too much to bear. "Please," she said, her own voice ringing in her ears as a whine. What the hell was she doing? Was she begging him for *that*?

"Please?" he taunted. "Please what?"

She writhed about in shame and tension.

"Tell me what you want, baby," he said.

When he said that, it put a tremor through her very depths; the word was both affectionate but also how he'd said it back at her apartment when chiding her, 'Don't be a baby.'

Then he'd bent her over her sofa and spanked her, and thinking of it now made her skin flood with heat. "I want to come," she breathed. Then she added, "Please." And she cringed, having been made to say it.

"Come here then," he said. He took his hand away from where she needed him and she cried out at the loss, but then he pulled her in close, so that her body pressed to his deliciously. As he did, he leaned back, until she lay full length on top of him, straddling his hips, and through the layers of their clothing, his hardness pushed insistently against her pussy. She stifled a moan, to feel his thick rigidity beneath her. He bounced her playfully against it, his hands spread out on her bottom, a half-smile flickering on his face. Then he began to grind himself against her, and the smile vanished.

The girth of him intimidated her; thank God he didn't seem about to put it inside. All the same, the thought of him doing so made her heart race, to feel his cock bearing up against the split of her and think that he could do just that if he wanted. She pushed her face into his shirt, the rib of it rough on her skin, his scent musky and pleasing. She pressed her nose against his shoulder, into the muscle made hard by tension, and reveled in its implacability.

"You want to come all pressed against me?" he said, just next to her ear, and she squirmed.

To her joy, he held her there, his hands gripping her bottom as he kept on grinding her rhythmically. His cock pushed hard on her clit through her shorts, and she felt herself soaking the fabric of them helplessly. She was just at the cusp of it, and yet… and yet she couldn't quite… couldn't…

She whined in frustration and wriggled, trying to take it for herself, pushing her body along his bulge. He slid his hand into the cleft of her buttocks, stroking the sensitive places there through her shorts, prodding even at that tight, intimate ring of muscle with his finger. She yelped at that, and then the shock of it, the pleasure it gave mixed with the… just the wrongness of it, pushed her over the edge. Pressed down on his rocking hips, she came with a loud wail, biting at his shirt as she did, grabbing fistfuls of it as her whole body spasmed in ecstasy.

He ground her all the way through it; he pushed his fingers onto the back end of her through her shorts, teasing at that private spot, crowding her on both sides so there was no escaping him. The pleasure peaked and rang all through her, like nothing she had ever felt. Her legs stretched long and rigid and then, just as swiftly, relaxed, dropping to the sides of him as she was left sensitive and spent. Her legs collapsed into his, wrapped around them. She felt the intractable hardness of his right leg, the titanium one, and she shivered with bliss.

Now his thrusts against her grew faster, rougher, somehow less aware of her presence. His hard cock smashing up on her just orgasmed, sensitive clit made her shriek and thrash against him, and when he did not stop, she came again, a piercing sharp climax that stiffened her legs until she fell limp once more, barely sensible to what he did. After a moment, he slowed, and his gruntlike panting softened; she felt his cool breath as he brushed his face over the crown of her head. Had he kissed her there, in a rush of tenderness from his own orgasm? The whole of it had dazed her too much to tell.

Her mind and body fell still, as though she'd woken from a deep sleep, a dream, and was no longer certain about reality. Drifting in that space in which reality counts for little, and she held the precious fading dream in her head for as long as possible.

He moved first. He shifted beneath her, and finding her

limp, he pulled her up slowly along with him. He scratched her head playfully, making her feel rather like a puppy. "Ready to go to bed?" he asked, and she nodded dazedly. Oh, shit, wait. Did he mean, go to his bed? A panic shot through her. What she wanted, suddenly, was to be alone, in the dark of her own little bunk, where he could not see her.

He stood, helping her up to her feet, and she found herself shaky. They walked that way, with him holding her arm, out into the corridor, where he turned toward the barracks. Thank God. She wanted to hide, couldn't bear to see him after what had just happened, or to have him see her.

At the door of her room, she said curtly, "I can get to bed myself, thank you." She kept her head bent, face out of sight, but caught a small jerk of surprise from him when she said it.

"All right. It was fun, kid. Goodnight." He gave her an awkward pat on the shoulder, almost playful, before walking off back up the hall. She was too exhausted to ponder on it, or to even want to. She stepped into her small room, grateful for its compact comfort, and dove into the bed as she ordered the lights off, to be enclosed by the sweetness of the dark.

Chapter 2

Four weeks earlier...

R hys leapt up against the pink haze of a Martian sky. One long bound from the crumbling hilltop, he grinned as he remained airborne for an impossible stretch.

Then his heel clipped the rocky scree and he leapt again from the touch point. The buoyancy of Martian gravity intoxicated him, distracting him even from the problem at hand. His legs raced under him of their own volition, one flesh and one titanium, and carried him to the bottom of the hill where he skidded to a stop in a cloud of caramel-colored dust. Just barely, he kept his footing. Probably thanks to the titanium.

The rusted terrain spread out to the horizon, unbroken by anything save the tall, distant Pylons. They shimmered, magnified and distorted by the dust and wind, as hollow in appearance as they had become, the massive structures abandoned, the soy fields gone. How long had it been since he'd seen them? Not since the Mutiny, when the fields had been set ablaze. The memory of the war, of his own part played, left a bad taste in his mouth. They'd called him a hero, but he had his doubts; he'd tossed the medals some time ago. The metal leg, he was stuck with.

It didn't matter now. Only saving Callie mattered. A kid sister he'd neglected too long and somehow had failed to protect. There was no time to waste. He picked up his pace, checking the coordinates as he did. He was close. The ship should be arriving any minute. He had only to stay put and watch for it.

From the east, a ruddy cloud smeared the sky. A sand-storm was headed his way.

"I hate these kinds of jobs," muttered Sydell. A burnt orange haze occluded the cockpit view, and she could see nothing.

"Yes, you've said that," Walter replied. "But we have to take what we can, until we get our rating up."

She waited, but he said no more, though she swore it showed on his long, lank face, *your fault*. Fair enough. He piloted; she planned. She would have been a pilot herself, but it hadn't been in the cards, so she dealt with the clients. He flew the transport ship like a champion. On her end, things hadn't gone so well. She never could quite get along with the customer base.

The narrow cockpit had only been designed for two people; she wedged herself now in the tight entryway. They'd not considered comfort back when they'd built these ships; it had been a different era, when one suffered through the journey in wonder at being able to travel through space at all. Probably, it was the run-down ship itself that had failed them as a taxi service. But it had been what she could afford when Dad died; it had gotten her off Earth, and really, what else mattered? He would have been proud; he always had been one to appreciate the big picture.

"Hail him again," she ordered, shifting her body between the hard pillars of the doorway, as if she could really find a comfortable space.

"My last hail's on queue. He'd get it if he could. That storm's blocking it, most likely." Walter spun around in the chair, locking his fingers behind his bouffant of blond hair, staring her way and looking just as anxious as he had when they were kids and she'd been about to do something stupid.

"I should have said no," she growled, "that's what you're thinking, right?"

"It's a weird one, for sure," he said with a shrug. Any criticism he had could only hang in the air unsaid, which she hated, and she wished he would just say what he thought. This had been an unusual job from the start. That two line, encrypted message from "R.C", to meet out in the middle of nowhere, on Mars no less. Wanting transport to Earth, no cargo, but all the same could it be anything that wasn't criminal? No, it couldn't.

But she had responded, and here she stood, waiting, willing to turn a blind eye if only for the money. No ship, he'd said; he'd be on foot. On foot from where? And now, the sandstorm, and he had to be out in it, somewhere, but they couldn't hail him. Maybe they shouldn't hail him. Maybe they should just leave.

"Goddammit," she said under her breath. She squeezed out of the entryway and started back for the airlock. She couldn't lose this job, not now. Losing the job meant losing the ship, and no way in hell could that happen. Any fear she felt simply didn't count. She wouldn't be run aground, wouldn't get sent back to Earth.

Walter called after her, "What are you doing?"

"I have to go get him," she shouted from the hall.

"You ought to let *me* go." Barely audible as she raced away.

"Nope, I'm going." She didn't know if he'd heard her, but he didn't follow, and she didn't expect him to. She adored Walt, they'd been friends for ages, but she knew him well enough to expect complacence on his part, where a call to action was needed. Besides, he was only out here piloting as a favor to her, and she wasn't about to let him get hurt.

Stupid, this was stupid. But better than sitting around thinking about how stupid it had been to take on the job at all. She stripped off her tank top and pants and dropped them in a scattered line down the narrow path to the airlock as she moved along, the grating on the floor pressing little squares into her bare feet. She was better insulated in an old, bulky spacesuit the less she wore, though it always had struck her as counter-intuitive. She kept on only a pair of white underwear, merely for comfort in a suit which was, like the ship, not at all designed for such.

Her suit hung like a butchered animal in the crew ingress, holding its stiff bipedal form through the shoulders and tapering from there like a deflated balloon. Bright orange synthweave over the plastoid shell, practical on the moon but nearly camouflage on an iron planet. A chill passed over her now that she was headed out, which she chalked up to being undressed, and quickly she waded into her suit, as if it could insulate her from her mounting dread.

Over the ship's comm, Walt said something, but she

couldn't hear him as she depressurized the room and locked her helmet into place. Offhandedly, she recalled that some of the suit's features had bugged out last time she'd used it; namely, the thermostat and the Nav. No time to think about it now, and she hardly wished to. She jammed her fist into the broken panel and the door churned noisily as it opened. A cloud of dust overcame her instantly, obscuring everything save for the violet sky overhead. A blue star caught her attention. Was it Earth?

"You shouldn't be out walking in that," came Walt's anxious voice through the speaker in her helmet.

"Our client shouldn't be, either." Her teeth were set, and the words came out terse.

"Hey, he wanted to meet like this."

"Yeah, well." She stayed in place next to the ship. God, she couldn't see anything. If the Nav wasn't working, she could be lost until the storm passed, which might be hours or more.

"Walt, where is he?" she called, going shrill at the end despite her best effort to control it.

"I'm doing another scan right now."

She grunted an acknowledgment. Nothing to see now but a dull peach "fog", and even that obscured by the scratches on her visor. Sometimes when she bought discount, she *really* bought discount. No, this had been a bad idea for sure. But she had to find the client. Possibly save the client.

"I'm picking up movement three clicks from you, northeast," said Walt.

Northeast. She checked the visor's compass and reoriented herself. With reluctance, she set off away from the ship and toward the target. Money, she needed the money. She would pay the ship off if it killed her… and fuck, maybe it would.

Walt said, "It's someone on foot. Too slow to be anything else. Gotta be our guy." But his casual tone made her inexplicably anxious. What if it wasn't "R.C."? Hell, it could be anyone. And, even if it was him, they knew nothing about him. Why had he wanted to meet like this, out here, in a dead zone? For all she knew, he'd kill them once he got where he wanted to go.

You're escalating things. Just focus on the here and now. The here and now being a blur of Martian dirt. She glanced backward. No ship in sight. She stood in the swirl of dust, unable for a moment to get her bearings. She shivered. Yes, the heating. That had been malfunctioning too. No way to tell if it lagged, either, not until an alarm went off, and it'd be too late by then. If the alarm still even functioned.

Don't think about that, either! Her rapid breaths echoed around in her helmet and fogged the visor even worse.

"He's moving right toward you! Must have a ping on the ship."

"Of course, he does," she said, relieved to hear it, because she was terrified to move any farther out into the dust storm. Walter didn't respond, either because he didn't want to, or because the outbound had failed. She should have checked on it before she came out, along with everything else.

"Ten feet. Moving directly to you."

Shit, he probably had a ping on *her*. Her heart throbbed in her throat and heralded a queasy wave, along with a sudden flash of heat. Fear? Or her body trying to compensate for a drop in temp? She struggled to look down at her thermostat, placed obscurely to one side of her helmet. Core read as within safe parameters if you could trust it. She thrust forward, stumbling in the opaque cloud toward…

Thud!

She bounced back as she hit, but just as she did, someone caught her from the front and held her at the elbows, in an unbreakable grip that was just shy of painful. The shape in front of her, what she'd slammed into, was a person, likely *the* person, and now that he had her in his grasp, he held her still. Vaguely, she saw the outline of a tall, masculine shape, broad through the shoulders and tapering to square hips and long legs. He had one of those cutting edge suits, form fitting rather than bulky, and exorbitantly expensive. If he could afford that kind of thing, why the hell did he need her ship?

She had no way of communicating with him, not from her suit. "Walt! Hail him again!" she cried.

Walt did not respond. A moment passed, in the clutches of this stranger, and then he turned her around and propelled her along in the direction of the ship. A rush of relief hit her, if only because he seemed to know exactly where he was going. She would get back to the ship at least. Along with the relief, a sensation of heat flooded her veins, and a wave of dizziness made it difficult to keep her steps in a straight line. Did she have enough oxygen? The O2 regulators had never given her trouble before.

The ship popped into view as a jagged maroon lump. The other spacewalker kept fast hold of her arms, but with her hands, she brushed against the paneling until the familiar ridge of the airlock door rubbed against her fingers. She worked the latch, which stuck as usual, but after a moment it creaked open, and she punched the pass code into the stiff buttons. She sighed into her helmet as the door hissed open.

He released her, and she rushed inside. The lights powered on, and the door closed. The reflective tint of his helmet obscured his face; the time for the airlock to repressurize stretched out impossibly. She felt she would never see who had followed her in.

Then the green light flashed on, and he pulled off his helmet as she still struggled with her own, her arms oddly weak, her head light. The latches on the seal tended to stick.

He had dark auburn hair, over a tall forehead, and snapping hazel eyes; yes, angry eyes glaring right at her, and his thin, straight mouth was set tightly. She stepped back as he reached out for her.

Chapter 3

Barely aware of the person in the suit, Rhys grabbed him by the shoulders and spun him around to get a look at the dials on the back of it. The chunky helmet clattered to the floor.

"Stop, what the hell—" came an angry protest, but he'd seen the gauges on the back, and he started at the pressure latches at the sides and waist.

"You ought to have died out there in this piece of junk," he scolded, and with one rough motion, he pulled the suit away from her so it gathered in a bundle at her knees. "Your gauges are shot to hell. Your suit was cranking up and overheating you."

She turned herself sideways, her long, chocolate-brown hair covering the sides of her breasts even before she swiftly curled her arms around her chest. Briefly, she reminded him of a mermaid. She wore nothing save for a pair of white panties stretched over her full hips.

"You didn't need to rip my suit off," she snarled.

"I thought that's what you were trying to do. Couldn't you tell it was too hot?" he said. He glanced around.

"Haven't you got your airlock stocked? A blanket or anything?"

She shook her head, her tawny skin flushed and her lips pressed tight together.

"No med kits, either," he grunted in contempt, as he finished looking the room over. Who didn't stock a single med kit in their airlock? Warm irritation pulsed through him as he tried to keep his eyes averted from the nearly naked woman only three feet away. He gestured at the sorry heap of a suit at her ankles as she stepped out of it.

"That relic should be destroyed." He crossed his arms, frowning at her. "Look, I didn't know you weren't wearing anything." It was the closest to an apology he would offer.

She huffed. Her dark eyes were opaque but bright with anger, and their shape reminded him of a cat's. Her full, round cheeks were still rosy, and though her mouth pursed tightly in disapproval, it had a bowed tenderness to it that appealed to him. With effort, he kept his gaze up, on her face. "Are you Miss Rivas?"

She nodded, still turned away from him. "You're my pickup, I assume?"

"You shouldn't assume anything. But, yes, I'm Rhysling Canton."

She narrowed her eyes. "All right. Well, let me get to my cabin and then we can get moving."

He watched her for a moment more and then stepped out of the doorway. She stormed ahead of him down the hall, then sped around a narrow corridor. He followed on her heels, taking in the back view of her offhandedly as he also admired the ship. She had a long, slender waist, almost serpentine, and her hips flared out with a breadth and depth just a bit too large for the rest of her. Disproportionate, but not unattractively so.

As for the ship, it was an old, steadfast model, with all

the charm of white plastoid siding and interface terminals every few feet or so. He couldn't help but notice all the unnecessary wear and tear. These older ships could go on for years, but most people who bought them anymore just burned them out. Such a shame.

She stopped in front of a room with a half open door. It seemed to be jammed that way, broken. She darted in and said, "Don't follow me."

He remained in the hall but glanced in after her. Probably the largest room in the ship, and with a broad stretch of visiglass over the bed, he guessed it was the loft, usually used as a captain's cabin. Did that make her the head of this operation? If so, then the sorry condition of the ship and her suit started to make sense to him. He'd already figured her for a total amateur.

"How long have you been in the transport business?" he asked. Dammit, he'd wanted a transport small enough to stay off radar, but not something this casual. This joke of a captain was going to end up being a risk to Callie if he didn't get things under control quickly.

"Why does that matter?" she retorted, reappearing from the shadows of the room wearing a dark-gray thermal jumpsuit, soft and form-fitting. She'd tied all her hair up behind her head, leaving long strands of messy layers around her face and eyes, including one streak dyed absurdly emerald-green. He kept his stare leveled on her until she frowned and bent over a pair of heavy boots, shoving her feet into them clumsily. "Three years," she answered finally. "After I bought this ship."

He nodded slowly. He remained at the doorway when she made a move to exit.

"You're in my way," she said, glaring up at him. She wore too much dark eyeliner; it made her look sulky. He kept his eyes fixed on hers, and after a moment, her eyes dropped. He waited, trying to size her up. She'd bought this ferry, but she couldn't take care of it, couldn't even be bothered to have her awful spacesuit repaired or replaced. Clearly, she was in over her head.

"Listen," he said, "this is a very casual business you seem to have going here."

"If you're dissatisfied, I can give you a lift to the station, but I'll still need the deposit."

"No," he said in a low voice, "I've got somewhere to be. I just need you to understand, this isn't going to be like most of your jobs. Someone's life is at stake."

She met his eyes again, hostile this time. "You know this is just a transport service?"

"Yes, and I needed something small, something that wouldn't catch any attention. That's why I couldn't meet you at the station. I can't be spotted here."

"My listing insists on no criminal activity—"

"This isn't anything like that. Not on my end anyway. We're here to rescue someone who's being held hostage."

"I'm a *ferry* service," she stressed, squinting hard at him, but she blinked several times, spasmodically, some kind of an anxious tic, maybe.

He crossed his arms over his chest. "No kidding. And a bad one. But can you handle ferrying me to a location on this planet, wait for me, and then ferry me to a station? Or is that too much for you?"

Her eyes flashed. For a split second, he thought she'd try to hit him. Good. Let her. She'd be sorry and then they could get on with rescuing Callie.

Her face went stony, and she said, "I'll need to speak with my pilot. Excuse me."

He stepped aside. He kept up with her as she ducked down a hatch to the lower deck and ended up outside a small mess kitchen with a three seat bar and a table. At the bar, sat a wiry young man with a red leather duster and silver-rimmed glasses, eating from a plastoid bowl. As they entered, he spun the bar stool to face them, noodles dangling from his mouth.

"You're the pilot?" Rhys asked. The young man nodded, the noodles rapidly disappearing.

"Can you fly this thing over rocky terrain?"

"I can fly anywhere, on any terrain," he replied, not boastful at all, just stating it as a fact.

"Hold up," she interjected. "Walter, there's something weird going on here. He says there's a hostage, so I assume there's risk involved—"

"Risk?" Rhys said with a dry laugh. "Where was your fear of risk going out in a sandstorm in that museum piece of a spacesuit? Or are you just too ignorant to know what a risk that was?"

"Jesus Christ! Let me talk to my pilot," she snapped. "*I'll* be the one to decide if we keep working with you, got it?"

"It's already decided," he said. "You agreed to transport me. I arranged to be dropped out here to meet you. I don't have time to find another ferry. My sister has been kidnapped and held, and the only way I can get her, the only way to guarantee she won't vanish, is if we make this rescue now. On your ship and by a specific plan. I need your compliance for it to work and I *will* have it."

He caught a strange contraction on Walter's face, almost like the start of a grin, as his eyes darted toward her. Her jaw dropped slightly. Then she opened her mouth, but Rhys spoke quicker.

"I'm prepared to triple your fee if you're able to cooperate perfectly. Call it a bonus."

Her eyes darted about in conflict. It nearly amused him, how easy she was to read. She wanted the money. But she didn't want to give in to him. What she didn't know, was that she didn't have a choice. He had no time to make other arrangements; this had to happen now. Every second wasted, the window was sliding closed. This so-called captain could either comply or get dragged along for the ride.

"Take the money," he pressed. He stood tall, took a half step closer, barely noticeable, just enough to be daunting. He wanted to intimidate her; he needed to win easily right now. She didn't know what she was doing, and as per usual, he would have to take over for someone else's incompetence.

She let her breath out in a slow huff. "If anything happens to my ship…"

He snorted. "Lots of things could happen to your ship, judging from the state it's in. When you get paid, you'll take it to a repair shop if you really care about it. Now, if you're finished with lunch," he looked at Walter, "I'd like to get moving."

Walter set his bowl down on the bar, nodding affably. He seemed almost excited about the turn of events.

She sat down next to Walt in the cockpit when Rhys had stepped out. The brief excitement over being offered so substantial a bonus by that jackass was fading swiftly.

"It's like he's commandeered the ship," she said, furious, but spoken under her breath.

"Hardly," said Walt. "Besides, it's hard to blame him. It's his sister."

She shrugged. "Seems like something the Rangers should take care of."

"This guy doesn't seem like the type to let the Rangers take care of it."

"Right. He's a goddamn vigilante. Last I checked, that's a felony."

Now Walt shrugged. "Okay. Do you want to tell him to get off the ship? Because I sure as hell don't. I don't think he'd go anywhere."

"This is *my* ship," she said through her teeth and made a kick at the bulkhead. "If he thinks I'm just going to go along with this, he's dead wrong."

Walt said nothing, but she sensed his disapproval. Though the AI Nav did the piloting right now, he still kept his seat at the controls, never one to leave anything to chance. Through the narrow visiglass, the flat, rusty desert grew darker as they skimmed along, shifting to an eggplant purple, the surface rockier as they climbed toward the mountains. The land had changed as they drew closer to wherever Rhys was taking them.

After a few more minutes, the rocks around them grew taller, and soon enough they were flying through a narrow canyon. Was this one of those "dark areas" of Mars she'd heard about? Where crime-lords took haven, and the Rangers didn't bother, or couldn't bother, to patrol?

She stole a look at Rhys from where he now stood, wedged in the entryway of the cockpit, his dark brows drawn low in concentration as he watched out the visiglass. Probably, he'd had no choice but to do this himself if it were such a lawless area. She admired him, for about four seconds, and then remembered that it would likely get them all killed. He'd tricked her into this. And triple her fee or not, he'd all but forced her to go along once he had.

"*There.*"

She tensed at the sound of his voice, which had a sort of calm menace to it. *He's dangerous*, she thought. Just an instinct, but nonetheless, her anger chilled a bit. She followed his gaze out the viewport; the ravine had opened into a small clearing surrounded by rocky cliffs.

"What the hell's that?" Walt breathed. At the top of one cliff, in the distance, some sort of edifice rose, too complex to be natural but too large to be man-made. Or was it? She squinted, trying to make out what she was seeing.

"Slow down," said Rhys, "we're nearly in range." He pulled something small out of his jacket, a tiny black cube, no larger than his fingertip.

"Jesus," said Walt, staring at it.

"What's that?" she asked sharply.

"Um," Walt stammered, his eyes on Rhys. "That's a jammer, I think. Isn't it?"

"An exclusive," Rhys replied with the shadow of a smile.

A jammer? Tech like that, hell, it could be worth a million credits or more. "Why did you hire *me* if you could buy that?" she snapped.

"Settle down," said Rhys, staring at the piece with an admiring glitter in his eyes; he pinched it ever so slightly and it came to glowing blue life. Then he smiled. "I hired your ship, Miss Rivas, not you. It's old, its registration is, well, substandard." He raised an eyebrow at her, as if to implicate her in some way. "It wouldn't tip anyone off at the station when you arrived. Just like the one that brought me here a few days back. This ship raises no flags. And now," he set the jammer on the console, in front of Walt, "it's not even traceable."

"What's the core life on that thing?" asked Walt.

"I'd say thirty minutes?" Rhys shrugged. "But it's all we'll need to get my sister and get out."

And then, the edifice on the rock all at once came into

focus, at first, like an illusion, like seeing a castle in the clouds. But this… this had been *made*. Built into the rock, from the rock. Carved pillars, half the height of the cliff, flanking a door so tall, it could only be the entrance for some kind of god. Or demon.

"What the actual fuck," she breathed.

"Yep," said Rhys with savage pleasantness. "A monument to a megalomaniac."

"Who would make something like that?" She did not expect him to answer; it was more rhetorical than anything. Clearly, they were dealing with a criminal of a different order.

"My brother," said Rhys with a grim smile, "Parsons."

Chapter 4

Parsons. Parsons the Pale. Drug lord. Human trafficker. The Devil himself… she could not speak, though her brain screamed with questions. How the fuck were they going to get someone back from in there?

Walter said, "Your brother kidnapped your sister?"

"Yes," sighed Rhys.

"Why?" She spoke finally, anger and fear straining her voice. This whole thing felt like some kind of a sick joke.

"He wants her support." Rhys scratched the back of his head, stepping backward to the hall. He was too broad to fit well in the entryway. "Wants her shares of some of my father's investments, which he left to her. It would make things better for him."

She pointed at the dragon's lair of a fortress. "Better?" she said snidely. "For *him*?"

"No one ever stops wanting more," said Rhys lightly.

She screwed her face up, disgusted. The disgust did not exempt Rhys. "You're clearly rolling in it. There must have been a better way to do this?"

His eyes met hers, two sharp hazel points boring right into her, and she grew warm under his gaze. Was he angry? Or just trying to figure her out? After a moment, he shook his head. "No. No better way." He sighed and went on, "And I'm not rich. Not like they are. I'm a bastard."

He said it casually, with no resentment. *How does that matter?* she almost said aloud but stopped herself. No point. Anyway, he *was* rich, she knew. Maybe not as rich as someone who could build that thing into the side of a cliff, but he had more money than she would ever know what to do with, judging from the tech he had.

"Turn into that crevice on your two o' clock," said Rhys. She opened her mouth to ask what he meant, then toppled away from the bulkhead and right into his chest as the ship lurched into the turn. He caught her in his arms; his touch shocked her with a weird thrill for an instant before he propelled her back onto her seat.

"Why aren't you strapped in?" he demanded.

"You aren't strapped in," she pointed out.

"*I'm* not stumbling around the cockpit," he said, and then he leaned forward, towering over her as though he would put the straps around her himself, and she inched back with a panicky breath. Then he looked out the view-port and she followed suit. They'd turned into an impossibly narrow corridor; if she didn't trust Walt as she did, she would've thought they couldn't clear it. All the same, it made her tense.

"There will be ledges," said Rhys, still leaning over her, though now speaking to Walt. "You'll need to watch closely. We're going to land on one."

She straightened up in her seat, Rhys being close enough in the small space that she could feel the heat coming off his chest. But he didn't seem to be aware of her now. He pointed. "There."

Walt slowed the ship at the word and hovered over a ledge she had not seen. It was one of several lips sticking out from the canyon wall but set apart by a cave-like entrance where it met the cliff side. Walt swung the ship and landed neatly, and Rhys blinked. Was he surprised? Possibly impressed? She felt a surge of pride for her friend and pilot, but also wished it had been *she* who'd landed it, she who had made him impressed.

"What can we do from out here?" she asked.

"You don't need to do anything. *You*," he glared down at her, "can buckle yourself in and stay put. Walt, be ready to fly. This is an old entrance, it probably isn't guarded. But I might be spotted inside and if that happens, we could have pursuers."

Her skin bristled at the way he'd spoken to her. "You seem to know this place well," she said sourly.

"I do," he said. "That's why he couldn't know I was coming. I'm the only one who knows how to find her." And with that, he left the cockpit in the direction of the airlock.

———

She paced down the hall from the cockpit to the hatch, then climbed down the hatch and paced the hall in the crew quarters. She glanced at the timepiece lit at intervals along the bulkhead. Only twenty minutes had passed. It felt like hours. She climbed back up to the cockpit. "When do we cut bait?" she blurted the moment she saw Walt.

"Are you serious?"

"Yes! When can we make an educated guess that he failed and get the hell out, before we get ourselves involved with the fucking Devil himself?"

"I hate to say it, be we are kinda already involved."

"No thanks to you. You were fucking gleeful for the chance to do something like this."

"Look, I didn't know it had anything to do with… with Parsons." His voice dropped on the name, as though afraid of being heard. "The way I hear it, he's barely a real person. Like a myth." He rubbed his chin.

"Not myth. Real. With a lot of family issues, apparently."

"So, a Greek myth."

"Ha," she said, deadpan, "glad you're amused. We're working for the drug lord of the century's brother, doing god knows what at his base."

"Getting his sister."

"Maybe. Who's to say? He knows this place, Walt. Like, *knows* it. Doesn't that disturb you?"

Walt didn't answer. After a moment, he said, "Sy, do you really want to leave him here?"

She pressed her lips together. No, she didn't really. Just discussing it, made her feel shitty. But every minute they stayed, the twist in her stomach grew tighter. This could all blow up worse than they could imagine, and right now her mind was cranking overtime, imagining just how bad it could go.

"*Sy.*" Walt's tone drew her attention sharply. She swallowed when she looked out the viewport. Two figures in red spacesuits had emerged from the dark entrance that Rhys had gone into. Strapped across their chests, were what looked to be ionic weapons. Contraband.

"I think they're confused," he said, his calm tone negated by the white knuckles of his fist as it gripped the throttle.

They don't know who we are, she thought. Yet, they weren't hailing. "Can we hail them?" she asked.

"I've been trying. They aren't responding."

"I'm going out there."

"What? Why?"

"To try and make this seem, I don't know, like a legit visit! Throw them off, buy us time. If we stay in here, they'll probably send out more, and Rhys will never be able to get out."

"Or, we fly now."

It did seem like the smart thing to do. "Urgh, I can't," she moaned. She set off once again for the airlock. Her suit sat in a heap in the corner, just where Rhys had left it. She pulled it on, her shaky hands barely able to snap closed the clasps. She cranked the heat down to zero and hoped that it wouldn't actually be zero. Anyway, the ionic blasters were much more of an immediate concern.

She slammed the airlock button and it closed, then opened the hatch to the outside and popped through, refusing to think any longer about everything that could go wrong.

The instant they spotted her, she waved her arms frantically. She found herself grinning absurdly, though they would not be able to see her face. In the next moment, she was jumping up and down like a fool. They did not reach for their guns or approach her. Instead, one looked warily at the other, and she could only guess what it was he said over the comm.

A burst of static piped into her helmet, and she thought for an instant her heart had exploded.

"Identify yourself!" They'd hacked into her channel somehow! What should she say? She clipped the general "out" button with her chin. What to say to a couple of ion wielding gangsters? Of a warlord, no less?

"I'm here with payment!" she shouted. They glanced at one another and a moment more went by. Had the outgoing audio even worked?

"Who are you?" blurted into her comm. "What payment is this regarding?"

"I represent Halifax Corp!" she cried. Where the hell had that come from? "I'm here to pay, pay the debt they owe."

"Why didn't they just wire the credits?"

"The payment's solid," she said. She could almost sense their surprise. Solid. *Gold*. Now that meant something.

"Halifax. Solid. Okay. Follow us; we'll find someone who knows about this."

No, she'd no intention of going in with them. She needed to buy time for Rhys to get back without more guards being alerted. "I will not," she said, amazed to hear how confident her voice sounded echoing in her helmet. "I demand a representative come out to meet me."

She flinched on saying it. A representative? Now they'd have to tell someone she was here. Likely, though, they had already. God, what the hell was she doing? Walt ought to have stopped her. Why the hell did Walt never stop her?

Then Rhys came out of the cave behind them; she recognized his figure instantly. Two pulses of something fired from a weapon in his hand, and the suits standing there before her crumpled, one onto its knees, the other right to the ground, face first. The pulse had been sound-less but the vibrations from it lingered in the air around her.

Behind Rhys, a petite figure trailed along in a green suit like his own. At the shots, this person had stopped, but Rhys took her by the wrist and headed directly for Sydell. He snatched her shoulder in his free hand and propelled her once more toward the airlock.

After the airlock had re-pressurized, she cracked off her helmet, glad to see Rhys distracted by the newly rescued. He was helping with her suit, much more gently than when he'd dealt with her own. Then he unzipped his own, now covered in dark brown dust, and let it slip to the floor. Beneath it, he wore a tank top; she blinked at his wide, rounded shoulders and glanced down, embarrassed, but then her gaze caught on his legs... the right one had the narrow pants tapered off short at the thigh, from which sprouted a deep gray titanium synth-limb. Its matte, metallic beauty fascinated her, but she forced her eyes away. She set her suit on the floor as quietly as she could and started for the door. Rhys moved away from his sister and blocked her path.

"You left the ship," he said in a tone that made her stomach tighten. "I told you to stay put."

"I bought you time," she shot back, glowering up at him.

"You did nothing of the sort. You would have been safe on the ship. I dealt with them myself. All you did was very nearly die."

The ship lurched upward, and she stumbled to the floor. Rhys caught his sister by the arm. She was a sweet-looking sort of girl, with round eyes and a small, pert mouth like a child, and she said, "Rhys, it's hardly the time to argue."

"Yes, right," he said. "*You.*" He pointed a finger at Sydell, much too close to her face. The urge to bite it rose strong. "Get yourself strapped in somewhere, now."

Then he ushered his sister along down the hall. Sydell bounded past them toward the cockpit, wanting to get her seat next to Walt before Rhys tried to take it.

They'd been flying for perhaps twenty minutes when a ship popped up on the scanner. "Might want to come up here," Walt said over the comm to wherever Rhys was.

"No, don't call him here," she whispered, but it was too late. Rhys appeared in the doorway within a few seconds and crowded in behind them in the little cockpit space.

"We've got someone on our tail," said Walt.

"Jammer's probably done," said Rhys, shaking his head. "They must have caught a visual on us somehow." But he sounded doubtful.

"Who else could it be?" she asked.

Walt gave her a somber look, and she held her breath. "We would have been listed at the station," he murmured to her.

"No," she said tersely, "they wouldn't come all the way out here. To Mars? And anyway, we paid them this month."

She spoke in an extremely low voice but, all the same, could feel Rhys' eyes fixed on her from where he stood. For the moment, the new fear, that it could be *them*, the creditors, replaced her concern over him. God, what if they had followed her to Mars? If they had, it could only mean one thing. They didn't want any more late payments. They wanted the whole sum. The ship.

"It's not them," she whispered. She wanted more than anything to believe it.

"Either way, they're catching up," said Walt, louder now.

"Can we evade them?" Rhys asked. Who knew what he'd heard?

"Maybe," said Walt. His forehead shimmered with sweat.

"It's all right. So long as Callie's on board, they won't fire on us," said Rhys, still thinking the ship was from Parsons. She did not know which was worse, that Parsons' guns had caught up with them, or that the creditors she had been evading for a while now, had. They had a reputation for violence in their methods, same as Parsons did.

"They're hailing," said Walt.

Rhys' mouth flattened. He frowned, puzzled. "I guess I'll talk to them."

"It's audio only," said Walt as he flipped the switch.

A burst of speech flooded the comm, "Sydell Rivas. This is Jugen Reclamations. You will surrender this ship at once. We have legal precedent to repossess it. We will shuttle you to the nearest station if you comply. If you do not, we have authorization to fire on you and take it by force. You have three minutes to respond."

Her mouth went dry. She stared at a spot on the control panel where a flashing light indicated the message had been received. She hid her face low behind her messy hair, ducking her head.

"This isn't your ship," said Rhys. He did not sound surprised. No, his words were just a low drawl of scorn that made her cringe.

She spoke through gritted teeth. "This *is* my ship."

A silence followed, which Walter broke. "There was, uh, something of a lien remaining on it."

"It's mine. I paid them for over two thirds of it," she said in a ragged whisper. Everything she'd had, everything left from when Dad had died. They wouldn't take it, she wouldn't let them, no matter how long she had to run or how far…

"They seem to think they're entitled to it," said Rhys.

"A few payments were missed," said Walter, as she stared at him hatefully. He ignored her, folded his arms, determined. "For a while. A year."

Goddammit, whose side was he on?

"I see," said Rhys. "Then, yes, they're within their rights to take it. You probably have bounties on you if it's been that long." He leaned into the doorway and stared at her long and hard. "I guess it would be pointless to tell you how stupid it was to go on running a transport service with this on your back."

"I had to make money somehow," she muttered, looking at the floor.

"It counts against you that you didn't tell me about this, back when I explained the sensitive nature of the job," he went on, his voice calm but unrelenting, his nearness to her bordering on oppressive.

She glared up at him. "If it would've gotten you off my ship, believe me, I would have." A tense moment passed, and her whole body braced for something as the silence stretched out, her every muscle and nerve sharply alive, though Rhys did not move.

Walt broke the tension, thank God. "What's the word, Sy?"

"Land," said Rhys, before she could speak. "I'm going to talk with them. And *you*," He looked straight at her, his gaze gluing her to her seat. "If you leave the ship again, I will make you sorry."

Her heart pounded in her chest. What the fuck did he mean by that? He was threatening her, now?

With this said, he left and headed in the direction of the airlock.

Chapter 5

When he returned, the mood on the ship had become strained. Callie had gone over to the hall outside the cockpit and her eyes widened with concern when she saw him. As for Sydell, she'd not moved from her seat, but she had that hostile, sulky expression he'd come to expect from her. Cute girl, bad attitude. He couldn't help but think it high time he step in and deal with it. For now, though, he ignored her. The association was almost done, thank God.

"Walt," he said slowly, "get us to an exit trajectory. We're getting out of here and back to Earth as quickly as possible."

"Oh, thank heavens," said Callie. He patted her shoulder offhandedly. She'd been physically unharmed in the ordeal; of course, Parsons wouldn't have *hurt* her. But she'd spent almost a month as his prisoner, likely with attempts made at mind-breaking her, and by her own brother no less. Callie had practically worshiped Parsons as a kid. He would have to get her to a deprogramming therapist as soon as they got to Earth.

"They're letting us go?" Sydell cried with a hopeful catch in her voice. Her dark eyes brightened, and for a moment, she was not at all unpleasant looking.

He shook his head. "This wasn't your ship to command, Miss Rivas. You owed an exorbitant amount on it."

Her face screwed up. "I paid an exorbitant amount on it."

"That's called a loss," he said, keeping his tone emotionless, refusing to show just how angry he was. The fear had been total, for a moment, that Parsons might have caught them. "We're heading back to Earth now, and you can get off the ship once we get there. I'll pay you your fee, but the bonus I offered won't be happening. Your irresponsibility could have jeopardized my sister's safety."

"I don't understand. Why aren't they taking my ship?"

"Because I've paid them for it. I'm not risking being here any longer when Parsons might find us, so my hand's been forced."

"You bought my ship?" She stood, started to step toward where he blocked the entryway, then seemed to think better of it and stopped.

He folded his arms. "It's not your ship. You were on borrowed time, and you know it. You would have lost it today, whether to me, or to your creditors."

"Then you owe me for the money down." The sulky turn of her mouth grew even more unpleasant, almost petulant. A spoiled, entitled brat she was, if she really believed that.

"That makes no sense." He kept his tone as reasonable as he could. "*They* weren't going to give you that, because you missed almost a year of payments. They would have taken it and sold it. I just sped up the process. I owe you nothing. Now get out of this cockpit and prepare for escape velocity."

She shook her head emphatically. "You won't take my ship without giving me my cut, asshole, and you'll pay what you promised for my services!"

"I'll pay you the original fee and that's it. You transported me on a technically stolen vessel, you deceived me about it, and you put this whole operation at risk. I told you at the start that this wasn't a game. I could have lost Callie completely. And if Parsons had gotten ahold of you and your friend, believe me, not a soul would have ever heard from either one of you again."

Her scowl became hateful now, and when she started to speak, he cut her off. "You've put nothing into this ship, and you'll get nothing for it. You don't deserve it. Insult me again, and I'll be happy to not pay you at all." He spoke slowly, keeping his temper in check but almost relishing the cruelty of what he said. Her recklessness had put them all at risk, and she ought to suffer some consequence for it. If she kept it up, he'd be happy to dock her pay, as he'd said, though at this point he'd much prefer to have it out of her hide. She had it coming, for damn sure.

Her hands trembled at her sides now and the whites of her eyes had gone red. Something crazy had gotten into her head; he could see it by the way her eyes darted about, wild as a cat's. She took a step back toward the dash and leaned for the storage compartment between the two seats.

"Sy, no," Walter said, which alerted Rhys, and he rushed forward just in time to grab her wrist as she lifted a small pistol out of the container. He wrenched it out of her hand.

"This is robbery!" she shouted.

He wouldn't argue anymore. She'd been about to pull a gun on him, and so she'd lost all further rights as far as he cared. He snatched her at the elbow with a grip that made her yelp, and pulled her out of the cockpit, past where Callie stood in the hall, and toward the crew quarters.

"*Let me go!*"

Spoken through her teeth as he impelled her into the crew barracks, he ignored her completely and looked around for what he would need. This was an older ship, but the bunks should still have straps for take-offs and zero-G flight. He pushed her toward one of them. She tried to jerk her arm out of his grasp, and when he pulled her closer, she went dead weight on him, like a fucking toddler having a tantrum, and plummeted to the floor.

"Oh, no, you don't," he growled and hiked her back up. He pinned her arm behind her and, with his free hand, delivered two hard swats to her rear. It felt better than anything he'd done in a long time.

She hollered, "*Ow!* Hey, what the fuck?" She sounded more shocked than anything else. He dealt her several more decent smacks, until her curses came as cries and she danced in place, unable to break from him. Really, he'd love to have spent about twenty minutes doing the thing properly, but it was time to get the fuck back to Earth.

"Be still," he ordered and sat her down on the bunk. She stared up at him, horrified. He reached over her for the safety gear. She wasn't going anywhere for the rest of the trip; she would stay right on this bunk, strapped in until they landed on Earth, and he could finally give her the boot. "Lie down," he said coldly.

"You can't do this!" She shoved at him, but he caught her arm and held it.

"Stop it," he said, "or you'll be really getting your ass whipped, like someone ought to have done a long time ago."

For the moment, this stilled her; he caught a glimpse of

the silent astonishment on her face as he wrapped the arm restraint around her torso. He pushed her onto her back, along the bunk, and clipped it to the side of the bed. The straps had been designed to keep a sleeping person from floating away during zero-G travel, but by looping them about her limbs—and not without a struggle, for his threat had already worn thin on her and she wrestled against him as he worked— he had her at last secured. Though not completely immobile, she wasn't going anywhere.

He sighed. Seeing her bound and helpless, he felt immensely better; the anger that had been twisting around in him since the creditors had appeared, lifted. Having just exerted himself in the struggle with her left him energized, pleasantly so. "We'll be on Earth in about twenty-six hours," he said, his tone almost upbeat.

"Twenty-six hours? How? You'd have to turn off the gravity for the whole trip!"

He cracked a smile; he couldn't help it. "And you don't?"

She blinked her eyes rapidly, anxiously, as she had earlier. "No, I don't. I can't. I can't do zero, it makes me really sick!"

He sighed, exasperated. "It makes everyone sick. Don't you have an implant?"

"I…" She glanced away. "I haven't wanted to pay for one yet."

"If you're a spacer, you get an implant," he said. He searched along the wall panel and found a vomit tube. "It's gonna be a tough couple of days for you," he said, not unsympathetically.

"No! I can't fly back in zero. Please don't." She was pleading now, so unlike the brat who'd spent the whole mission arguing with him. Her eyes were huge, shimmering. Her lips twitched.

He sighed. "This isn't a vacation for me, Miss Rivas. I have business back on Europa, and I don't have time to just cruise around with the gravity on. I need to get Callie somewhere safe, too, and quick. I'm sorry. I swear, I'm not doing this to make you miserable." He chuckled lightly at the last sentence, a habit he had whenever he did feel bad about something. All strapped down on the bunk, she looked sort of pathetic and cute and he even felt sorry for her. Really, who wasn't trying to outrun creditors these days? She'd lost a lot on the ship, and though he considered it her own fault, he knew it had to feel like a tough break to her.

He brought the mask at the end of the tube to her face, but she bit at him. He whisked his hand away agilely and gave her a light slap on the cheek. This startled her just enough to give him time to buckle the mask behind her head. He stood and took a step back.

"I'll check in on you in a few hours," he said. "Or, I guess, I'll have Walt do it. Somehow I don't think you'd want *me* helping you to the toilet."

She barked something at him, muffled by the mask; judging from how red her face had gone, he guessed it was along the lines of a "Fuck you."

———

"Who doesn't get an implant for zero these days?" Rhys asked, eight hours later in the mess with Callie and Walt. Walt caught blobs of something edible out of the air, while he and Callie stayed tethered comfortably to their stools. The lights in the mess ebbed a dim gold; all power in the ship had been diverted to the thrusters.

"Well," said Walt, between bites, "where we grew up, there are stories, you know," *gulp*, "of those procedures getting botched. Like, bad. Kids getting their eardrums ruptured. They ran the test clinics in the shitty neighborhoods."

Yeah, he had heard about that, maybe fifteen years back? Just before he got his ticket off Earth himself. Pretty fucked up; it made sense she'd be afraid. "But you have an implant, right?" he asked Walt.

Walter nodded. "Yeah, I got one before college. I went to school to be a pilot. Money ran out, and none of the corps picked me up." He shrugged.

"You're a damned good pilot," Rhys said. "You should join the force on Io City. They'd run you through the Academy on their dime, with a referral. Europa needs pilots right now."

Walt smiled distantly. "I'll have to think about that one. I'm not sure when I'll make it out that way. Looks like we're grounded for the time being."

We're. So, he planned on staying with her. What was she to him? Were they a couple? Somehow, he just couldn't see it. "I'm heading back to Io City right after we stop on Earth. I'm taking this ship, too, once it's tuned up. I'd be happy to have you as a pilot, and I'd write you a referral to the Academy myself if you like."

Walter stared for a moment. "Wow. Thanks." Then he dropped his head. "I'll have to think on that too."

Rhys couldn't help it anymore; he had to know. "How did you end up flying with *her*?"

Walt smiled again, enigmatic. "She's an old friend. Grew up near her in, well, you'd probably call it a slum. I got myself into some trouble when I was a teen, trying to sell contraband. She helped me out, she and her dad. Her dad was a… gambler, and he knew people."

"A gambler?"

"I think he fenced stuff too. So, he knew the round of

criminals. Anyway, it was a few years after I dropped out of school, and I got a wire from her saying she has this ship. I never got through my four years, so it seemed like my only chance to fly again."

Rhys nodded. It was clear Walt had more than a passing loyalty to Sydell. Even if it had tanked his own ambitions. "She really ought to have an implant," Rhys said finally, simply because he could find nothing else to say, or that he ought to say. His opinions were much more than that. Walt was a fool to go on traipsing after a train wreck; he should take up his offer to go to Europa if he knew what was good for him.

"I don't think she'll be in space again any time soon," said Walt mildly.

Callie spoke up, her voice bright and querulous. "I wonder if you couldn't find something for her to do here."

Rhys blinked at her. She'd been so vague, so subdued since the rescue, that it shocked him to hear her speak on something so directly, and about Sydell no less. "Here? On the ship?"

"Yes, when you head back to Europa."

He waved a hand at her, dismissive. "This isn't a good place for her. Obviously. She's impulsive."

"So are you," said Callie, giving him one of her slow, sweet smiles.

"That may be," he agreed, as always finding himself humble with his little sister. "But I know what I'm doing out here. She doesn't. Being ignorant and impulsive on a ship, is a death warrant."

"Maybe you could teach her some things."

"She would *not* like me as a teacher," said Rhys, shifting in his chair. Teaching someone like Sydell required more than stern words. She needed discipline, the real kind, the kind he'd learned to dole out back in the dark days when he'd worked for his brother. He'd only given her the briefest taste of it. No, she would not like it at all… and he would like it a little too much. Best to avoid that. But really, why should Callie care about what happened to Sydell? He couldn't recall his sister ever being the charitable sort.

"She did save us," Callie said, firmer. "Those guards would've hailed the top of the chain. She stopped them."

"All the same, it was stupid," said Rhys.

"Maybe, but she *was* brave. She could have just flown off and left us too."

"If I owe her anything, it's getting her to someplace safe," he said swiftly. "And this ship is not that. Enough, Callie. I'm not going to discuss it anymore."

But Callie, as he recalled with annoyance, had never been cowed by him. "At least make her comfortable. Last time I checked on her, she was miserable."

"Yeah, she's not keeping anything down," said Walt.

He sighed heavily. "It's not my fault she doesn't have an implant."

"Can't you give her something? An anti-emetic?" Callie asked.

Where did his sister learn that word? He'd been the field medic; she, well, technically, she had a degree in home design, but she'd never had a job. With her money, she'd never need one.

"Callie, please drop it," he said. "The trip will be over soon. We need to figure out where you're going to go. Walter, would you mind letting my sister and me have a moment in private?"

Walt nodded and floated gracefully out of the mess.

After a long talk, Rhys decided that Callie hadn't been brainwashed or psychologically damaged; Parsons had just attempted to tenaciously convince her to invest most of her money in his "businesses". Tenacity may move mountains, but it hadn't moved Callie.

When they were done, he went to the medical supply closet. No anti-emetics to be found. But there were some sedatives that might do the trick. He grabbed what he needed and headed for the bunks. He'd imagined Sydell had fallen asleep by now, but she had not. She lay, weak and retching dryly into the soft whirring of the vacuum vomit tube. Her eyes were dull, exhausted. She turned her head from him when he swooped in.

He used the handholds to traverse the room and swung in to the bedside next to her. He checked her pulse at the wrist; she started at his touch. Her heartbeat was rapid and faint; she was definitely dehydrated. If she couldn't keep anything down, then that was a problem.

"I'm going to give you a fluid tap," he said. She ignored him. He pulled out the bag and I.V. he'd taken from the supply room and hung the bag on a hook next to the bed, to keep it from floating away. He tapped gently at her arm for a vein. She flinched when the point went in but otherwise disregarded him. He unclipped the mask over her face. "I can sedate you if you like," he offered. "You'll sleep the rest of the way."

"If I puke in my sleep, won't I choke?" she piped. She'd actually answered. It surprised him, and he tried not to smile so she wouldn't know it pleased him that she had.

"It'll relax all your muscles. You won't puke."

"Okay." Her voice came out small and weary, and he felt a small jerk of sympathy for her. He tried to keep the syringe out of her sight as he prepped it; the kit was older and the needle large. But she glimpsed it out of the corner of her eye and started to protest. He shifted her onto her side, pushing her against the straps while she wriggled. As he'd guessed, her jumpsuit had snaps at the waist, and he unfastened them swiftly.

"No, not like that!" she yelped. "Put it in my arm!"

"You don't want this in your arm, believe me," he said, and then wished he'd phrased it better, because now she squirmed around, frantic.

"Don't move," he said sternly, "or this could really hurt you."

He swept the suit down past her rear and yanked aside the thin cotton of her panties, exposing just enough cheek to stab. She'd ceased moving but made a petulant moan, which had an effect on him, a bit stimulating and not unexpected. He disregarded it and went on with the routine, swab of alcohol, then the jab. She whined a curse, and it was over; he pulled the needle out and gave the spot on her bottom a quick rub, before he could think on it. Then he snapped her suit back into place.

"Listen," he said suddenly, as much a surprise to himself as it must be to her, "I'm flying this ship to Europa once I've taken Callie home. You ought to consider staying on board here as one of the crew. You know the ship well enough, and I'll find something for you to work on. You'll be paid. I'd expect your compliance, of course. You'd have to do everything I say. But you wouldn't have to leave the ship."

God, had he really just made her that offer? Why? He almost hoped she'd refuse. But before she could, he said stiffly, "Just sleep on it before you make a rash answer."

She rolled over onto her back again, wincing when her bottom pressed on the bunk. With the light above shining straight into her eyes, they were a topaz brown, not opaque at all, and rather pretty. But they narrowed at him in fury.

"You could have just put that in the I.V.," she said through her teeth.

He frowned. Then he chuckled. Really, it had been an honest mistake on his part, an oversight from having not been in practice for so many years. And having gone a bit too long without sleep. But no sense having her think he didn't have a mean streak, because after all, he did.

"You're right, I could have," he said with a smirk, and her face flushed red, her brows tightening together. Then, within seconds, her face relaxed; her eyes rolled up and her lids sunk down over them, as the drugs pulled her into an irresistible sleep.

Chapter 6

Opening her eyes, she quite expected to feel like hell, but other than some grogginess, she didn't seem too bad off. Must have been the fluid tap. Something had awakened her, and she lay blinking on the bunk, not sure what it had been. Oh, yes. The utter silence of the ship, engines off. They'd arrived on Earth.

She sat up, unhindered; someone must have taken the straps off her. Rhys? She flushed warm, suddenly angry, and hoped not. Her last memories of him were not fond ones, nor were any of them, really. But what had he been saying, before she passed out? Something about the ship. He'd offered to let her stay on and work for him, hadn't he? *You'd have to do everything I say.* A flood of hot, seething anger flowed into her veins. Fuck. That.

She had to get off this ship. It was his now, and so she hated it, as she did him. She had to get out before she saw his face again. An ache came up into her chest and throat, when she thought about leaving it, leaving behind all she'd been for three years. But it didn't matter now. She needed to find Walt.

She rushed up to her cabin, her eyes darting into every room in search of Rhys, so as to avoid him. The ship, however, felt empty. Would they all have just left, with her still onboard? Even Walt?

The loft was vacant, but her bed had been made neatly, an alien occurrence. Someone had slept here. She hurriedly packed up the most important of her things into a worn leather rucksack. She tried not to think about all the nights she'd spent here, looking up at the stars through the visiglass. That was done with. Now, it was back to Earth, back to the streets of that stagnant cesspool she'd been fighting to pull herself up out of. Hot tears prickled at her eyes.

Someone walked past the loft, out in the hall. She froze, dead certain it was *him*. She tightened up, crossed her arms over her chest. They stopped and circled back.

Walt stood in the doorway. "Sy? What are you doing?"

"Packing. I'm getting the fuck off this tin can. You coming?"

He smiled, but his eyes were sad. "Sy," he said gently, "I think we both need to take a minute and think about what the future's going to be."

God, he annoyed her when he talked so slowly, which he always did when he pandered to her. And she hated when he did that too. "I don't have a minute," she said. "I'm getting out of here before I have to see that septic ejection of a man again."

Now, he only looked bewildered. "Who, Rhys?" he guessed finally.

"Yes. *Rhys*." She said his name like it was the foulest of curse words.

"He's offered us both positions on the ship, Sy. I think you ought to consider it, at least."

She snorted in disgust. "Are you kidding me? After he

took over our ship, then stole it right out from under me? Then he went back on his word about giving us a bonus."

"Do you really believe all that?"

She scowled, unable to tell him "Yes" in all honesty. But it was how she felt about it all. Besides… "He's an asshole, Walt. He strapped me up with a vomit tube for half a day. And he hit me."

"You were going to vomit, Sy. What do you mean, he hit you?"

She suddenly didn't want to say. But she'd already brought it up. "Well, I was trying to get away, and he… he slapped me on the ass, like I was a fucking child."

Walter sighed. "Shit, I'm sorry, Sy, but you did try to pull a gun on him. And you know," his tone changed, becoming short with exasperation, "you do act like an awful child sometimes. Maybe you should just let it go."

She was stunned. Walt was taking that wolverine's side of things. "Are you actually thinking about staying?" she asked finally, sick of talking about what had happened. Partly because it embarrassed her, and partly because the more she was forced to dwell on it, the worse her side of the story started to seem, even to herself.

He scratched at his eyebrow. "I've already thought on it. I'm going to stay, as a pilot. It might be my only chance to have a career as one. He's going to give me a referral to Io Academy."

She swallowed as a pain flickered in her throat. She'd done next to nothing for his career; their time together had been near stagnation for him, probably. Rhys could actually do something real for Walt, and it made her hate him all the more for it. But she didn't have the heart to give her old friend grief for trying to better himself.

"I think you ought to stay too. It would be good for you." Walt sounded firmer than he normally did. Did he think less of her now? If so, she could only blame Rhys. There was no way she could stay on a ship where everyone looked down on her, and still be able to stand herself.

"That will never happen," she said, with enough intensity that she saw all the arguments die on his face. Gratifying, even if it made her unreasonably sad.

"I can't say when we'll meet again, then," he said. "I wish you the best."

It was so generic, she had to fight back tears. She murmured something equally bland and correct and then he left. The room blurred and she sat down heavily on the bed. She never thought she'd find herself estranged from Walt, not in a million years. She knew it was her own fault, but it was easier, for now, to shift the blame onto Rhys. She lay back on her bed, one last time, before she could think the better of it. The gray skies of Earth hovered over her through the skylight.

What would she do now? She didn't know anyone on Earth, not anymore. Her father hadn't been on the best terms with the gangs when he'd died. The only contact she had still was Ricky, and that had ended poorly, even if he was staying on at her apartment. She could try landing a job in the only unskilled professions left, caregiving and sex work. Both were corporatized and miserable. It was why she'd gotten off Earth in the first place, no prospects. Hot tears ran down her temples and splashed into her ears. She'd been kicked back to where she'd been three years ago, just like that.

But why should she submit to it? Rhys owed her for the ship, for the job. If he'd paid what he promised, she might have a chance to claw her way up again, somehow. Suddenly, she sat bolt upright, both elated and terrified. She was so certain of what she must do next, that she dared not think on it.

The halls of the ship were empty now as she made her way to the cockpit. It grabbed her attention the instant she walked in, still attached to the control panel; that small, black square, so inconsequential. The jammer.

It had used its charge up, but it still had to have a value, if only for a look at the tech alone. As valuable, at least, as her down payment, as her bonus. Maybe enough to get her another ship. Rhys owed her that much at least. He could afford another jammer, while she had lost everything. It was stealing. Of course, it was stealing. But she could live with that. Every other option was worse. She grabbed the jammer off the control panel and dropped it into her ruck-sack. She checked the storage compartment for her gun, but it was gone.

The second she had the jammer in her bag, the familiar tingle charged through her, made her all at once alert and alive. An old rush she hadn't felt in a long time. It was why her father had banned her from picking pockets for him, even when all the neighborhood kids did it and used him as a fence. She'd been left out, useless. But he'd probably been right to do it.

"It's an illusion," she remembered him saying. "Every-thing seems brighter, sharper. But it's not. If you feel that way, then you'll steal when you shouldn't, and you'll get caught for your arrogance."

She took a deep breath to cool her head. How would she get caught, anyway? Such a small item, and Rhys probably didn't even want it anymore. He wouldn't come after her. Would he? Another thrill surged up in her again, more potent than the first; in fact, she couldn't place it as a human feeling, it wasn't like one she'd ever had. A new kind of fear, exhilarating but terrible. Thinking of Rhys actually coming after her made her legs go weak, made her stomach pitch brutally in her belly. But what else could she do? No risk, no reward. She raced out of the cockpit and off the ship, listening to her boots clomp on the ground so as to drown out the rising doubts.

The station docks were a chaos of shuttles and speeder traffic, as they always were. Wedges of faded, cloud-filtered light made its way down through the shafts of the skyscrapers, and in the shadows, children rambled around the cargo bins. It would be a mistake to assume they were playing, though it certainly seemed that way; a thief's childhood had taught her otherwise. Most children in Neo York did not simply play. She clutched her rucksack tightly in both hands.

A monstrous flock of pigeons surrounded a vagrant as he ate a stale bagel near the docking waste bins, and she stopped as she approached him. She took one last look at her ship, her heart contracting at how small, how eccentric a contrast it made to the newer models docked around it. Like her spacesuit, it looked like a museum replica. She whirled away from it and took off rapidly down the street, scattering the pigeons as she did.

She had to sell the jammer as fast as possible. To do that, she needed a fence. It would have to be Ricky; he was the only one she knew who wouldn't have it out for her, who owed it to her even. So, she headed in the direction of her old neighborhood, expecting a long walk. To use a taxi, she'd have to engage credit, and that would put her on the grid. Rhys was bound to notice it had gone missing, and she didn't want him having any way to find her when he did.

Rhys stood for a long moment in the cockpit of the empty ship. Of course, she'd taken the jammer. Hardly a surprise.

She was a thief's kid, she was reckless, and she was desperate. He smiled. Having the tracker put in it at purchase hadn't been a waste after all. He got someone on her tail and went on with his business, finding a safe place to leave Callie until he could be sure she was stable, and then getting a crew up to the ship for repairs. It still tickled him to have had it fall into his lap like this; these older models had gone scarce of late on the market. It would be liberating to have his own little vessel; the larger ships could be slow, and with the newer serials everyone knew where you were all the time. Not ideal.

Sydell's location pinged up after about an hour, in a message from his contact. Making her way to the old state-sponsored neighborhoods, possibly going home. He should have been more annoyed by it; this cost him even more time, time he needed to get back to Europa. But the idea of catching her intrigued him. He'd catch her, and she'd learn painfully fast that she couldn't cross him, and really hadn't he been wanting to teach her that since almost the moment they'd met? It would be a good lesson for her, and of course, he would enjoy having her at his mercy. Callie was safe now and he would allow himself this indulgence.

He hired a cab at the docks; when he gave the driver the location, the man said, "There's no good sex out there, mister." Rhys ignored him and they drove off. Fifteen minutes later, they were on an empty street of seemingly abandoned buildings, and the driver said, "Watch yourself. It only *looks* like no one's out here."

"Oh, I know," said Rhys, smiling. He tipped the man well and stepped out onto a street caked along the edges with a paper-mâché of garbage. From the corner of his eye, a quick movement alerted him to a group of kids behind an old stoop; they watched him quietly, like hungry birds.

The taxi had left him next to a high rise, where he'd tracked her. It looked as though it had at one time been a hotel, back when people would have still come to this part of the city for any reason. Hotel converted to state housing, and then finally to an abandoned slum when the funding ceased. The main door to the lobby had been smashed in, but the interior still had carpet, though it peeled away from the edges and had gone waxy gray with filth. Infinity lights shone their hideous blue-white, while hall windows had been broken and "repaired" by cardboard wedged in and now reeking damp.

The ping on his holowrist told him she would be up on the fifth floor. The elevator door was gone, just a gaping entryway with no car. Next to it, a man in a crumpled black shirt stood with his back turned, having a smoke and dropping the ash down the shaft to the basement. Rhys headed up the stairs.

How could anyone still live here? Is this where she had grown up? No surprise she'd been desperate to leave, would do desperate things to avoid going back. But her decisions were going to get her somewhere even worse if she didn't learn quickly. Hopefully, he could scare some sense into her. Or, more accurately, smack it into her hide.

Many of the apartment doors hung open or had no doors; most occupants had tacked up sheets or clothing. But her door, the door to the apartment shown on his device, was a sturdy one, complete with an intact knob and lock. The door stood cracked open by about a half an inch, and before he could think to question his good luck, he pushed it open as quietly as he could.

The room he stepped into was at variance with what he'd seen in the rest of the building. It looked like a home. The carpet was worn, and the large sofa sitting square in the center had ragged holes, but nothing was overly filthy, and the place had a semblance of dignity to it, even. Next to an open window, sat a ping pong table, stacked high with books, and a variety of old photographs graced the broad spaces of walls. He made his way around the sofa in a silent search and peered into the room along the wall, what appeared to be the only bedroom. The window there had also been opened; inside, an old hospital bed, along with an I.V. stand. Otherwise, empty. An unused room that made him think instantly of death.

"Ricky, did you stock the fridge at all?" came Sydell's voice from the kitchen, flat with complaint. He rounded the sofa, trying to get a peek into the kitchen, to be sure she had no exits. He stopped next to the ping pong table and was standing there when she stepped into the doorway.

She froze. Her eyes grew enormous, and she looked near as she had when he'd told her they'd be going back to Earth in zero. Just horrified. She wore her jumpsuit still, but over it now was a blue moto style jacket in stiff silicone.

"Miss Rivas," he said with a politeness he hoped would unnerve her. She flinched when he said her name.

"You let yourself in," she said, the words stretched. The muscles on her neck stood out and he could hear the strain of it in her voice. He really scared her after all. Good.

"I have," he said, taking another step in her direction, hoping to make her run, admit her guilt, show him if there were another exit in the house. And if she ran, then he could catch her.

She stayed put. "To what do I owe your visit?"

That's how she would play it, then? He smiled; he knew just how scared she was and admired her a bit for her attempt at cool carelessness.

"I've been led here," he said, "by a tracking device I had installed on a valuable piece of property."

Her face drained of color, and some flicker of desperation passed over her face, something in a spasm at the corner of her mouth. He readied himself for her to run.

The door opened behind him. Oh fuck, she wasn't alone here. How could he be so stupid? Of course, she wasn't. She'd mistaken him for someone else when he'd come in. What was it she'd said? *Ricky?*

He turned and saw the man who'd been having a smoke down by the elevator. "Ricky, I'm guessing?" he said, grinning in a friendly way as he ran his eyes over the man for any sign of a weapon. Ricky had curly dark hair and a handsome but jowl heavy face; his movements were slow, and he didn't reach for his pockets.

"You don't know me," Ricky said, not stepping into the room. Scared, like Sydell. Scared and looking to jump ship.

"No, I don't know you," Rhys agreed. "And as long as you don't have my jammer, I don't care to."

"She still has it," said Ricky, gesturing heavily toward Sydell.

"Goddammit, Ricky!" she cried. "Don't you dare leave! After all my father did for you—"

"Don't." Ricky held up a hand, his face stony. "Your father's dead, and I don't owe a dead man a damn thing. Fuck knows I owe enough to the living."

"You've been staying at my apartment, you ungrateful shit!" she yelled.

He caught Rhys' eye, and Rhys nodded. Ricky glanced once more at Sydell, with just a touch of doggish guilt in his round, dark eyes. Then he shuffled off.

A sound escaped her, like a sob, but when Rhys looked back to her, her eyes were dry, and she faced him with as much cool hostility as before. If she hated him now, she was really going to hate him soon. He found himself engaged, for a moment, with the ping-pong table beside him, having seen it was complete with two wooden paddles and a ball. Perfect. He took one of the paddles up and said, "You didn't think this one through, did you? Like everything else you do."

"That's not your problem," she said, scornful. That's right, after what she'd done, and him catching her, she showed no remorse, just scorn. He would change that for damn sure. He grazed his thumb along the rubber handle of the paddle.

"You've made it my problem, I think." He met her eyes. She blinked swiftly in little jerks; it was her tell, he knew that now. He really had her wound up. She glanced at his hands as if she had some idea of what was coming.

"Your property is right here." She reached into her jacket pocket and took out the jammer, then tossed it his way. He caught it in his free hand, not even bothering to look at it.

He went on speaking as though nothing had happened. "You fucked with me, and you don't get to do that without answering to me. So. Tell me. Were you just being stupid, or did you want to get caught? Does going to prison seem like it would be any better than whatever life you had before you got your ship?"

She stepped back now, fully into the kitchen. He matched her step but got no closer than that. She shook her head, dismissive. "Where are the police?"

"No police. You'll be dealing with me, Miss Rivas."

"I gave you the jammer. If you haven't told the cops, then we're done here—"

"Are you really so foolish as to think you could steal from me and I wouldn't find you and personally make you pay?"

"You've taken everything I have. I can't pay you anything."

"Please spare me your self-pity." He turned the paddle

over in his hand; her eyes stayed glued to it, wider than ever.

He smiled. "You've grown up in the ranks of thieves, haven't you? What happens if you steal from a criminal? Does he call the cops? No. He tortures you, probably kills you. Right?"

She said nothing. He didn't expect her to. "Consider yourself lucky today. No cops, no jail, and you get out of this alive. As for the torture, well, it depends on your definition, I guess. Because right now I'm going to spank you, and I'm going to do a good job of it this time, too. It's what I've been wanting to do since you brought your problems down on my head and then pulled a fucking gun on me."

She turned red now, a slow, deep flush, all the way up to her forehead. "You won't touch me," she breathed. "You don't have any right—"

"It's you who has no rights here, brat. You've crossed the wrong man today."

He stepped toward her, and she slammed the kitchen door. The lock clicked behind it.

Dammit. "Sydell," he said calmly, "open the door. I'll still get in there if you don't, and then it'll only go worse for you. Grow up for once and take your punishment."

She spoke, too quiet for him to hear. But she wasn't talking to him. He leaned over, next to the door. She spoke tersely. Who was in there with her?

"Get away from the door," he warned. He gave the door one swift kick next to the knob and it snapped open. He charged into the kitchen and found her on the phone.

When she saw him there, she spoke up. "Yes, I've stolen it. He's still here, I don't know if he'll press charges. No, I—"

Rhys slammed his hand down on the screen, ending the call. She smiled at him, almost smugly.

"You little idiot," he growled.

"Why didn't you want to involve the police, Mr. Canton?" she asked with an arch sweetness. "Because the only reason I can think is that you aren't such a good citizen yourself."

Fucking hell. What had she done? "I didn't call the police because I wanted to deal with you myself," he snapped. "I didn't want you to go to a field prison for the rest of your life, which won't be a long one now, by the way. What the hell is wrong with you?"

He'd been utterly calm before, enjoying himself, but now anger swelled up in him, quick and hot. His hand tore out and he snatched her by the jacket, yanking her toward him. The move shocked her too much for her to struggle at first, and by the time she did, he already had her arms pinned to her sides and had dragged her out into the living room toward the sofa. With a shove, he doubled her over one side of it, so that she sprawled across it, her rear pitched high on the arm. He held her in place with one hand tightly gripping her jacket. She bucked back against him, but he kept a firm grip, so that she couldn't move but a few inches as she struggled.

"Stop it; let me up!" Her pitch rose in panic. "Stop!"

"Stop being a baby." He had the inkling to rip down her jumpsuit and thrash her bare ass but decided against it. Save her a shred of dignity, now that she was going to prison. Goddammit, how had he let this get so out of hand?

He landed the paddle square in the middle of her backside, and she gasped.

Twice, and she shouted something and tried to shield her bottom from him with one flailing arm. He gathered her jacket up behind her, so that her arms were confined by the taut material; they dangled helplessly beside her. He had about a half dozen in when she started squalling about it, and he paused.

"Do you know how much you've fucked yourself?" he scolded. "You've called in and confessed to stealing something worth over a million credits. They don't care if I don't press charges. You've committed a felony and you're going to jail now."

She burst into tears, as if on cue, but he hadn't finished yet.

"This is hardly fun now that you've wrecked your whole life," he said. "But I never punish someone by half. On principle."

He paddled her steadily, ignoring her kicks and shouts, holding her still as she squirmed, her hips writhing helplessly on the sofa's arm. When she finally shifted into sobs, he stopped. Considering she'd be heading straight to prison from here, he figured she'd had enough.

He let go of her jacket and stood back. "That's it, I'm done," he growled. How dare she do something so stupid and ruin her life, just to spite him? Thinking of her on the phone with the cops, made him want to grab her up and paddle her all over again.

She'd crawled over to the opposite end of the sofa and curled up on one end of it, hiding her face in her hands, twisting in her seat, he knew, to ease her burning rear. Her quick jerks of breaths ended in sniffles. How could he fix this? He couldn't, of course. She cried for a few minutes more, while he stood there thinking of some way she could be salvaged. She'd go to jail, definitely. Could she avoid field prison, though? Was this her first offense?

"How old are you?" he asked.

She peeped at him, frowning, clearly puzzled. "Twenty-six."

Right, no way they'd show any leniency for youth. He

stepped over to the sofa and sat down next to her on the edge of the cushion, not sure what to say. She buried her face deep in her jacket collar, broke into fresh tears, and without thinking on it, he reached over and rumpled her hair at the crown of her head, with a sigh. Before he knew what had happened, she'd leaned in and he was embracing her under one arm, her hot, wet face pressing into his neck. What the fuck was he doing?

"Dammit," he said under his breath. After a few minutes, her sobs softened, and her breathing slowed down.

"You're right," she mumbled.

"What?"

"You're right. About all of it. I didn't deserve that ship. My dad left me everything he had, and I tanked it on something I knew nothing about."

Deserve the ship? When had he said… oh, yes, just before she'd pulled the gun on him. So, she *had* been listening. And he'd finally broken through to her, now that it was too late. Something about her tone put him in mind of a criminal confessing to a priest the night before his execution. Not far off from the truth, really.

"He thought it was enough money to send me to school." She shook her head and leaned back against the couch. She kept her head lowered, her eyes hidden under her mess of dark hair, but the tears still ran down her cheeks and dripped off her nose in blobs.

"He had no idea what school costs. He may have been a thief, but god, he was naive." She laughed bitterly. "He died thinking I'd escape this place. And I thought I had. I thought it would be a great adventure. I know I was bad at it. And I dragged Walt down with me."

She turned her head fully away, saying in a low voice, "Thanks for doing what you are for Walt. He's a good pilot and he deserves it." She peeked up at him, then blushed bright red again and hid her face once more in her hands, though she made no more sound of crying. She went on, muffled. "You might be right. Maybe I did think it would be easier to go to prison than to have to work things out for myself here." She shrugged. "Some of us fail. That's just life, I guess."

"Hush," he said in a low voice. Hot anger crept up into his chest, at what they would do to her. But why should he be angry? She'd done all of this to herself. Why would he care enough to still be angry?

"Sydell, what you need…" And here he stopped, because it didn't matter. What she needed, he couldn't give her. He had to get back to Io City. A long moment passed, his mind racing, but he stayed silent.

Then the cops arrived. They spilled into the front door, four of them nearly on top of one another, with ionic pistols and shock sticks at the fore. Sydell gasped and backed up into him; for a moment, he caught her in his arms and held her close. Then she broke away and stood.

"I'm the one who called," she said, defiant, but her hands trembled. Within seconds, they had her on the floor and barked orders at Rhys. He stood, hands vaguely raised, as they wrapped a null crown onto her head. She gave him a look of pure terror just before her eyes blanked out.

"We'll need you to come down with us, too, for questioning," said one; he wore the gleaming gold weave jacket that the captains did.

"Mmm," Rhys grumbled, looking out the window.

"You can come with us willingly, or like her," the captain said, apparently really needing to assert himself. Rhys rolled his eyes.

"I understand," said Rhys slowly, as though the captain

were a small, stupid child. He followed them as they made their way out, with Sydell held and carried between the four of them, a limb for each. Something about them carrying her like that infuriated him.

He glanced back once more into her sad little apartment as he left. He knew what he would have to do.

Chapter 7

A line of dazed men and women in hideous tomato red jumpsuits trailed infinitely back along the domed cement corridor. "You'll meet with an arbiter," they'd told her, "and then the judiciary. Then you'll be assigned your sentence." The sentence itself did not seem to be at all in question.

With the null crown removed, she was left temporarily dulled in mind and spirit. What little mental energy she had, she spent ruminating on everything she had heard about field prisons—large, open clearings, surrounded by electrical fencing and some sport shooters, but otherwise no interference with the inmates, a frigid mud pit in the winter, a parched desert in summer, with concrete barracks to sleep in, food dropped by air—and never enough of it. Prisons did not get overpopulated. The prisoners took care of that.

Of course, that had all been hearsay. Most people didn't talk much about field prisons, except perhaps to grumble that they'd become "a necessity". The aftereffects of the null crown spared her some of the abject terror she ought to be feeling, whether the tales were exaggerated or not. It blunted the shame, too.

She knew she should feel ashamed after what had happened with Rhys. He'd turned her up and paddled her like she was a naughty student at some old-fashioned boarding school. Too ridiculous; the memories returned almost the way dreams did, surreal and distorted. She remembered how much it had stung, the swift escalation of pain only slightly eclipsing the radiant humiliation of it. To make it worse, she'd gone all blubbery on him, telling him what must have seemed like a sob story. Yet despite it all, she had ceased to be angry with him, inexplicably. She hated no one but herself now for everything that had happened, and he must hate her too; thank God she would never have to see him again.

Her thoughts slowly roused her from the dulled state, as the wait stretched out. Crammed tightly in line, corralled like cattle for the slaughter, she had an urge to scream. The row of infinity lights above drilled into her skull.

At long last, she arrived at the security gate. A guard with a black plastoid baton gestured her way, with a jabbing motion.

"Name," he demanded, as dull as the rest of them. He differed only in having a touch of dangerous impatience, which she could sense at the tip of the baton as it hovered closer to her ribs.

"Sydell. Rivas."

He typed it onto an old holopad. "Larceny, class one. Oh-kay. Plea?"

"What?"

"What's your plea?"

"Don't I see my lawyer first? Doesn't this part happen at trial?"

The guard rolled his eyes. "The judiciary doesn't have time for that. We do preliminaries here, then trial. Then you see your arbiter. Now, *your plea*."

"What's the charge again?"

"Larceny, class one. Don't waste my goddamn time."

Was there leniency for a guilty plea? Or would it be better to say she hadn't stolen it, that it had been a mistake? They had her confession, on the phone, probably a statement from Rhys as well. No point lying about it. With a resigned breath, she said, "Guilty."

He gave a satisfied nod. "Proceed."

She entered the security gate. The corridor ended and opened into a massive steel enclosure, flooded with more infinity light than she'd ever seen. The dirt floor made her think of a cattle auction. She began to shake, her jumpsuit growing damp with cold sweat. Prisoners flooded into the enclosure from all directions, separated by a labyrinth of chain link fencing. She was a drop in this ocean of people. She was nothing.

Over a local speaker on the fence, bursting through with static, sounded, "Sydell Rivas!" and made her jump. She'd been crumpled in the dirt, as far from others as possible, and nodded off at some point. Now her heart jerked into a raucous beating that made her sick. The clusters of chain link had some sense after all; they separated the mass of the enclosure into smaller "courts," complete with floating screens. After a moment, the judiciary came into view on the hovering holoscreen. She was an older woman, with a pale white face and a round, red nose, as though all the blood had been squeezed into the tip.

"Ms. Rivas, you will convene with your arbiter," she

said, her voice metallic, as one's gets from smoking too much. Another floating screen flickered to life on the chain link, near her shoulder. She backed away as a squirrelly man with a long, dark ponytail appeared there, life-size, clearly sitting in a cluttered room somewhere. Deep lines showed beneath his bored, weary eyes.

"You pled guilty," he said in a monotone; it was obvious he thought that this was a waste of his time.

"I had no counsel," she hissed. "Besides, they have evidence, testimonies… isn't there some leniency for a guilty plea?"

He shrugged. "If you've got anything to offer."

"What, like money?"

He rolled his eyes. "Names. Like, of people who may have helped you, or other criminals."

Ricky. It would just be Ricky. He had helped her, or offered to, just before he'd abandoned her. And for all she knew, he might have gone back to her apartment right after her arrest. Piece of shit.

But she wasn't a rat. "May I change my plea?" she asked.

"Stupid, at this point." He ate a spoonful of something. Cereal. This mosquito of a man was eating a bowl of cereal, right now.

"How professional you are," Sydell muttered, loud enough to be heard, but he didn't react at all to her sarcasm. "Do you have *any* incentive to help me?" she said acidly.

He looked her dead in the eye. "How could I? I'm employed by At Peace, so is the judiciary. But it's traditional to have an arbiter." He waved his hand. "Part of the Bill of Rights and all."

At Peace? She racked her brain. Wasn't At Peace the name of the largest prison corp? Yes, that was it! And that's who they *worked for*. "In that case, fuck off," she said with disgust.

He coughed on the cereal but recovered quickly. "Is that what you want?"

"Is there nothing I can do to improve my situation?"

He flinched impatiently. "No. Serve your sentence. Best case scenario, a corp picks up your papers and impresses you. It's not always an improvement, though."

She fell silent, engulfed in despair. At some point, the arbiter logged off.

"Sydell Rivas," said the judiciary. "With a guilty plea, this process is sped along, and no evidence need be admitted. Since this is your first offense on record, I hereby sentence you to twelve years at Neo York State Field Penitentiary. Your name has been submitted to eligible corporations for a work release, but as this is a class one offense, you have no possibility of parole."

Twelve years? A dull, terrible pain rose in her throat and stuck there, refusing to become tears. She should cry, but she couldn't. She should scream, curse this hologram of a human being. But it would be pointless. She couldn't think on it now, on the idea of *years*. She would lose her mind if she did. She just had to get through the end of the trial, get through the day without losing it completely. At some point tonight, she would be alone, in privacy; she could weep in the darkness with no one to see her. At some point, she would have solitude. Wouldn't she?

"Take her to the bunker," said the bailiff. The guard sidled up next to her, his stun baton humming threateningly.

"What?" she cried. "Am I going to the prison now?"

"No," said the guard with ragged impatience, "The bus only runs in the mornings. You spend the night in the bunker."

Herded in with the crowds who had finished their trials as well, she made her way out of the huge building, to a flat waste she could not recognize. Some buildings in the distance might have been Neo York. If so, she'd been brought much farther out of the city than she'd supposed.

She and the others were moved into a cylindrical steel building, smaller by far than the last. At the door, a guard issued her a new jumpsuit, ordering her to change right there. She fought back tears, but seeing the apathy of everyone around mollified her. They did not care, or were too wrapped up in their own sufferings to care, for now.

Her new jumpsuit had a stiffness to it and a strong chemical smell. Something dark had stained the lower midsection. Blood? Yes, and around the stain, the fabric had been re-stitched, further suggesting violence. A sweeping cold wave of nausea crashed over her. Tears spilled onto her cheeks beyond her control; she was too scared to care. Another inmate slammed into her, and she stumbled to her knees, where she remained, too frightened to move or check to see whether it had been accidental or deliberate.

"*Rivas!*" The guard had shouted, but sounds came distant and muted, as though she were underwater.

"Rivas!" A hand grabbed her hair, standing her up painfully. "This way."

He gestured to a tunnel leading out of the silo, to God knew where. He wanted to take her away from the others into some dark spot… her mind could only light upon hideous reasons. But it did not matter. He wielded the stun baton and seemed willing, even hopeful, to use it. She moved off into the corridor.

He pushed her into a room behind a swinging metal door. Lit by a single infinity bulb, the room appeared to be an office, in miniature. The desk stretched nearly wall to wall, the man behind it just small enough of frame to fit there. He wore horn-rimmed glasses and held a blue folder in his hands.

"Sydell Rivas?" he asked mechanically, like he was checking a box in a column.

"Yes," she creaked, barely audible.

"I have some things for you to sign." He pulled two sheets of paper out from the folder.

"What is it?"

He waved a pale, thin hand. "It's out-processing paper-work. You've been flagged for recruitment."

"Recruitment?"

"A work release," he said with a fatigued impatience. "But we have to have your permission. Believe me when I say, you should sign it." There was no spark of concern for her when he said it; it was a factual assessment that he made and relayed, only.

She peered down at the papers spread on the desk. The words crowded around each other strangely, making her dizzy. "I-I can't read that."

"Have you had a null crown on?"

She nodded.

"All right. I'll sum it up. It says, essentially, that you're to become a recruit of Canton Excavations for as long as their terms require. There's no term stated here, which isn't unusual. They may intend to keep you longer than your sentence. But you won't be serving it out at Neo York Field Penitentiary. Your debt to At Peace has been paid."

Debt. So, some company had bought her? "Excava-tions?" she breathed. Would she be working in mines? Where?

A man stuck his head in the door and said, "The repre-sentative is here."

"Very well, send him in. Really, we need to wrap this up, I have thirty-six more today."

Thirty-six more what? Did he mean people to process, for recruitment? She had no chance to ask, because the door swung open all the way and then Rhys stepped in.

Rhys. Rhys Canton. Canton Excavations. A wave of relief and, well, *joy*, hit her the moment he appeared. It blotted out everything else that she remembered she ought to feel. She should hate him, for how he'd treated her. But right now, she couldn't and didn't.

She'd not really noted before how tall he was, perhaps it was the ridiculously small room. He seemed out of place here, even dressed in casual clothes, a plaid shirt, attractively tight around his broad shoulders and arms, and fitted jeans. His auburn hair seemed darker, his hairline higher than she remembered, and his eyes kinder. He gave a curt nod to her as greeting, and all the gruesome shame of breaking down in front of him overcame her, and she caught the back of an empty chair so as not to topple over with light-headedness.

"Are you okay?" he asked, stepping in closer, the familiar irritated expression returning to his features, his eyes sharp again, taking over what had been that open look of… had it been anticipation? Concern? She couldn't be sure now. She nodded, forcing herself to stand upright.

"Have they told you what I'm offering?" he asked.

"They said I was being recruited. By Rhysling Excavations."

He gave her a small smile, which made her heart pound.

"Canton Excavations," he corrected mildly. "Which is the company I own. I'm making you the same offer I did on the ship, before you stole my jammer. You'll work for me on the ship until we get to Io City. Then, you'll be working for me there, for my company. The terms are the same as before, except now you'll legally belong to Canton Excavations. You'll answer to me. You won't be in prison, but you won't be free, either. You have to obey me and my team. Do you understand?"

She bristled at the terms, physically so. A weird, prickly heat crawled through her, from her face downwards. "How long?" she asked through her teeth. No term had been stated, but surely it couldn't be longer than her twelve year sentence?

"Until I think you're ready for your freedom."

Her blood went hot under her skin. The fucking arrogance of it! No surprise, though, not from him. She caught her tongue, as she remembered that he owed her nothing. Yet he'd come here and done this. Why? Could he still be angry with her for stealing from him? Did he want to make her pay, himself? Would she be able to escape him if it got to be too hateful? She glared into his eyes, thinking on it, and she felt he must know her thoughts. Held by his gaze, a dark sensation of falling overcame her, the fall one has in a dream, slow and eternal and breathless. No. She had more chance of escaping the field prison, than she did him. She knew it in her bones.

He went on, his tone cool, almost businesslike. "Honestly, I don't foresee you being obedient. You haven't been, not in any of our dealings. So, I'll reserve the right to discipline you, just like I already have. With a paddle, or any other way I think fit. Just putting it out there."

The room grew smaller, somehow? Pulsated? She stepped back from him, but the floor seemed to move beneath her, like the floor of a ship at sea. She clutched the back of the chair again, as a blurred darkness swarmed her head, a hot vertigo. One of the guards sniggered. The realization of having an audience as Rhys so casually discussed it, burned into her, brought her back to herself. Her muscles tensed. What a pleasure it would be to laugh and spit in Rhys Canton's face. He'd lose, in a way. So would she, but she was willing to make the sacrifice.

"Who the fuck do you think you are?" she groaned, some demon of rage giving her courage. Courage to face him, the guards, all twelve years of prison life, or death in prison if she had to.

He sighed, his jaw relaxing a little, and he tilted his head. The lines at the corners of his muddy green eyes softened. "I'm someone who cares just enough to help you out. You might not like every minute of it, but I promise it will be better than if you stay here."

This set the world rocking once more. Her head felt light, like it was floating off her body. What the fuck was going on? Was it the null crown wearing off? No, she couldn't believe he cared about what happened to her, after everything. Why should he? Yet his face... he almost looked like he was making an appeal.

"Ms. Rivas," said the man from behind the desk, his tone so injured, one might think he'd been waiting several hours for her to make a decision.

She'd been overjoyed when Rhys had first stepped in. If he were to leave here without her... no, that couldn't happen, she couldn't bear it. The instinct to go with him outweighed the urge to blow it all to smithereens, though that urge was strong too.

"All right," she said stoically, "I'll go with you." All at once. she felt buoyant, like a great weight on her had evaporated. For a split second, she could swear he looked relieved, too, and did a smile trace his lips? But just as rapidly his mouth set somberly, and his brows pinched together.

"Then let's go," he said. "We'll be making a stop to fit

you with a zero-g implant, then we take off. You can rest on the ship."

"Wait, what—" But she stopped herself, partly because his eyes narrowed, threateningly, and partly because it would be stupid to argue. She couldn't spend the whole flight strapped to a vomit tube. She signed the paper for the little man behind the desk, avoiding the glances of the guards.

"Come on," said Rhys impatiently. "Let's get out of this hellhole." And then he pushed open the metal door, and she followed him out.

———

Sitting at a wrought iron table at a cafe in uptown, he watched as Callie nibbled at her croissant. She'd never been a big eater, but something about her interaction with the food disturbed him, as though it were unreal to her or, more accurately, that she was not real enough to eat it. Was she changed, somehow, from before?

He tried to shake the strange impression and stretched out his arms under the sun lamps. They could almost fool his brain into thinking it was a fine summer day and not overcast, as every day on Earth had been since he was five years old.

"This is a nice place," she said. "Reminds me of that trip to Paris, before the fires."

"Yeah, we were lucky to see it before that happened," he said dryly and sipped his coffee. After a few moments, he said, "It's all going to be very normal, don't worry. You'll have your own apartment, ocean front. You'll be free to go about as you please, on the grounds."

"On the grounds," she said, with a smile and a shake of her head. She'd tied her delicate peachy hair back, and a swathe of freckles stood out on her round, pale forehead.

"I just want you to be looked after. You'll have access to care staff twenty-four seven. You'll have a personal therapist—"

"Rhys," she said. "It's okay. I get it. I think *you* feel guilty about it, though."

He shrugged, uncomfortable. Of course, he felt guilty. He'd missed this somehow, his people who kept tabs on Parsons had missed the fact that he'd been planning to take Callie. And now that he had her back, he had to leave again, and leave her at a sanitarium. Albeit an incredibly upscale one, more of a luxury retreat than anything else. The security couldn't be beat. But still, it didn't feel great.

"Do you think she'll try to run away?"

"What?" His head snapped up as she shook him out of his thoughts. Would who run away? Oh. Her. He laughed lightly. "She's unconscious right now. Getting the implant. But, no, I don't think she will. Outside of my custody, she's a felon."

"I hope you can trust her."

"I trust her to be impulsive. But she won't be stealing from me again, that's for sure. When we get to Europa, she'll have a job there, and she'll settle down." Getting her settled would be trying for them both, in different ways, but it would happen. It would bite her some, but she really was getting the better end of the deal, all things considered.

"How is Canton Excavations?" She leaned back from her plate. "I haven't heard a thing about it in ages."

"I know, I'm sorry, I haven't been able to write. I don't trust the wires. The Council has some idea of what we've got under Io City, even if they pretend not to."

"Under the city… you mean the ruins?"

"Yes. Dad bought up most of those caves from the city, back when no one cared. Claimed them as excavations. But now Europa Council's getting curious." Not simply curious. Greedy. Like all governments.

"I mean, the aliens lived down there." She wrapped her little hands around her teacup. "Well, not aliens, I guess. Europans. I'd think Io City would have been more interested."

"They were, a bit, but there wasn't anything down there. Nothing as big as the city shell. Really, they were a lot more interested in getting Dad's money at the time, so they let him buy what he wanted."

He stirred his coffee and lowered his voice. "Callie. There's something down there. In the caves. We found a chamber with markings all over it. Like, gashes in the rock. *They* put it there and it has to mean something."

"The aliens put it there?"

"We know nothing about them. They left this giant shell that we use as a city, and as far as we know, they just disappeared. This stuff I found, this, like, writing or, or really, it seems more like a mathematical pattern. It might tell us why they left, or better still, *how*."

Now that he'd said it to someone, out in the open, it felt unreal.

"How?" she asked.

"I mean, where they went and how they went there. It might explain faster than light travel."

"You think they left the system?"

"We haven't found signs of them anywhere else. With some of the things they were able to do to Europa, I think they had the tech."

She nodded. She looked less incredulous than his business partner had been when he'd first told him about it. But she also did not seem entirely coherent. Maybe he shouldn't have told her. She really just needed to rest, not be bothered with things like this.

"Will you go that far away?" she asked.

He frowned. What did she mean by that? Then it dawned on him. "No, Callie, of course not. Even if we figured it out, faster than light would take a long time to develop. I'm just hoping to be able to uncover it."

She smiled. "I hope you figure it out."

"I'm going to come back soon. You know that, right?"

She nodded vaguely. Probably didn't believe him, and he didn't blame her. If it wouldn't be so easy for Parsons to take her again, he would bring her with him to Io City. But, no, she was much safer on Earth. After all, she'd been kidnapped during spaceflight. Parsons had methods of getting around the system that spun the heads of all three governments.

It's safer here, he told himself again. He just couldn't shake the feeling that she was different, somehow, than before the kidnapping. But he wasn't the best judge. He hadn't even spent this much time with her in several years.

They finished breakfast in a relaxed silence. Callie never had been one to prattle for the sake of filling air. Just as he finished his food, the alert went off on his holowrist.

"This is goodbye, then?" she asked.

"Well, it's just the alarm I set. I want to be there before she wakes up. She seemed pretty convinced everything would go wrong." She didn't trust people, didn't trust authority. But she would learn to accept authority, learn that she couldn't elude it forever. He'd make sure of that.

"I can't blame her," Callie said.

"This isn't a slum clinic. Jesus, I booked her at the best surgeon in the city."

"Good. Be there for her when she wakes up."

He laughed. "I just want to be there when she finds out it all went fine and that she was wrong."

"Well, I want to get to my new apartment."

He sighed. She was trying to make it easier for him.

He ordered her a cab and they said their goodbyes. He left before it arrived, moving at a clip along the street in the direction of the surgeon. When he went around the corner, he glanced back and saw her at the table, small and strange and still handling the croissant as though it were an alien object.

Chapter 8

"Sydell," he repeated, sharper this time.

The drugs from the surgery hadn't quite worn off her yet; he could tell by her dazed expression. Her large, dark eyes were still unfocused as she took in the ship confusedly. He'd changed a few things, sure, but the substance was no different. In fact, most of the crew he'd hired had been disappointed that he'd kept much of the original materials and not changed the interiors to the sleeker, more modern designs. Those, he insisted, would have looked terrible in such small spaces. And why change a classic?

"Come on, you're going to your quarters," he said. She looked like she could use about a day and a half of sleep. She trailed after him, peering into the rooms and dodging the crew as they bustled about. Her discomfort was palpable.

He stopped at a narrow door. She stared up at him. "This is a storage cubby," she said.

"It was." He opened the door. He'd converted it into a room on the off-chance of having a passenger who wanted to bunk separately. The bed lay wall to wall. "I thought you might like to have a space to yourself. Some privacy."

She gazed up at him oddly, her eyes wide. Had he horrified her? Maybe so, maybe she thought this was just an attempt to make things hard on her. Well, things would be hard on her, yes, but honestly, he had intended that having a separate room would make her feel better.

"Okay," she said, then bent her head. "Thanks."

He'd definitely not expected that. He kept up his stern tone, however. "Get as much sleep as you need. When you wake up, you're to report to me. I'll give you some work to do. Got it?"

She nodded. He would've preferred a verbal response but given her state, he let it go. "I'm set up in the captain's loft," he said and waited for her reaction. It was her old room, after all. Her eyes darted to him, and her lips pressed together. But she only nodded, again.

He said, "There's a pair of grav boots under your bunk. I installed a generator on the ship, but we'll transition in and out of using it, so be prepared to lose and gain gravities without notice. You'll get used to it quickly. Goodnight."

He left her abruptly, stepping back into the hall. She'd already slumped down onto the bed, staring at him with wary exhaustion as he shut the door on her. Then he made his way to Walter, in the cockpit.

They left for Europa within the hour, on what would be a six week journey. Jupiter and the moons were not at an ideal distance for it, but the ship was fast, though he hadn't upgraded the engines yet. He could get better tech on the moons.

Sydell came up to his loft after about sixteen hours. Her hair hung loose about her face now, but at least she'd brushed it. The emerald streak curved under her chin like the claw of some strange sea creature. Much of the haggard horror on her face since her imprisonment had vanished, and she looked well rested, though her eyebrows were drawn together in a peevish frown.

"Good morning," he said with a sincere cheerfulness. Nothing made him feel better than getting going toward his destination. She spoke little as he led them down into the sub-engine rooms at the lowest level of the ship.

"If you're going to be working here, I want you to know the ship well, every little part," he said. The lights in the hold snapped on as they walked in.

"I know this ship pretty well," she said. Her voice was soft, but her eyes narrowed.

"Do you?" he asked, leaning toward her, his arms crossed. He gestured toward the oxygen scrubbers. "What are those?"

She shrugged. "I know the ship. I don't know exactly how every little thing works." She said it in such a way that made it sound as though it were too dull for her to be bothered with it.

He smiled. "These recycle our breathable atmosphere. Without them, carbon dioxide builds up and we die. Is that too boring for you?"

She regarded him now with a gleam of hatred in her eye, which he found oddly satisfying.

"You'll be cleaning out all the filters," he said cheerily. "You need to do them one at a time."

Her lips curled down. The hate gleamed brighter, but she said nothing.

"Come on, I'll show you how."

As he'd instructed, she returned to him in his loft once she'd finished, having taken considerably longer to do the job than anyone he'd known. No surprise there. She gazed around the room, taking in the changes. He hadn't done too much, put in a larger bed, with a better mattress, and he'd added in a desk at the center of the room and a drafting table along the wall. Both the desk and the table were cluttered with his various projects, but he'd made the bed with military precision.

He remained seated at his desk when she stepped in. "All right. Now I'd like you to go through all the bunks on the ship and run the bedding through the dry wash. Do you know how it works?"

"Yes," she said, barely moving her set mouth. She lowered her face, so he couldn't see her eyes under all the messy pieces of her hair. Maybe he should just get out his scissors and chop the layers short, into fringe, right now.

"You can start with what's here," he said, waving at his own bed, and then he settled back to his papers.

"Oh-kay," she said, drawing the word out mockingly, as though he were being ridiculous. Then she went about pulling the bedding off the square of mattress, huffing and tugging at the tight tucked corners, and muttering a little to herself. After a few minutes of this, when he caught a few elaborate curses from her, he said, "I'm sorry, I missed that. What did you say?" He spun the chair so that he faced her.

"I was talking to myself," she grumbled.

"You're not alone and it was loud enough for me to hear. It wouldn't be polite of you not to share." He spoke lightly but put an edge to his words and noticed her muscles tense as she rose from where she'd been bent. The resentful pout on her face wavered as she looked up at him. Then she dropped the bedding she'd been holding and said, "Fine," in the tone of someone ready to pull the pin on a grenade tied to their chest.

Here we go. He crossed his arms, straightening up in his chair, and waited.

"I think it's petty of you to take me on like this, just to

punish me for stealing from you. As revenge goes, it's just sad, really." Her head swayed as she spoke. "It's pathetic."

"You want a more substantial punishment?" he asked. "That seemed to make you cry."

She grew silent, her cheeks flooding pink, and he could practically smell the rage wafting off her. He shook his head. "Revenge. Don't be absurd. I only took what you might call revenge, once. And that's done. What you did doesn't figure into anything that you do here. I don't even think about it. Let it go."

At his last words, her face flinched, like he'd slapped her. "Then why are you singling me out to do all this grunt work?" she asked.

He sighed. "Because you need something to do, and it's the only work you're qualified to do here. That's not my fault."

"I know this ship far better than you think I do."

"Then prove it. Prove that there's something else you can do here that's useful, and I'll gladly have you do it. In the meantime, you should reconsider throwing insults around. I don't think on the past much, but I do make a habit of avenging fresh injuries. And you know my methods."

She shrunk away from him, like a coiling, angry snake. Cautious, but still considering the success of taking a strike. *Go on, do it*, he thought. See what happens.

Instead, she went back to tugging the sheets off his bed silently. The contention had not ended, just been postponed. She'd test him soon and he'd be more than ready for it when she did. He had a paddle in his desk drawer with her name on it, figuratively speaking, and this one had holes drilled in. Part of him wanted to use it on her right now, but he'd rather she forced his hand.

He smiled at her scowling face and took up his holoscreen, going back to studying the pattern from the cave under Io City. He'd taken to calling it "the code" and of late, much of his free time was spent in trying to crack it if such a thing were possible. It so absorbed him that he didn't even notice when she left.

———

She hated every part of the ship, now. Everywhere but that little room which used to be a storage closet. He was making her sleep in a goddamned closet. Yet, the small, enclosed darkness of it calmed her, and she liked to retreat there when she finished with whatever new, dismal task he'd given her.

She didn't want to see or talk to anyone on the ship, not even Walter. She could sense his cool disapproval at what she'd done with the jammer. The crew Rhys had hired were all strangers, and who knew what they'd heard about her, about how she'd come to be onboard? Besides, they were all Rhys' people, best avoided. Most of all, she wanted to avoid Rhys himself, but it wasn't possible, as he insisted that she keep checking in with him daily, so he could give her things to do. She tried as best as she could not to run into him at any other time.

Sometimes, though, alone in her room, she could remember feeling almost comforted by him as he'd held her on her sofa. That flood of warmth, the memory, came to her some nights just before she fell asleep, so that she never had to really think on it. If only she could just forget all of it.

At three weeks into the journey, as she lay sprawled out on her bunk looking at pictures of Io City on her holo-screen —or more accurately, the holoscreen Rhys had lent her— she became aware of an eerie silence. Then the grav shifted, slowly, giving her a sinking feeling and a dull nausea at her core, one which no ear implant could ever fix. But her weight was back, and it felt so strange! And the silence, the engines. The constant hum of the engines had ceased. They'd halted thrusters, so the grav generator had come back on. But why?

She sat up, her mouth dry and her heart racing. What was wrong? She switched on the overhead lights and found they'd downshifted into the red glow of low power, and it did nothing to comfort her. The intercom crackled on. "This is the captain," Rhys said. He sounded weary, but not at all alarmed, and she leaned back on her bunk, letting out her breath as her stomach muscles relaxed.

"We seem to have been side-swiped by a solar flare and our engines were disabled. We're on the ionic backup generator for the time being. If you have any experience with older reactors, please report to me on C deck. I could use a hand."

Didn't apply to her, thankfully. She'd never messed around with the engines; sometimes Walt had, but the computer system had been pretty good at keeping everything in tune. What did it look like, now that it was powered down? Would anyone even notice if she just walked through and took a peek? She didn't want to sit alone in this closet through the power down, anyway. She leapt up, snapped off her grav boots and headed for C deck.

She ducked into one of the bunk rooms in the hall, so as not to be noticed. She peeked around the doorway, but Rhys saw her immediately. He gave her a cursory nod and went back to what he'd been doing, kneeling at the wall panel next to the engine room door. He'd taken the panel door off of it and had his hands wrist deep in the wiring. After a moment, one of the crew appeared at the hatch from the level above and jumped the short distance into the hall, ignoring the ladder. A short, bald man with a long nose and safety glasses; vaguely, she recalled seeing him perhaps once before; he was the technician.

"Sealed?" he asked pleasantly, as if he'd expected it.

"Yeah," said Rhys, a bit short, and frowned at the panel.

"It's a computer override. Some kind of older security measure. You can't fix it from this side."

"Can't really get to the panel on the other side."

"No, we've got to get in through the system. Came by to tell you I was on it."

"Okay," said Rhys, standing. "Thanks." He gave his wrist a shake, as though he'd hurt it in some way.

She had stepped out into the hall, her mouth open, and had been about to tell him about the other way to get inside, but instead, she just grinned at him foolishly. Why should she tell him? He didn't deserve that information. But what if… what if she got the door open herself? She ducked off down the hall, afraid he would get some idea of what she was up to. Yes, she could get the door open herself; that would show him. Show him she knew the ship and could do something about it. She pictured announcing that she'd gotten the door open herself, and she smiled. Too sweet to resist.

She jogged toward the airlock, hoping they didn't know about the vent. Why would they? From what she remembered, it had only been installed on this sub series. It wasn't even on the posted blueprints of the ship; she only knew about it from her own explorations. It really was just meant to be.

A little voice piped up in her, said that maybe going into the reactor through the vent could be dangerous, and of course, Rhys wouldn't want her doing something dangerous. The vent was in place for emergency overheating, in which case, the airlock, which it opened into, would lock down. But with the reactor disabled, that couldn't happen. Really, the gains were too great not to do it. Showing Rhys up was too alluring.

In the airlock, her bulky suit had gone, and all around the circle of the room hung more of those lightweight, expensive green models. Rhys had put a lot of money into this ship. He'd really made it his own. But he still didn't know about the vent.

She slipped off her jacket and hung it on one of the hooks atop a suit. Even in just her jumpsuit, it would be a tight squeeze. Some kind of new cabinet had appeared in the airlock, the perfect height for getting her up to the shaft. Curious, she opened the cabinet door and found it had med-kits, gauze, and, of course, blankets. She sighed and hoisted herself on top of it.

Once up, she stretched toward the vent opening, at the ceiling, shoving both arms in and trying to wedge her body into the mouth of it. She kicked her legs madly, trying to boost herself up on anything. She swung her leg to the left and caught on what felt like one of the hooks; she curled her foot around it and pushed, managing to boost herself by about an inch, which was all she needed. Then she jammed her arms against the siding and wriggled until the rest of her body followed. A tight fit, but she could move forward.

The air smelled strange, metallic; it made her throat tingle. It felt almost charged, like the air during a lightning storm. Compacted in the small space, she began to grow warm, and then after another moment, almost hot. So hot, she could swear the vent had been heated if she didn't know better. Could the reactor have vented before it shut down? If so, it wouldn't get any hotter. Time to do this.

She scooted along with all the power she could muster. Something about the heat spooked her and she wanted to get through the shaft as quickly as she could. She'd grown sweaty now and felt as if she'd swollen, and the vent had grown smaller. She pictured the map of the ship in her head, visualizing the tunnel as it spanned the airlock to the engine room. Not any longer than the distance she'd come from where Rhys had been at the door. Of course, she'd jogged that; now she wriggled like a snake.

God, it was taking forever! And it had gotten smaller, and… hotter? How? Sweat poured down into her eyes, burning. Tears flooded to clear them. This had been a terrible idea. Something had gone wrong, something she couldn't understand but could no longer deny…

Oh, fuck.

The backup generator. Oh fuck, oh fuck. Her breaths came short and quick, and her heart galloped. The backup ionic engine didn't need to vent, no, but it was between the engine and crew decks, which located it at some point beneath the vent, she wasn't sure how far. It had to be what had heated up the vent. Was it close enough to kill her? Might be. But she couldn't go back now. It would take longer. She pushed herself forward, trying not to think. Oh, God, what if she died in this vent, frying over the engine like a sausage?

The panic moved her faster as the adrenaline surged. Finally, the vent dipped down some, and her weight could help her as she moved along, almost sliding down. She kept her hands and face away from the metal, which had started to heat through her thermal jumpsuit, and felt nearly unbearable on her forearms and belly.

A square of light appeared ahead, and she cried out with relief, and also fear that she wouldn't make it. In her excitement, she ignored the burning on her arms and thighs, though tears streamed down her cheeks. She cursed, her shouts echoing madly in the awful metal tunnel.

Finally, she reached the opening, the beautiful red light of the engine room, and slid out with searing pain, face first, not caring how she landed. A large cooling container broke her fall; she rolled off the final six feet and collapsed onto the floor. It knocked the wind out of her, but she still managed a weak, relieved laugh of pure joy that she'd made it out alive and was no longer burning. She unzipped her thermal and pulled her arms out, which hurt the most. She held them out, letting them cool. With the lights so low, she couldn't see how badly they were burned. She couldn't see blisters.

The reactor emitted a dim red light, the one which filled the room, and it soothed her. She didn't know how a solar flare could have shut it down; it looked perfectly fine, just silent. She'd owned the ship for so long and yet understood so little about it. And now her ignorance had almost killed her.

She fastened her jumpsuit back up and stepped to the override panel on the door. She held down the switch. She started in surprise when the door hissed open; just like that, it had worked. On the other side of it, stood Rhys; his eyes widened in a similar, stunned surprise, and then his lower eyelids tensed, raised in a squint. His hands were still buried in the panel.

"*What did you do?*"

She spoke quickly. "I got the engine room unlocked. Engine still needs to be fixed, though. I can't do everything around here." She gave him a playful grin, but he did not laugh. The second she saw his face, she knew she'd been stupid to have ever thought this would be a good idea.

"How did you get into the engine room?" His eyes ran

over her, as though her appearance could answer his questions. And she knew she had to be a mess.

She spoke lightly, carelessly. "Oh, there's a vent that runs there from the airlock. I just went through that. Like I said, I know the ship pretty well." She shrugged. Could he tell she was shaking? Nope, this was not going as she'd imagined. Instead of getting to poke at him for underestimating her, she was under interrogation, and after what had just happened, guilt had to be written all over her. But then, how would he know what had happened?

The technician thrust his head into the hallway from the hatch in the ceiling. "Hey, I just saw the door opened. It wasn't me."

"It was *her*," said Rhys, his jaw tight. "She went through a vent."

"Ah, the emergency cooling vent. I didn't count that as an option, because it runs right over the backup."

Goddamn it.

The tech looked her over, nodding. "You're lucky. If you'd gone through it any later than you had, you'd be dead."

She swallowed down her panic. "Yep. Had to act fast."

"So, you *knew* it went over the backup engine?" demanded Rhys.

She opened her mouth, but for a moment, nothing came out. How had this gotten so out of hand? At last, she said, "I knew I could make it to the engine room."

He glared at her, silent. She did her best to stand still, not squirm, and play very cool, like what she'd done had been perfectly fine. She even scowled back at him after a moment and said, "Here you thought I didn't know my own ship."

"This is not your ship."

Somehow, she kept her tone light, even after that. "Slip of the tongue. But you know, a thank you would be nice."

He barked a laugh, a humorless, furious laugh. "A thank you," he mocked, his eyebrows up. He shook his head, smiling unpleasantly. "No. Go up to my quarters and wait for me there."

Her stomach plunged; for a moment, she thought the gravity had downshifted again. "What? Why?"

"You heard me. Get off this deck. Now." His eyes flashed brilliant, the only thing alive in his otherwise stony face. She started to argue, but his expression terrified her. He stepped away, moving over to the hatch to speak with the tech. Her ears buzzed; whatever they were saying, she had no comprehension of it at all. Dazed, she walked away, not daring to stay on the deck he'd ordered her off of, but not wanting to do as he said and go up to his quarters. What would he do? He was pissed.

Where else could she go? Could she hide? No. He'd find her. She was trapped here with him on this ship, and she had no choice but to face him. Unless she shot herself out the airlock. She rubbed her temples with her fingers, finding her hair soaked with sweat. Her legs felt as heavy as lead as she made her way up to her old cabin, which was now his quarters.

Chapter 9

She'd been sitting in his office chair for about twenty minutes, spinning back and forth anxiously and making kicks at the legs of the desk, when he stepped in. She stopped, grappled the arms of the chair, and forced herself to look at him. His features were stony, his skin smudged with grease and creased with lines of fatigue. All the same, he seemed determined. In his hands, he held a steel cylinder. He unscrewed the top of it and set it down on the desk in front of her.

"Drink it," he said. His tone did not bear arguing with, so she took it and drank. The instant the cold, sweet water touched her mouth, her thirst overcame her, and she gulped it greedily, until she'd finished everything in the thermos. His eyes stayed on her the whole time.

"Are you hurt?" he asked finally.

"No," she said. He raised his eyebrows, clearly not believing her. She pulled up the sleeves of her thermal, showing him. "It's just pink, like a sunburn."

He nodded. Who knew what he thought? It took everything she had not to crumble under his hawk-like stare.

"Get out of my chair," he said.

She stood hurriedly. "Sorry. I was tired, and I didn't know where else—"

"It's all right. But you're going to stand now."

Shit. Shit! Was he going to punish her? No, she could fix this, she just had to explain. "L-listen," she stammered. "The o-only reason I—"

"No." He held up a hand to silence her. "No. You ought to have known better. And from now on, you will. Now turn around and face the desk."

She stamped her foot, tried to summon anger to obliterate her fear. "You told me to prove it! Proving means doing something, right?"

He stared at her, puzzled. Then he said, "Do you mean when I told you to prove that you knew the ship?"

"Yes!"

"You didn't think to tell me what you knew?"

"That's not proof, just more talk! Isn't it always better to ask for forgiveness than permission?"

He chuckled and ran his hand over his head in a kind of fatigued exasperation, rubbing at his eyes. "That saying happens to be, 'better to *beg* for forgiveness', you know. So, you can tell me which is better after you do just that. Now turn around."

His words cracked like a whip, and his eyes lit up slightly. She couldn't argue anymore. To do as he said terrified her, to not do as he said terrified her. She jerked in place like a broken automaton.

"Sydell," he said, his voice low. She turned and clasped the edge of the desk. She couldn't see what he was doing, and she twitched nervously. She heard the desk drawer creak as he slid it open, and she twisted her head around to see.

"No," he said calmly. "Face the desk like I said. Lean

forward over it. I'm going to spank you with a paddle, and you aren't to move until I'm done."

Her ears burned when he said it. She started to cover them even, to hide herself from this heinous humiliation, but how could that help her? She'd ceased breathing; with effort, she set her hands back on the desk but did not lean over it. She could not do it. From behind, he planted his hand between her shoulders and firmly eased her forward, so that she had to set herself on her elbows. A squeak of fear escaped her, and she went hot with shame and swore that she wouldn't make another sound.

He made a move behind her, and she piped, "No! It's not fair!"

Whap! The sound of it stunned her, even before the sting seared into her consciousness and she gasped. Somehow it hurt worse than it had before, at her apartment. She peeked back before she could stop herself and saw the length of the paddle in his hand, just as she'd felt it across both cheeks. With the smattering of small holes across its wooden length, it was a wicked looking thing.

"I told you to turn around," he said and followed with another swipe at her.

"Jesus!" she yelped, shocked by the bright pain of it, which intensified even as he took a pause.

"This is a proper one, with holes drilled in," he said, his tone light, almost pleasant. "I'm going to do right by you this time."

"Guess we can't have your arm getting tired," she said through gritted teeth.

He laughed, sounding genuinely amused. He followed up with another rapid fire hit, pausing just enough so that the searing raised to a point which was nearly intolerable. And then he fired two more.

"Mmrph!" She tugged at her hair and squirmed about

the desk, anything to keep herself from crying out. She shifted her hips around, as if it could somehow assuage the terrific smarting that somehow only escalated, even though he'd stopped.

"You're moving more than I'd like," he said.

God, really? He was tearing her ass off and then criticizing her for moving? Too much, it was too much; anger rocketed up and she snarled, "If you need your target to be still at such a close range, then you're just bad."

Whap, whap! He'd not hit harder, but faster, and then took that awful pause, so the pain could double up on itself, and with it, the adrenaline rose steeply; it shot through her with the panic and sting.

"Ow… fuck, ow, ow!"

He landed another and she gave a war cry and swept her arms across his desk, knocking most of what was on top of it to the floor. Books, papers, a container of pens; all of it clattered about, the pens bouncing all over the room. She raised herself up by her arms. He put his hands at her shoulders and set her back down, this time with force.

"*Bad girl*," he said in a smooth growl. She could swear he almost sounded satisfied. Some place between her belly button and her crotch throbbed when he said it; some dark, internal place she'd never been aware existed. The feeling was… wrong. Wrong, to be made to feel as if she were melting when he said that. She took in her breath quickly, becoming aware that she'd not been breathing.

"Do you need to be *really* punished, then?" he asked ominously. Instinctively, she started to scramble away, sliding against the desk, but he caught her hips. The strength of his hands shocked her; it didn't hurt, but she knew she could not break that hold no matter how she struggled.

"This is going to feel a lot worse straight on your skin,"

he said, and in the next instant, he'd unsnapped the back-seat of her jumpsuit and yanked it down her hips, taking her panties down along with it.

She gasped in mortification, and in a voice bright with rage, said, "You asshole, you'll be sorry—"

He laughed at this. *Laughed*. She froze, astonished. It left her helpless to the next smattering of slaps from the paddle. Holy hell, but it hurt, as he'd said, direct on her bare skin. The peaks of the pain pierced into her very soul; no part of her escaped him.

Before she knew it, she was shouting heartily, pounding the desk with her forearms and fists. She'd sworn not to make a sound, just to save face; now she was having the most intense tantrum she'd ever known, her throat hoarse from screaming out "fuck" and "fucking bastard" and "I hate you!" Christ, would he never stop? Her curses melted into sobs, and she pressed her forehead into the desk, her tears running down her nose shamefully.

After a few more swats, he ceased. "You are my crew," he said, "and you won't endanger yourself again." He didn't sound angry, only extremely serious. "Do you understand?"

She sniffled and gulped, unable to speak. Now that he'd stopped, it somehow hurt even worse, climbing toward some pinnacle of fiery pain she couldn't predict. More than anything, she wanted to rub the awful sting from her cheeks, but she would not stoop to it, not now, not right in front of him.

"Do you understand, Sydell?" he repeated, calm but with the same dire tone.

She nodded her head against the desk, cool and strangely comforting. She tried not to think about how she looked to him, doubled over, ass bared; it could not be borne right now.

"Sydell. I want to hear you answer."

"I'll try," she said.

Behind her, he snorted. "You think *this* hurts?" he said and swiped one more hit.

It was too much; she shrieked; a short, hoarse sound, then forgot her pride completely and blubbered, "Please, please stop. Please."

"Do you know what it would feel like to roast alive in that vent?" he snapped.

"I-I have some idea," flew out of her mouth before she could stop it. She swore she could hear him shake his head disapprovingly.

"You will not endanger yourself on this ship, or anytime while you're my recruit. You will ask my permission before you do anything that comes into your head. Is that clear?"

"Okay. Yes."

"Do you know what it would have been like to find a roasted person in a vent on my ship? Do you think I would enjoy finding you like that?"

"I don't know," she breathed. "You're… you're a little sadistic, so maybe…" She braced herself for his response, couldn't believe she'd said it. A stupid joke, not worth the price. But he did not spank her again.

Instead, he grew quiet, almost as if he were reflecting. Then he said, "You don't know what I am, and you don't need to. All you need to know, is how to behave. And what to expect if you don't."

What a strange thing to say. It perplexed her, so that she forgot her burning ass for a moment and could only wonder at him. She'd not bothered to think about him before, on who he was, other than how he treated her, but it dawned on her suddenly that he was, in fact, something of a singularity.

"All right," she breathed. "I'm sorry." This last came out before she could think on it and, as such, sounded so sincere that it surprised her. Was that her own voice, so contrite?

His hands relaxed their hold on her instantly, and then he swept her pants back up over her flaming rear and snapped them back into place. Something about this last step proved too much for her, whether too intimate or too kind; she broke into a shudder of sobs and slipped away from him, dashing down behind the desk. She wanted to leave, to go to her room, but knew she couldn't, not until he gave his permission.

He did not stop her from curling up behind his desk on the floor, however. He only said, "Before you go, you need to put everything back on my desk that you displaced." He sounded a little out of breath. The desk drawer squealed open, and the clatter of the paddle being put away relaxed her. Now out of his sight, she rubbed at her bottom vigorously, until the roaring sting subsided a little. He quietly took his seat in the swivel chair and opened his holoscreen, evidently allowing her time to collect herself.

She cried as quietly as possible into her arm, wiping all the wet from her face into her sleeve. A spike of anger rushed up in her and she asked, "Why do you do this to me?" but she did not dare to get up and face him when she spoke. Her voice came out tearful, whiny, and she hated it.

"Because it will work," he answered placidly. "I intend to break you of your habit of being impulsive and rushing into things that will get you hurt."

"It will *work*?" she repeated with a disgust she couldn't hide. "You can't just do things like that because they work. How do you even know it will?"

"I'm a pragmatist. I don't see the point in wasting time with things that don't work. You need to change your behavior quickly, so I'll correct you in ways that will make you change it quickly. The danger you keep putting yourself in puts to rest any misgivings I might have about how I train you."

"Train me?" she said, horrified.

"Yes. Sydell, I used to train people. I used to work where humans were trained and sold off for the pleasure of others. Some came in willingly, some not so much. My father and brother were human traffickers. Parsons still is, but you probably knew that. I broke with them, but I don't deny what I did, and having done it, I know what will work for you and what won't. You'll be happiest if you comply with me and if you don't underestimate what I'm capable of."

Holy shit. He was a slaver. Had *been* a slaver. She'd been going to prison, but now she was in the power of someone who spoke so casually of training her, like she was an animal. The weight of his words glued her to the floor, and for the moment, she had a sense of drowning, of not being able to breathe. She was fucked.

She closed her eyes. Clearly, he was a monster. Thinking of him this way, she could regain a shred of her dignity. It strengthened her and she stood, slowly. He glanced up at her. He did not look monstrous, only tired, and maybe a little curious as to what she would do next. She noted shaded lines under his hazel eyes and ruddy stubble grown out around his face. But this did not fool her. He was a monster of the worst order.

She began wandering about the room, picking up the books and papers on the floor, and even the pens, taking care to find every last one. She put it all up on the desk, while he went back to looking at his holoscreen, fully absorbed in it. At last, the desk looked at least close to how it had been before. "Can I go now?" she asked, more meekly than she'd intended.

"You may," he said stoically, though she got the feeling he tried to mask that it pleased him. She moved to the door, and he said, "You should stop by first aid and get some burn spray for your arms. It'll help you get to sleep."

The last sentence, the kindness of it, shocked her into silence, and she could only nod. Then he shrugged and added, "Might work for your ass, too."

She could have no response to this, except to feel her blood burn up her neck and into her face, scorching her ears. She raced out the door without another word.

———

She lay on her bunk. She would never sleep after all that had happened. Never.

She'd retrieved the burn spray, as he'd said, and finding it worked so well on her arms and along her thighs where the heat of the vent had burnt her, she went ahead and sprayed her bottom too. It helped a good deal, and somehow this, his helping her feel better after what he'd done, was the most mortifying part of the experience. With the burns, and her burning rear end, she was uncomfortably hot, so she stripped off her jumpsuit and left it crumpled on the floor. She rolled onto her stomach on her bunk and closed her eyes, trying to shut out all thought.

She slipped into the fretful sleep one has after an ordeal. And she'd had not one, but two. As the night progressed, her sleep only grew more restless, almost fevered. The burns perhaps? She dreamt of Rhys, standing behind her with his hands on her hips, their grasp hot and unyielding. Nothing more than that, did she dream, but in it, she heard him say, "Bad girl," and she woke, her heart racing.

The small, dark room, which usually comforted her, now felt too warm, even stifling. A needy pulsing called her attention to her groin. Almost as if the heat that clung still to her bottom had spread out, made its way lewdly into her more tender parts. She rolled onto her side, pushed a pillow between her bare legs, and rubbed herself up against it, her usual method to release this sort of tension. The pressure both relieved and stimulated her. Rhys flooded again to her mind, with his dark eyebrows and high forehead, repellent yet also inflaming her. With it, came a hot suffusing of desire throughout her body which she could not deny the nature of.

"Turn around and face the desk…"

She shuddered, and that tiny, sensitive hub of pleasure seated over her pussy throbbed in demand. She rubbed harder against the pillow, her breaths growing ragged. A little chill passed over her with the heat, and her nipples stood up against the pillow; she pushed her face into it and muffled a moan. She would come any second now, come the fastest she ever had in her life, just lying here with her bottom warmed and the memory of him holding her by the shoulders, then his hands unfastening her jumpsuit…

No! No, she could not do this, not think of Rhys like this. It might make her feel better now, but tomorrow? When she saw him again? Jesus, she would have to see him again. Why the hell was this happening? What was the matter with her? Did she… did she *want* Rhys now? Could it work that way, like a switch flipped on inside her, and someone she had hated, since almost the moment she had met him, became someone she desired, even without her willing it?

What the hell was happening to her? What was he doing? And how could she face him again, like this?

She managed to avoid him the next day. With all the engine repairs still going on, it was not difficult; everyone was too wrapped up with disassembling the core to take much notice of her. She stayed in her little room, growing restless.

When he called up over the comm, summoning everyone to the engine room, she was almost grateful. Hiding out in her bunk had become unbearable. But the feeling was still with her, the strange melting heaviness in her limbs when she heard his voice. No way could she be normal around him, with whatever this was. She had little choice but to go, however. As she dressed, forgoing her thermal for something less drably professional, she was plagued by the alarming desire for him to notice her when she arrived.

Chapter 10

Present...

'All right. It was fun, kid. Goodnight,' he had said, swiping a hand over her head like she was a favorite cat, and then he had just left her at her bunk.

The ionic generator was still running, and it was still swelteringly hot. Already, she regretted having the coffee; it only frazzled her nerves further. She jumped at every sound and turned toward the mess hall door; was it him? He typically came in at the start of every day for coffee, and her stomach went shaky at the prospect of seeing him now. She braced herself for it during her whole meal. But, as it happened, he never showed up.

It was fun, kid. Goodnight. What the hell did that even mean? Was that the sort of thing he did for fun? What had happened with him in the engine room could hardly be called fun, nothing so casual as that. Rhys had crushed her body to his and made her feel things utterly alien to

112

anything she'd ever felt, feelings and sensations too intense to belong to the world as she'd known it.

She had little experience with sex, but not zero experience. She'd *done it* at least, with Ricky.

Back in the last few months of Dad's illness, Ricky would come to the apartment and bring liberal amounts of weed, to help her dad with the pain. Then the two of them would smoke some of it on the couch and talk about the old days as if they had been friends. Really, she'd always seen him as a rival, someone Dad let do the jobs which he wouldn't trust her with. She'd never really liked him. But he'd been the only one to show up once Dad had been bedridden. She couldn't remember anymore how it had come out in conversation that she was still a virgin. But they decided it would help get her mind off things to change that.

Turned out, the world's obsession with sex was overblown. Inferior even to masturbation, which was never great, either. After a few goes with Ricky, she was over it and it had never happened again. That said, she'd thought it would have given her a yardstick of sorts, to compare. But, no, what had happened with Rhys couldn't even be compared. The closest thing she had to link it with, in experience, was the electric rush she got when she stole something, but it was more than that, too.

Well, what had happened after with Ricky, might at least give her a clue of what to expect now. Ricky had been distant with her afterwards and even sent a proxy to bring the weed for the next few months. He hadn't even asked about moving into her apartment until he'd known for sure that she was leaving. And so, when Rhys did not show up in the mess, she didn't let herself feel anything about it at all. It was par for the course.

Yet, once she'd eaten, she realized she would still need

to report to him. How could she do that, like everything was normal? When Walt came into the mess, she asked what he was doing.

"Re-calibrating the object detection system," he said.

What was that, exactly? God only knew, but she offered to help. Rhys couldn't get mad if she were working, could he? And then she wouldn't have to see him herself.

Except, as soon as she got into the cockpit with Walt, his voice came in over the comm, sternly, "Sydell. You're to report to me in my office."

"No worries," said Walt as she left, in a way that told her he would rather be working alone anyway. A feeling of uselessness hit her, of being unwanted by anyone. She fairly trudged up to the loft, as though walking through four feet of water.

In his cabin, he'd opened the visor shutter and the reverse inkblot of gleaming white stars dazzled her. She gazed at them, awestruck, while Rhys waited, sitting quietly behind his desk, and only after a moment, did she grudgingly look his way. He wore a fresh jumpsuit, nicer than his other and olive green; it passed cleanly over the lines of his body, showing his muscular form while still just shy of clinging to him. Goddammit, he was handsome. His dark-lashed hazel eyes drove into her, and she glanced away.

"You never reported," he said.

"I thought I'd see you at the mess," she replied with a slight shrug. At the shrug, his brows knotted.

"But you didn't." His voice grew lower, and her stomach tensed.

"No. I was going to help Walt with..." She couldn't remember, not with him staring like that. "Mmm, the calibration of the... detection..." She trailed off into a mumble. Not good.

"Sydell, you report to *me*. Nothing has changed."

She cringed, her ears roaring, now that he'd referenced it, even if indirectly. But she nodded.

"I need discipline on this ship," he said. "Otherwise, shit goes wrong. You're my recruit, and I expect you to report to me just as I've directed you. Nothing has changed."

Her head snapped up at the repetition. Something about it seemed awkward.

He went on quickly, smoothly. "What happened last night was fun. I enjoyed it, and I hope you did too." His voice ran light and cool. "But it wasn't surprising. We've been working together closely. I've punished you, well, intimately. Your desires for me were natural. Even predictable. Believe me, I know." His elbows rested on the desk, his hands pressed together at the fingertips.

Her mouth went dry, even as the whole of her grew hot. If he had sat in here all morning deliberately constructing something to say which could most offend her, he could not have done better than this.

He continued. "It's natural in our situation here, that we should want to blow off some steam."

"Blow off steam?"

"Yes. That's what you could call it. I only brought it up, because you failed to report this morning. Maybe you thought that now I would let you slack off that requirement. But I still expect exactly the same from you as I always have."

No, he could not have fathomed how awkward she felt, or how vulnerable, could he? Because he was a monster. Her desires were "predictable" to him. Right, he was a slaver, and that's just how he trained people. "You're the one who didn't show up at mess this morning," she said. It was a shot in the dark, assuming that he had not done so because of what had happened. But she felt it to be true.

"I had my coffee here, which is none of your concern."

She pressed her lips together. "Fine. What do you want me to work on?"

He blinked, as though he had expected her to prolong the subject. But he was done with it, clearly, and as far as he needed to know, she was too.

"Whatever you were doing to help Walt sounded sufficient. He might need a hand."

"Seriously? You called me here to tell me we blew off steam, and to go back to doing what I was already doing, but only because you told me to?"

"Careful." He drew the word out, warningly. He leaned back in his chair.

"Okay, then. I will make sure to come up here every day so you can shit on me. I get it, this is *your* ship. It must be true if you keep saying it every five minutes."

"Don't think for a second that because we've fooled around, I won't turn you up and paddle you again."

"Fuck you," she growled, from something deep inside herself that hurt. Hurt more than what he could do to her physically. Her fury blotted out all thought of the consequences, anyway. His eyes pierced into her, and she waited for him to do it.

After a moment, he said, "Get out and cool your head. Last chance."

She left swiftly, a choking heat rushing up into her throat. She managed to escape the room without crying, but only just.

Goddammit.

He had handled that badly. The awareness of it sat with him like a bad smell. But he wasn't about to give her a pass on things, as if what they'd done had changed her position on the ship. It hadn't.

No point regretting what had happened. Maybe it had been a mistake, but it was done. Trying to avoid it, had perhaps been unrealistic. He'd wanted her since, well, honestly, since he'd tied her down to the bunk, back when they were on Mars. But he'd wanted more than that to mentor her, break her of her stupid habit of jumping into danger, and find something she was good at. Give her the discipline to actually do it. This would muddy the waters some. At least, he hadn't fucked her.

Since his time working for Parsons, he'd handled all his sexual needs professionally. No emotion, no drama. Io City sex work services were almost clinical in this regard, and they'd been enough. Adequate. Not intoxicating. But intoxicating was dangerous; the word itself could tell you that.

Intoxication was wanting to possess someone. A feeling that had been awakened in him when his first experiences of attraction had been with people who'd given him total power over them. *Exhilarating*. What a person shared in that kind of relationship was electric.

But Parsons used those bonds to break people, expecting him to do the same. When he left, it was with disgust for his brother, and for himself too. He accepted the tepidity of the legal sex industry as one accepts dry toast after a night out on a bender.

This thing with Sydell was different, though. She was so responsive to him. What a rush to tease her, to watch her come apart in his hands. But he had control here. She was indentured to him, legally, and so she belonged to him, and he liked that. Yet it made him responsible for her, and that grounded him, made him consider what he did with her carefully. At least most of the time.

He'd hurt her, her pride and maybe her feelings too. They'd been intimate and it hadn't changed her place on the ship; he wouldn't let it make her special. He hoped it was mostly her vanity he'd hurt, that she'd been lewd with him, and it had gained her nothing; his requirements were the same. With any luck, once she knew that for certain, she'd settle down. That's why he had to be tough with her now. It had been damned hard. He was sure she'd been going to cry. When she'd cussed at him, he'd wanted more than anything to spank her, but knew if he did, she would break down, and then, well, who knew what would have happened then.

He found his way back to the engine room and got to it, putting his ship back together.

He refused to think on it any more all day. He had dinner in the mess and didn't see Sydell again. He needed to let it go. He'd been harsh, yes, but what she needed was harsh. He couldn't let this give her any power.

But after dinner, he stopped at her little room on his way from the mess, almost as if he just found himself there. *What the hell am I doing?* he thought as he knocked on her door.

Complete silence. But he knew she was there; the occupied light shone on the door panel. "Sydell. Open up, I need to speak with you."

"No."

He hit the override code and the door slid open. She lay on her bunk, facing the wall. Her back tensed when the door slid open. The low red light made it hard to see her well. "You don't get to disregard me," he said. "Once more, and we'll go up to my office. Understood?"

"Yes." The answer came strained, muffled. Was she crying?

"Sydell, I know you see me as an enemy. But I'm trying to help you. I'm trying to help you become someone who can survive, thrive even, and not have to live your life trying to outrun creditors." He paused, squinted into the darkness of the cabin. "I know this is difficult for you. But you need it. I hope on some level, you understand that."

Her shoulders moved, slightly, either in a shrug or a shudder, he could not tell.

All right, time to get it over with. "As to what happened with us… I didn't want it to happen, because in some ways, it was taking advantage of you. You're my recruit, I'm here to teach you to be responsible and I, well, I guess I was disappointed in myself. That's why I, I don't know, made light of things."

A long silence. Then she breathed, "Oh." She rolled onto her back but stared at the ceiling. Had he made progress?

She said, "You said it was predictable. That I would do that. What did that mean?"

"Predictable?" he repeated. Buying time. He didn't want to answer, wouldn't have, not before. He'd owed her no answers. But now, that didn't feel quite so true. And after all, he *had* said it.

"Why was it predictable?" she pressed.

He sighed. "Well, some people respond strongly to… being disciplined. I've known for a while that you needed me to punish you, asked for it on a level you can't understand. And people like that often respond to it sexually."

"I don't get off on you spanking me," she said with a snort.

Not yet, you don't. He pushed the thought away. "No. But

you respond to me, for being the one to do it. You can't help it."

She huffed. She folded her arms around herself. Then, after a moment, she bent her head to him. "Okay. So, what about you? Why did you do it? Was it predictable for you?"

"It's in my nature, yes. I enjoy having that power over you." He said this in a monotone, and then changed the subject swiftly, away from himself. "But you have to accept your place here on the ship. I don't say that out of any spite for you. Simply that you have to learn some basic discipline, have to be able to do some things day to day that you don't always love. That's why I said, nothing's changed. My plan for you is the same."

"Plan for me? So, I'm like, training to be a maid or something? Or like someone's slave? Why didn't you just sell me to Parsons?"

He laughed, deep and long, putting a hand to his forehead. "Damn, but if you don't know how to dramatize the fuck out of everything."

"This isn't who I am!" She threw an arm out, shook it at him. "I don't scrub floors with toothbrushes. That's why I didn't go into the goddamned army, didn't become a nurse. Maybe I wouldn't have been running from creditors if I had. But that's better than doing grunt work all day, every day."

"What is it that you want, Sydell?"

She frowned. A cute frown, genuinely bemused. "What?"

"What do you want to do? Pretend you can do anything. What is it?"

"Well," her voice trembled, embarrassed. "I would like to pilot a ship."

"Have you flown one?"

"I flew this one, with Walt, sometimes. But you have to go to school to get a license."

Of course, Walt would have just let her fly it, wouldn't he? He said, "Yes. And that takes work. It takes a lot of day to day grind. And if you don't learn to deal with that, then you'll never be able to do anything you want. All you'll ever do is dream."

"Okay. Yes, I get it. Can we just go back to you telling me what to do, instead of these moral tirades? Because I do understand. But I'm telling you, I can't be what you want."

"You don't know what I want. Stop making your stupid assumptions."

"Can't you just let me do something that isn't mind-numbingly boring for once? Because, I'm not gonna lie, you say it's not spite, but I feel like you enjoy it. You enjoy making me do things I hate. I can feel it."

He smiled, smothered it, didn't want her to see. "I wouldn't concern yourself with that. You'll get used to things. And once I see you can handle some responsibilities, your duties can change. There will be all sorts of things you can do on Europa. You won't be my recruit forever."

She shrugged. "Okay." She turned her face back to the wall. "Until then I'm just your whipping boy?"

He laughed again. He shouldn't; she was being a smart ass and it would reward a bad attitude. But he couldn't help it.

"If that's what you want, then, yes," he said.

"It's what you want, too. You already admitted as much."

He sighed. "Goodnight, Sydell. I'll see you in my office tomorrow."

After four days without moving, the engine had been restored to full functionality, but he hesitated to turn it on, even after the careful search he'd made of its parts. He needed to make a trip outside first. He called Sydell up over the comm. When she showed up, he led her out into the hall.

"Would you like to join me in doing something that isn't mind-numbingly boring?" he asked, his eyebrows raised.

She stared at him a moment and then said, with the trace of a smile, "That again?"

He stifled his grin. He needed her to know this was serious. "I need to go outside and check on the solar sail. It's showing damage. I'd like you to come along."

Her eyes grew wide, fearful, the pupils waxing for a split second. "Outside? On the ship? This ship has a solar sail?" Each sentence was a pitch higher than the last.

"It does now. Going outside for maintenance during a flight isn't uncommon. And it's perfectly safe, as long as you're smart about it. You'll be cabled into me."

She'd gone totally pale now; as he'd guessed, she was terrified, and when scared, she tried to throw herself into things without thinking them through. She wouldn't be able to do that with him along, literally tied to her. He'd start to teach her to control her fear, her reaction to it. Teach her to change her reactions.

"Why do *I* need to go?"

"I need someone to assist. I thought of you, since you asked for something more interesting to do. This will be exciting for you." He gave her no time to argue and started for the airlock. She remained some distance behind. He motioned her forward, into the airlock, and within minutes had her fitted into one of the new suits.

"You'll be clipped to the ship at all times," he said, as he attached a cable to the utility belt on her suit, already attached to his own. "You'll be tied into me, and one of us will always be clipped to the ship. You will not unclip unless I give you the clear. Got it?"

She nodded. He pulled on the cable lightly. "I like you better on a leash, I think."

"You're on a leash too," she quipped, which irked him, but he couldn't think of a retort. He went on as prepared. "If either of us *do* become detached, don't panic. We have propulsion systems built into the suit. We can move about as we need. But that likely won't happen."

She raised her arms, fit her helmet over her head, tucking her messy hair into her collar. He patted the top of her helmet. "Is that understood? I'd like to hear you, Sydell."

She nodded sulkily and muttered, "Okay." It made him want to shake her. Hadn't she only just been complaining of wanting more exciting work? He tried to stay friendly and not let her annoy him. He smiled, even, and said, "It's like climbing a jungle gym, underwater. Sort of. It's like nothing you've ever done. It's fun. Ready?"

She just stared, bewildered.

"I know you're scared," he said gently.

"I'm not," she said, then blinked rapidly and shook her head, as though trying to shake away the mannerism.

"You always blink like that when you're scared," he pointed out.

"You think I don't know that?" she snapped, giving her head another shake. Then she blushed, and he wished he hadn't said anything about it. He gave her a little tug on the cable, making her stagger as it pulled her toward him.

"You're tethered to me. I will not let you go. You'll pay attention to me and do everything I say. Is that clear?"

Her mouth turned down, pouting, and her eyes grew larger; a tenderness for her prodded at him, along with an exasperation. "I said I want to hear you. You will obey everything I say, is that clear?"

"Yes, sir," she whispered, without a touch of irony, and the tenderness in him became a flood of warmth and desire from his heart down to his groin. He checked himself from his first instinct, to embrace her. Instead, he gave her cable another tug, hoping she would recognize it as affection. Then he hit the button to de-pressurize the airlock.

———

She'd always thought of her ship as small. Out here, it rose —or fell—away from her like a great column of gleaming white. Her face plate had adjusted for the brightness of it as it faced solar side, giving it a surreal matte quality, like a tube of ceramic.

Rhys had clipped in first just outside the egress; she'd followed almost blindly and now hung in place, her arm wrapped about one rung in a line of many. The sudden loss of gravity left her feeling like her body had drifted apart; her legs floated out from under her into the stars and panic rose, hammering in her chest. Why had he brought her out here? Why had she agreed to come? She ought to have said no, have begged not to come, but she didn't want him to know how scared she was.

"Sydell, switch to the comm channel I just opened." His voice came in through her helmet.

A green light had flickered on under her chin; she nudged it to engage. "Okay, I'm here," she said. The panic ebbed away for a moment. Why had he made her get on a new channel?

"So," he said, "we're not actually out here to fix the solar sail."

"Uh, okay." The spot where her ribs parted in her chest tensed a little.

"There wasn't actually a solar flare that shut down the engine," he said calmly. "That's what I told the crew, but what happened is we were hacked, and the engine was shut down by something like a virus. Hey, clip in. I'm moving forward."

She clipped in two rungs ahead. A virus? Someone had hacked them and shut down their engine? And he seemed barely troubled by it at all.

He unclipped and moved along the rungs, then clipped and tugged at her cable. "All right, your turn. Go out ahead of me and clip in."

She looked out at the rungs before her, up at where the ship met the black expanse and formed something like a horizon. Suddenly, she had the feeling of being upside down and clinging to the ship to keep from falling, from being swallowed by the dark enormity all around them. She broke into a cold sweat, paralyzed.

"Hey. *Sydell*," said Rhys, so sternly that she lost a bit of the awful sensation. "Look at your hands. Nothing but your hands, or me. You got it?"

She swallowed down the nausea and said, "Got it." She brought her eyes down carefully to her gloved hands, clasping at the rung. She moved them one at a time along the rungs; her body felt to be flying with the motions of it. When she reached him, he put out a hand and steadied her, pulling her in and then helping her along as she moved past him.

"You are always clipped in," he reminded her. Gratitude overwhelmed her, just that he was there, helping her along, his voice holding the flood of panic at bay. She continued along the rungs until her cable went taut, tugging at her waist, and then she clipped in.

"Good girl," he said. Her heart fluttered, nearly as much as when he had called her a bad one.

"So why are we out here?" she asked, keeping her voice as stoic as she could.

"I picked up a rogue signal emission. Well, actually, Walt picked it up. It's encoded to look like static in our emissions, but he saw something was off. I think something might be attached to the ship and managed to hack in. That's what we're looking for."

"Why? Who would do that?" she asked finally, as he took his turn climbing alongside her. She braced her arm against him as he passed her, steadying him as he had done for her, and he said, "You don't have to..." Then he laughed softly. "Well, thank you." He cleared his throat. "It's Parsons, obviously."

She shuddered. He went on, "I foiled his plan; now he's doing the same. Trying to slow me down."

Parsons. How could he be so casual about it? "So, what, he's just having his revenge?" she asked. "That seems petty, for someone like him."

A silence followed, during which Rhys clipped and then tugged for her to follow him. Caught up in what he'd been telling her, she almost forgot to be afraid as she moved along.

Rhys said, "He wants something from me. It's why he really took Callie, I think. To find out what she might know. Or to turn her against me. We've been at war for a while now. I'm not sure exactly what his plans are, but hacking the ship seems to be part of it."

"Is he trying to kill us?"

Rhys laughed. "No. Parsons needs things from me, things I can't provide dead."

"Is he… can he hear us on the ship? Is that why we're on a private channel?"

"It's possible. This is an encrypted channel, so it can't be hacked, at least not for a while. He'd also be on a delay if he's hacked the comms. I'm hoping he didn't, but we still need to be careful."

She glanced over her shoulder, to see how far they'd come. Out in the distance, a crumpled asteroid, half in shadow, lurched along oddly and gave her the sense that she floated in the opposite direction, dizzying her. "Are we moving?" she asked, her pitch rising.

"We're drifting," he said evenly. "Now clip in right here. I want to go and have a look. You're doing a great job, Sydell."

She panted a little and then thought he must have heard it, with the comms being so sensitive. Why in hell should she react to his praise that way? She wasn't a dog. She clipped in as he'd said and closed her eyes, so that she couldn't see the movement of the asteroid. How fast was the ship moving? If she let go, would she drift along with the ship, or would it go on without her?

"There we are," said Rhys, and she followed his gaze to… to what? With the ship's curve, she could only just see his head and shoulders, but not what he was looking at.

"What is it?" she piped.

"Hang on, let me, there we are. I can't reach it. Sydell, you'll need to come closer."

She sighed. She wanted this to be over. She unclipped and started moving along the rungs.

"But don't unclip yet—"

What? She reached down to clip into a rung, but then something came floating around from beyond him and she gazed up. "That's what he hacked us with," said Rhys. "Attached to one of the exterior storage containers."

It was silver, shaped vaguely like a briefcase and of a similar size. She started to land the clip when something shook the line, and she lost hold of it. She grabbed out in front of her and then she saw what had happened. Something had hit Rhys; it propelled him now away from the ship; something about twice his size, white and blocklike. The storage container? He was caught onto it by the back of his suit, and it dragged him up, up and away from the ship.

She made one more frantic swing for the clip before the trajectory of Rhys and the container ripped her away from the rungs and into the void.

Chapter 11

She'd often been plagued by a dream in which, walking down the hall of her apartment back in Neo York, the floor would drop out from under her, and she would find herself in freefall down a dark chasm. Then all the things around her disappeared, grew small and distant as she fell, until she was alone in darkness, and the falling became more like floating. Floating, suspended in terror, her guts still at her throat, through a dark, unending nothingness.

Floating away from the ship into the endless maw of space, the nightmare had realized itself in a way nightmares rarely do. For a moment, she thought she'd blacked out from the terror, for everything went dark. But, no, she'd only spun away from the bright, sun-reflecting ship and come to face the endless.

Then she spun again, and Rhys appeared some distance in front of her, in a mad struggle with the storage crate. It looked to have caught onto his pack. She heard roaring in her comm, like a monster, like she'd been swallowed by a monster of the deep. After a moment, she recognized it as her own breathing.

Rhys wrangled now with his pack, which was what had caught onto the container, and she watched, dragged along, like it was some absurd film playing out in front of her. What could she do? She almost called out, but how would that help him? Finally, she tugged at the cable attaching them and found that it moved her closer. Or did it move him closer? She could not tell but kept tugging it. Once she'd gotten close enough, he motioned to the straps. Was the comm not working?

"Rhys?" she piped. He did not respond. She unclipped the straps from his pack as he bid her, and he threw his arms back so that they separated from the shipping container, losing the pack in the process as it drifted beyond his reach, toward the void.

He nodded at her, pushed his chin out. What? Oh, he wanted her to try another channel. She pushed at the wire with her chin. Sounds of his breathing played immediately into her helmet. "Rhys!" she cried. It was all she could say. A rush of relief flooded her at being able to connect to him again.

He gave her cable a small tug. "We're going to be fine."

"But your pack's gone. How much O2 do you have?"

"I have enough in my suit. But I can't spare any to use my thrusters, so you'll have to get us back. It will be easy. I'll walk you through it."

She clenched her teeth and started to tremble. Was she even cold? The temp controls on this suit should be working, right? What was the matter?

"Can't we just contact the ship, have them come get us?" she asked.

"I've hailed; they aren't responding. The link's failed, for some reason."

Some reason. Surely, he had to think it was more than that? Yes, of course, he did, he just didn't want to scare her right now, didn't want to let her know someone was out to hurt them—

"Sydell," he said slowly, "you need to listen now. When you start your thrusters, use the momentum to sling yourself toward the ship, using the cable."

"What!"

He laughed. A forced laugh, she thought, designed to keep her spirits up. It had an edge to it she didn't want to dwell on.

"Start your thrusters and give the cord a tug. It's easier to learn it by doing it. Go on."

He led her hand to the control on her belt. She tugged on the end of the nozzle; a rush of expelled air careened her forward, just for a second, from the center of her pack and straight into Rhys. She bounced off him lightly and he chuckled. "This time, arc your shoulders a bit, see how you can move yourself around. Get a feel for it."

The slowness of his words felt deceptive to her; he was masking an urgency she couldn't understand. She grasped the nozzle and tugged again, this time arching her back. She flipped onto her belly and zoomed away from him, then caught as the cable tugged, and dragged him along.

"There you go. Now just try to keep yourself aimed right at the ship."

"Oh my god, Rhys. We're so far away." She stared back at the ship, easily half the size it had been before they were launched clean of it.

"Not really. The thrusters will get us back pretty damn quick."

She held the nozzle in place and kept her back straight, so that she kept up a smooth trajectory toward the ship.

"Don't turn around now. Eyes forward. You could get disoriented. All right?"

"Yes," she said. She was so scared of messing it up, she dared not even tilt her head. She would get them back safely.

"Good girl," he said very softly. Her ears prickled. But something else too, a faint spasm in her middle, from just where her ribs parted. A pang of doubt.

"How much oxygen do you have left, Rhys?" she asked.

"I have enough. You just focus on what you're doing."

The cable shuddered, making vibrations around the belt at her waist. What? It shuddered again, harder this time. Her stomach clenched. Something was wrong; he wasn't telling her something. The impulse overcame her. She bent herself at the waist and peered back, taking her hand off the nozzle as she did.

Rhys' hand landed against the cable, shaking it. He held a cutting tool. Fuck, he was going to cut the tether! She grabbed the cable with both hands, yanking him in as close as she could.

"Turn around!" he thundered. "Goddammit, do as I say!" He swept the knife down over the cable again. She kicked out wildly, and her foot met his hand, hard. The tool glittered as it spun out and away from them. He made a swing for it, but it was well out of reach. She had triumphed.

"Fuck. Fuck!" His roars over the comm chilled her. His eyes burnt into her through his visor. She had never seen him so angry; if she had not already been at the height of terror, his gaze would have put her there.

Then he closed his eyes, and his breathing started to slow somewhat. "I don't have enough oxygen to use my thrusters," he said through clenched teeth. "And you don't have enough to get us both back to the ship."

"What?" she cried.

"Using the O2 thrusters is for emergencies. It uses compressed air rapidly. I didn't think you could get us both back, but now you are just going to have to try."

His control over his emotion bled over to her and she started to cry. "Why didn't you tell me?"

"You would have fought me, and there wasn't time."

"I fought you anyway."

"So you did." He sounded almost resigned.

"Rhys, what's wrong?"

"My pack's gone. There's a leak in my suit. I'm dead weight for you. I wanted you to get back. I don't know that you can now. Dammit."

A leak? "So, what, you we're just going to die? Going to kill yourself?"

"Don't be absurd. I'm dropping my core temp. It should let me survive longer without oxygen. If I'd cut my line, you could have made it back to the ship and sent them out for me. It might have worked."

"Can we not unclip?"

"No, the belt clips lock when we're detached from the ship, for safety. That's why I was cutting it."

"You were an ass not to tell me what you were planning, Rhys."

"Get going back toward the ship, you little lunatic. We aren't going to discuss it anymore."

Her heart throbbed at what almost felt like affection coming from him. She swallowed and turned away from him. Her O2 levels had already dropped by about half. She tugged at the nozzle. She cried softly, trying to breathe as quietly as possible, so he wouldn't hear. Her sobs choked her; no way he'd failed to notice.

He said softly, "Sydell, when we get back to the ship,

I'm going to spank the daylights out of you for this one." There was the trace of a smile in his voice.

She cried harder, but a knot in her chest eased, and she relaxed for a moment as they crawled along toward the ship. She tugged the nozzle as hard as she could, to speed them up.

"Ease up," he said. "You'll blow through O2 too fast. Just go steady."

"But you—"

"I'm going to start getting my core temp down now. I might pass out. You'll need to get us to the ship and find something to grab on to. Clip your cable on the second you can and try to contact Walt."

She did not ease up on the throttle. What was he going to do about it? He couldn't very well tug her back without wasting their momentum.

"Sydell, you will run out of O2—"

"I'm doing this, not you. You aren't the only one who gets to take risks. You're trying to get me back alive even if it kills you, and I'm not okay with it."

"I told you, you're to do everything I say—"

"Punish me later."

Amazingly, he grew silent. She thought she heard a sigh. Then he said, "If I don't make it, you need to be careful back on the ship. That storage crate may have been hooked up to release when the hacking device was removed, but it could be possible that someone onboard released it."

What? Well, yes, that would make sense, why else couldn't they contact the ship? Someone there wanted them dead, likely someone working for Parsons. Who? She went through the faces of everyone on his crew, as to who might be suspicious. She was pulled out of the chain of thought when she realized Rhys' breathing had changed, becoming thick, blurred. "Rhys?"

He did not answer. She began to cry again and kicked her chin against the comm wire. Nothing. It was like they'd been cut off completely. How could they be so far from the ship, when the time it had taken them to spin away from it had felt like seconds? She stretched out her back and legs, as if this could somehow get them there faster.

The alarm on her O2 meter sounded in her helmet. Already? Jesus. Rhys had been right. She'd blown most of her oxygen on the thrusters. She did not relent on the nozzle, however.

The ship grew steadily larger, its whiteness transfixing her. So bright, so different from how it had looked in the dock on Earth. So white, a weird blue spot appeared. No, wait. That was in her own vision, and on noticing it, dizziness rushed her. So, this was it. The beginnings of asphyxia. She kept the thrusters at full power. *I'm not getting back on that ship if he doesn't make it. Either we both get there, or neither of us do.*

He would not have approved at all.

Her fingertips tingled. Her lips felt numb, like that time the social worker had tricked her into going to the dentist and the man had stuck her gums full of lidocaine, to work on her teeth.

"Sy!" Walt's voice burst into the silence. Her heart leapt up and she gasped, "Walt! We need help…" She squinted at the ship; the blue at the center had encompassed her vision. Where was she going to land on it? That door ahead, which one was it? Oh yeah…

"I'm landing outside the starboard emergency hatch." Her voice came out sleepy, slow. "We need to be rescued from there and we need a medic. We're both nearly out of O2."

"We're coming out to you."

The ship grew larger then, with a sudden and terrifying rapidness. She aimed herself at the airlock door, concentrating her will on being ready for the moment she hit. She had to grab on, even if she hit hard. How hard would she hit? A weird blackness paused over her. Passing out. And he'd been out of oxygen for much longer. *He's dead as a door nail*, she thought. She didn't even know what a door nail was.

Then the ship rushed up and hit her, and she crumpled into it. She caught and wrapped her arm around a handle, just as Rhys hit and ricocheted off. The line jerked, and a pain tore through her arm as his weight tried to jerk her away. She screamed, the darkness drowned her, the blue circle becoming everything at once, the alarm shrilling in her skull. With her last conscious motion, she clipped herself onto a rung next to the hatch.

"Walter..." she murmured, like a prayer.

***

She awoke with something over her face, something pushed against her mouth, suffocating her. She reached up and pushed at it. Cold air rushed into her. They were giving her oxygen. She tried to move her head, to see Rhys, but she couldn't.

She rolled herself over, but a pain shot through her arm like a firework, and she forgot him for a moment, forgot everything but that pain. Was this the airlock? Where was Rhys? They needed to give him oxygen too... and then something stabbed into her shoulder, and she shrieked as the world blurred and disappeared again.

So achingly tired. But she peeled her eyes open.

Someone had spoken. Walter. "Sy?" The high pitched tone he had when he was anxious, or happy. Which?

Her arm. Her arm had been hurt, and she tensed, expected pain, but felt nothing at all. She glanced down. Still there. It rested flat against her, immobile. She lay on the bed in her own little room, attached to an IV bag clipped up to the wall. "Where's Rhys?" she blurted.

"What happened out there?" Walt's eyes were wide under his scrunched brows and lined forehead.

"Where. Is. Rhys."

"He's alive. He's in medical. The room they converted to medical, anyway. It's one of the barracks. Please tell me what happened."

The flood of relief made her think she'd pass out again, for a moment. She'd done it. She'd brought him back alive. Her body glowed with a deep warmth, like nothing she'd ever felt. But why wasn't he here already? He should be here, and of course, he'd be furious with her. She lowered her voice. "You told Rhys about that thing that hacked our ship?"

"Uh, yeah. It was attached to the ship, to one of the crates. Sy, someone released it from storage. I mean, someone was *in* storage. They had to be. That crate was triggered manually."

She shivered. Rhys was right. Someone on board was out to hurt them, kill them.

He went on, "I searched the place myself, ran scans. The readings were weird, though. I think whoever was down there used some kind of a jammer, like the one you… like the one Rhys had."

"You idiot, you went down there?"

"I brought a weapon. Don't you lecture me." His sternness startled her. Had Rhys given everyone the green light to curb her, then? He went on, "For right now, you ought to stay here, and keep the door locked. It's likely Rhys was the target but—"

"Of course, Rhys was the target," she snapped, and she told him of Rhys' suspicions about Parsons.

"Well," said Walt. "We've got him on lockdown in the med room, so no one's getting to him."

So that's why he wasn't here. "How'd you talk him into that?"

Walt stayed quiet a moment. Then he said, "Rhys isn't conscious right now. We thought it best to induce hyposleep, since we found him in a state of hypothermic shock."

She went cold. Hyposleep? They'd locked him in a room, almost comatose, helpless. Totally vulnerable. "Rhys wouldn't want that," she said coldly. She could not risk sounding emotional over this, not if she would get him to listen to her.

"Maybe not, but the medic said that Io City has better tech for getting him restored without anything being damaged."

Nausea gripped her at his words. How bad off had he been? And the medic? He could be the one working for Parsons; any of them could be! What was the point in having him on lockdown when anyone could break it?

"It'll be okay, Sy," said Walt. "We'll be on Europa soon enough. Just sit tight and keep your door locked. I'll come check on you again soon."

He exited, all while she tried her best to look helpless and obedient. The second he left, she ripped the IV out of her arm with a grunt. She had to see Rhys for herself. She had to try to wake him. Someone on the ship wanted him dead and he would not want to be kept like this. His room was locked, but that meant little. A vent led from the hold up to the barracks Walter had spoken of, and that's where she headed.

She squeezed through the vent into the barracks turned med bay, finding her footing on one of the tall cabinets. The lights in the room were drawn low. It had changed since she'd last seen it; all the bunks had been removed and replaced with two beds. Rhys lay on the one nearest the door. Small white wires were taped about his head and chest, and he had an IV but, otherwise, did not look much different. His chest and shoulders were bare under the blue blanket.

She leapt from the cabinet and approached the bed. The status panel over his head was alive with numbers and readings, none of which she could understand. But here was Rhys, and he only seemed to be asleep. Seeing him now after all that had happened, she started to shake, and her vision blurred over with tears. Why wouldn't he just sit up now and speak to her? Grab hold of her and spank her, even? She couldn't stand to see him like this. She needed him. She knew then that it was why she'd come here so quickly and that all the other reasons were secondary. But just the same, he couldn't stay like this. He wasn't safe. She had to wake him.

There had to be a way. She stepped over to the terminal next to his bed. She was determined to figure it out.

Warmth flooded him. His heart galloped in his chest, almost to bursting, and his eyelids snapped open just as he took a deep snatch of a breath. The heat rose up in him, transmuting into rage, a bright, energetic rage. He sat up, ready to punch something.

Sydell stood before him and she stepped back, her eyes wide and shiny. His heart slammed in his ribs once more on seeing her, but hot anger flared and obliterated whatever tender feeling he may have had. Last thing he could remember, she'd been towing him to the ship. She wouldn't pare down the thrusters. They should both be dead, because she was fucking crazy and wouldn't listen.

"What the hell's going on?" he barked, gripping the metal bed frame.

"It's okay," she said, her voice trembling, "I gave you a shot of hy-adrenaline. You were in hyposleep."

Hy-adrenaline. That would explain the heat and the rage. She crept in closer to him.

"Step back," he said, with deliberate menace, and she froze in place. She did not look to be as deterred as he would like, however. Her eyes stayed fixed on him, and they were wide, but it wasn't with fear. Not exactly.

"You stay right there," he ordered. "And you explain to me exactly what happened."

She told him. He fixated on her words, trying to forget her presence, until the anger passed.

"…and since the scans said you weren't brain dead," she finished, "I looked up how I could revive you and followed the instructions on the terminal. Someone on the ship wants to kill you and I couldn't leave you like that."

She dropped her head. She was hurt by something, but what? Fighting back tears, even. Well, he could certainly make her cry. He took a deep breath as the anger pitched to its peak. He would master it if it killed him. He closed his eyes. Mercifully, she said nothing.

She remained quiet, even as the minutes passed. Time to take stock. He'd lived; by some miracle, she'd managed to get them both back to the ship. And those fucking idiots had put him into hyposleep. Well, she'd done the right thing, waking him up. For that, he was grateful to her. But she would not be getting out of this unscathed.

"Wait," he said, "if they put me in lockdown, how did you get in here?"

She glanced over her shoulder. "That vent." She ducked her head, almost meekly.

He laughed coldly. "Another vent."

The pulsing and irrational rage had dissipated. Seeing her now with her hurt expression, almost bewildered, he felt that odd jerk of affection for her once again. It kicked through him, sharp and unexpected.

"Come here," he said. To his surprise, she did, her head lowered.

"Thank you for waking me up," he said. He put a hand under her chin and lifted her face up. Tears tore down her cheeks with the motion.

"What's wrong?"

"Nothing," she mumbled. "I was scared. Someone tried to kill you, and you were just lying there. And I didn't know if you'd wake up."

Her face scrunched up and she lowered it again, hiding it behind her wild hair. He reached out and touched her arm. It felt cold under her jumpsuit. She looked down at his hand. In a swift motion, he pulled her close and wrapped his arms around her, holding her body to him in an effort to warm her. She trembled, lightly at first, but soon it became more of a quaking, and he swept her up off her feet, sitting her on his lap on top of the blanket.

"We're going to be fine," he said. But he held her tighter. Her dark hair came to rest just under his nose, as though she'd nuzzled into him, and she smelled sweet, like butterscotch. He rested his chin at the top of her head, and she sighed and leaned into him. They stayed like that for a little while, until she had stopped trembling and no longer felt cold. In fact, she started to wriggle in his arms, to shift herself to get more comfortable, and he knew her spirits had returned. He held her in place.

"Rhys…" She stilled, again, and he found he liked hearing her say his name right now.

She said, "You're gonna spank me, aren't you?"

"Hell yes, I am," he replied softly, into her ear. Her breath caught in her throat and her skin, under his fingers, bathed over in goosebumps. He stroked her arm. At least she knew she had it coming.

"Now?" she asked, her voice breathy as he caressed her.

"You seem pretty eager for it," he teased, and then she started to squirm, trying to break away. Now that she had her vigor back, he reveled in wrestling with her, turning her over in his arms and pushing her down across his legs and along the hospital bed. Behind her back, he took her wrist in his hand.

"Don't! That shoulder was dislocated," she piped. Anger pierced again, that she'd gotten herself hurt, that she hadn't told him. He smacked her bottom, hard enough to make her gasp. But she didn't struggle.

"You ought to have told me that immediately," he said. Then he unsnapped the waist of her jumpsuit and yanked it down and, after a moment, tugged her white briefs down too, making her squeal. Her rounded ass, paler than the rest of her, trembled almost expectantly on his lap. He thrilled to have nothing between them.

Chapter 12

She whimpered in anticipation, since he'd yet to spank her again. He let it build. He moved her arm carefully to her side; it must have been numb, for she did not notice. It was this injury that got to him the most, and not at all rationally. They ought to have died; she was beyond lucky to be alive. Why should he be so upset she'd hurt her arm? Because it was his fault; he hadn't protected her like he should have, had failed to calculate how far Parsons was willing to push. His fault, but she would be punished. Punished, because she still wasn't listening.

She huffed, almost impatiently, and said, "You don't have your paddle."

"Do you want me to get it?"

"Not particularly," she mumbled.

"Good. Because I think I'll enjoy using my hand."

"Do it then!" she shouted.

"Hush." He rested his hand on her bottom, soft and cool. "I'm in control of this, not you." He went on calmly, "Do you know why you're being punished?"

She panted, exasperated. "Maybe because I said punish me later?"

"That's right. You knew what to expect. You repeatedly ignored my directions."

"You tell me not to endanger myself, and then you try to cut your cable and die. Maybe take your own advice."

No, this wouldn't do at all. He started in, one slap after another, tinting her pronounced rear a blotchy red and keeping firm hold of her waist as she tried to squirm off him. Once she was yowling, he paused a moment.

"You don't get to countermand me," he said.

He raised his hand to spank her again and she shouted, "You don't get to leave me!"

The personal nature of this startled him, and he stayed his hand for a moment and rested it once again on her rear. Still soft, not so cool. His palm and fingers tingled. "I'm not going to leave you," he said firmly. "The situation required me to take that risk. It was the best thing to do."

"Hardly," she seethed. "What *I* did kept us both alive."

Jesus. Still utterly unremorseful, wasn't she? He soundly covered the sides of her bottom and upper thighs now, until he had her thoroughly finger painted and squalling.

"I don't care, I don't care," she said through gritted teeth. "I kept you alive and I'm glad—" Her voice broke here, but then she went on in an exultant breath, "You aren't dead and you can't make me regret it."

No, he didn't expect he could. Only the crazy ones were as stubborn as this, only the ones who were the most trouble. He spanked her a few more times, simply because it felt necessary to do it. By now, she'd sort of curled up into him, with her good arm wrapped around his hip and her face pressed into his side, as though determined to weather through. He started to rub at her bright, angry red cheeks, and she gasped and then whined, pushing her face into him harder.

He swung her up quickly. He suddenly needed to see her face. He held her on his lap, one arm wrapped around her and gripping her hot rump with his free hand. She glared at him, defiant, her cheeks shining with tears, her mouth parted a bit helplessly. Almost pleading. It was clear in her eyes that she needed him. Needed him, and had refused to let him go, had been willing to die to save him. He did not approve, but pride in her charged through him, nevertheless. Pride, yes, that's what was surging up into his chest, filling up his heart, wasn't it?

Before he could think on it, he had bent her back, holding her between the shoulder blades as he kissed her firmly on the mouth, and she collapsed into him. Her mouth opened to him as he prodded it with his tongue, and she whined, pleased. He felt her heart racing under her warm breast.

When he pulled away, she made a low, plaintive sound, as though disappointed. God, she was adorable. No, this wasn't just pride he felt. Were that it was so simple. This was something he ought to go up to his cabin and think on, spend a few hours alone with before… She shifted her weight on his lap, her soft bottom and plump thighs grinding against him. Beneath them, he was rock hard. He rumbled, deep in his throat. She smiled and wiggled again, her eyes sparkling mischievously.

"All right now," he murmured, almost a warning. Not sure if it was for himself or her. He had to restrain himself here. Before, he'd hurt her feelings. He'd belittled what had happened between them. If it happened now, after what they had been through together, it could not be belittled. He knew that. Things would get serious, and she'd get to see his nature when things were serious. It was better not to go there…

She pushed her mouth forward again and closed her eyes. No, it was impossible not to kiss her. This time, he drank deeply, her moans moving through his lips as vibrations. He ground his cock into her thighs, and she squealed, delighted. He moved his face away, looked her square in her sweet, lusty brown eyes. "Sydell," he said, "this is going to change things."

She moaned in response, wrapping her arms around his naked shoulders.

"I will want you to be mine," he said. His voice sounded grim to his own ears.

"Then make me yours already!" she cried, next to his ear.

Was she serious, or simply impatient to get what she craved? She'd looked so helpless… Could she feel what it was he felt? Her demand both excited and aggravated him, it wasn't in tune with all that coursed through his veins. But her words were on the money. He had to make her his. She had no clue what she was getting herself into, did she? But maybe she deserved to find out.

He took hold of her thermal jumpsuit and pulled down the zipper along her torso, then at the snaps which remained at the waist and along the back of her. The material fell away at her chest, and she gasped, nearly bared on his lap, and he smiled. She curled her arm over her breasts, and he shook his head, pulling it away gently. Her breasts wobbled free.

"You want to be mine. It's only fair I should get to admire you."

The blush of her nipples went taut, and she whimpered as he brushed them softly under his thumbs. Then he ran his hand down the sweet curve of her belly to that tuft of curling hair at the delta of her legs and only just grazed at it with his fingertips.

"Sexy girl," he said, tickling at her lightly, running his finger down teasingly between her legs, to where they met tightly in her sideways pose on his lap. Her eyes half closed and her head lolled to the side; she took on that drugged expression she'd had when he'd touched her for the first time, in the engine room. The intoxication was his, too, as potent as the hy-adrenaline shot had been. It charged through him like an order, a command to fuck her now, and fuck her hard. Best to prolong it a bit, though. He reached back up and took her breasts in his hands, strumming at her nipples until she whined deep in her throat.

"Please," she whispered, and her hips ground on him again, rolling in slow, rhythmic circles on his thigh. He growled and pushed his cock against her bottom, letting her get a good feel of just what was in store. He brought his hands to her shoulders and moved her around on his lap, until he had her facing away, mounted on him like a chair; she made a little whine of confused protest at the position. He pulled her tightly to him, her back pressed to his chest, and opened her legs with his own, splaying her.

"There now, I've got your pussy all exposed for me," he said and then ran his hand along her inner thigh, just next to it. She moaned and writhed on him; he kissed lightly at her neck, at her ear, and he felt her shiver.

"Rhys," she panted. He teased around the split of her, just catching at the soft, wet curls where she opened.

"You got nice and wet," he said, right in her ear, and she cried out, as though shocked at the words. "You just need a firm hand, don't you, baby?"

She whimpered. He slapped lightly at the soaked cleft of her, and she sucked in all her breath.

"Don't you?" he repeated, deepening his voice.

"Y-yes, Rhys," she said.

Goddamn. She was so cute. "What do you want, Sydell? Do you want me to fuck you?"

She yelped aloud at this, and just as she did, he slid his hand over her pussy, running his fingers along the slickness at her entrance and gliding up to that sensitive bud above, spreading her juices up and over it. He stroked around it slowly, until she mewled desperately. He prodded a fingertip into her hot, wet cunt and she went rigid, then pushed her heated mound against his wrist. "Calm down, baby." He chuckled, ceasing to stimulate her for the moment.

"Please," she cried.

"Tell me what you want."

She groaned. Then she said, her voice shaking, "Erm… fuck me. Please."

"You want me to fuck this needy hole?" He stroked his finger along the slick mouth of her pussy, and she howled. He slid his hand up and rubbed at her clit in earnest, until he had her thrashing around on his lap. Then he stopped again and pulled away the blanket from over his thighs, shifting her weight. His cock bobbed free as he did and landed on her bottom with a soft smack. She gasped, as though knowing it instantly.

"That's going in your wet little pussy now," he growled and bit at her neck. He positioned her farther out on his lap, leaning her forward and holding her with one arm wrapped around her waist. Taking himself at the base of his shaft, he nudged his cock along the crack of her, searching for her warm, wet lips with his tip. It slid to the spot like a magnet, and he pushed the end of himself into her.

"Aaah! Oh, God, Rhys, it's—" He cut off her speech as he jammed the rest of it in smoothly, and reached around to the front of her, to where her furry mound now thrust forward, spread taut around him, so that each intimate piece of her became crudely available to his hand. He ran his fingers over every fold and crevice of her, possessively, and she howled. God, it felt good to be in her. He glanced down at his cock penetrating just beneath her thick, red-streaked ass, and groaned appreciatively. She responded with a squeak, her whole body gone tense on his shaft, and he took her pussy in hand once more as he began to slowly thrust in and out of her. He kept his arm tight around her waist.

She gripped him from her depths as he spread her over and over, and he savored the hot tightness of her. She panted ragged little breaths, and he rubbed vigorously all around her clit as he hammered inside her. Her body twitched and she begged senselessly and clawed at his forearm where he held her. At last, she came with a shriek, spasming on his cock while he pinched around her little bud until she screamed long with passion. Then she went limp, her legs dangling helplessly along his own, and he kept her held under his arm, supporting her weight. He now approached that juncture, in which to proceed onward would commit him to his climax. But a thought intruded.

"Are you shunted?" he asked, in almost a grunt.

She didn't respond for a moment, but he waited, keeping himself still, knowing she wouldn't be at her most sensible. After a few seconds, she wagged her head back and forth, swinging her wild hair. *No.* Disappointing, but he was hardly surprised. She did have that fear, that deep distrust of doctors. For now, it was on him to take care of things.

He thrust on, while she started to whine in time with his motions, getting more excited again as they grew more urgent. As he reached that peak from which he could not back down, he tore himself out of her and, cock in hand, came ardently all over her back and bottom, groaning as the bright burst of pleasure overtook him. She squirmed as the hot splatter of it landed, and he laughed, a satisfied rumble.

Taking her under her chin, he pulled her upright and pivoted her face so as to press her flushed cheek to his mouth. Her eyes were closed. He held her this way until he'd caught his breath. "Come on, get up. We're going to my loft," he said. He stood her up and wrapped a blanket from the bed about his hips, tucking it tightly. She watched him, her eyes wide, her head leaning to the side. On impulse, he wrapped an arm around her hips and then levered her up over his shoulder.

She squawked a protest, which he answered with a light, playful slap to her rear, and then proceeded to carry her out into the hall. "Someone will see me," she hissed.

"Doubt it," he said, though he cared little if they did. What better way to have everyone know how it was and save the tedium of having to tell it? She was his now, and he was carrying her back to his cabin, naked, whipped, and cum-covered.

She woke in the loft, now filled with an eerie, soft golden light. Her loft. Her bed... no, a new bed. Oh. Right. She was in Rhys' bed. She pulled the sheets up over her face, flushing hot to remember it all. *Jesus.*

It had been romantic, maybe, being carried up here, though she was naked and marked by him, and anxious someone would see her. Romantic when he'd opened the visor so that they were bathed in the starlight. But after that… he'd tossed her onto his bed and taken her, again and again, all while she kept begging for more. She blushed hot now, to think on how she'd begged him. He was rough with her, insistent, but he'd watched her like a hawk, as though to avoid pushing her too far with what he did. All the same, it had been a bit frightening. Exhilarating. Like nothing she'd ever known.

After such an end to such a day, she'd found herself falling asleep even as he'd been rousing her for another round. Then he had been tender, pulling her onto him and kissing the top of her head, and she'd passed out with her face on his broad chest, the hairs of which tickled her skin in a way that was oddly comforting.

And now she was here, next to him, and he would wake soon and speak to her. Shit, what would he say? What would she say? And what was this strange light in the room, not like sunlight but… she peered out the viewport, raising herself up on her arms. Holy shit. It was Jupiter. A deep throbbing gold and brown, a tiger's eye sphere, with a torrent of red at its side, like a stab wound. She made some sound of awe, and Rhys moved on the bed next to her. He followed her gaze upward.

"Nearly there," he said. "Now that the ship's actually moving. It's farther than it looks, though."

She blinked and looked down shyly as he fixed his eyes on her. He leaned in and took a handful of her hair, gently pulling her face close.

"Good morning," he said, and as he pressed into her, she felt his thick morning wood prodding her thigh. He kissed her roughly and she fell back against the pillows, her legs opening of their own eager accord before she'd even realized it. His mood was tender no longer; he pulled at her legs beneath her knees and drew her flat on her back, then leaned over to the alcove in the wall, to get another prophylactic shroud. Was it the third one they'd used already? Or the fourth?

"We're going to have you shunted as soon as we get to Io City," he said, as he rolled the shroud over his cock. She pressed her lips together to see it now, as she couldn't in the dark of the night before. Arrogantly large, it struck up from him nearly parallel to his abdomen. How had it fit in her at all?

"Why?" she asked, her eyes staying on his manhood.

"So I can fill you up with cum," he said simply, and she scowled, because it was so crass. Then he hiked her legs up to his shoulders, which was not exactly comfortable but… In this way, he impaled her, looking her right in the eyes as he did, and she flushed hot all over again. She felt her whole cunt soaking as he pushed in and out of her, doubling her against herself, and she yipped as he collided with sensitive spots inside her body she didn't know existed, in a strangely pleasurable pain. It titillated her every nerve, and as he came, in quickening thrusts, she cried out excitedly, though she did not reach climax herself.

After, he stood up and got dressed, while she stayed bundled in the bed, her jumpsuit still down in the medical room. He moved about briskly, with a bright look on his face that wasn't quite a smile, satisfied, and energized by what they'd done. But what was going to happen now?

He caught her gaze, and as if he knew her thoughts, he said, "I'd like you to stay here in the loft with me. I'll bring up your clothes for you later. Sound all right?"

"Um. Sure." She kept her happiness smothered in a dull tone.

"It's a small space, I know, but we only have a bit over a week left. And when we get to Europa, you'll stay with me." He zipped up his jumpsuit and then started rifling through one of the closets.

"With you?"

"Yes, at my apartment. It's not large, but it should do. We won't be there a lot."

A rushing up of joy within her made her fall silent. She would go home, with Rhys. But… but he hadn't asked, he'd *told* her, and a hot annoyance at this dampened the joy somewhat. He'd changed toward her, from acting like an overzealous boss to, well, acting like he owned her. His attitude made her want him all the more; didn't she respond to him with a rapid intensity every time he took her? Yes, but she couldn't approve of it. He ought to have asked her.

"So, you just say where I'm going to live now, and I live there?" she asked irritably.

He had a sock in his hand, but he stopped what he was doing and looked her dead in the eyes. Her heart fluttered. "Sydell, you're under my authority, legally. At least until your sentence is served. I certainly *can* say where you will live."

She squirmed under the twisted sheet, as if that could alleviate the hot prickle of annoyance this gave her. She snorted and said, "Is it normal, is it even legal, to dictate who a prisoner sleeps with as well as where she sleeps?"

His dark brows locked together, and she felt a throbbing in her depths, where he'd just been inside. Hell, even his anger stirred her. She glanced away and drew the sheet over her breasts, with the sudden instinct to not be seen. He shrugged, as though refusing to be baited. "I don't think there are any laws pertaining to it. But are you suggesting that you had no say in *this*?" His arm swept the room; he meant, in their sleeping together.

"No," she grumbled, "you know I wanted to. I just didn't expect to be told I'd be collected up to your apartment like I was to your loft."

"I won't strip you down and carry you there, if that's

what you mean. And I'm not forcing *this*, what's happened between us, to continue. Just say the word and we can go back to how things were. We'll find a place for you to stay. I'm not so desperate as to force you to be with me." He scoffed, laughed even, with the last words, and she grew hot with fury, even as a little pang tore at her throat. He could get bent. She'd live on the street sooner than she'd live with this asshole.

He spoke first. "But, as long as *this* goes on, you will live with me, and you will be mine. That's the way it is, with me."

He *had* said, he would want her to be his. She hadn't thought much on it when he'd said it, hadn't been of the mind to. She opened her mouth to tell him off, as she'd been about to do. But she didn't. She couldn't. She wanted to go home with him. She *wanted* to be his.

"We'll get you used to it soon enough," he said and dashed over to the bed. He tore the bedding away from her, so she couldn't hide from him. He snatched her legs up at the ankles and lifted them up against his chest. He landed a ringing smack on her exposed rear, then followed it with another. She struggled and swiped at him with her good arm. "Dammit, Rhys, stop it! Ow!" God, her butt was still sore from the night before; his slaps stung enough that she earnestly hated him for a moment.

"I know why you're so bitchy," he said, all at once ceasing. "You didn't get to come."

Her mouth hung open at this, outraged, while he took her calves in his hands and yanked her legs open, then loomed over her defenseless pussy. He leaned his face in so close that she felt his hot breath on her wet petals, and she had to stifle an excited whine. She ached with need, but she argued on, "This isn't the way things get settled."

"Settled?" he asked sharply, but with the twitch of a

grin. "What needs to be settled? You think now when we have disagreements, you can whine at me and just have your way?"

She reeled at this, even as something pulsed deep in her, made her pussy lips quiver uncontrollably, and he was so close, could he have seen it?

"You are mine," he said, more gently now. "You don't have to be, but as long as you are, you don't need to worry about settling anything. What I say, settles things. Got it?"

She felt as though she were being pulled into some kind of darkness, a black hole; yes, a massive gravity crushing out everything sensible. Her body trembled as every reality she'd ever counted on was warped by it and around it. She'd not seen him, somehow, until this very moment, and he was a dark star, and the star had trapped her.

He dipped his head down between her legs and she sucked in her breath, while his arms pressed down on her thighs, keeping them spread. He kissed her, tenderly, right on that aching bud, and she moaned. Then his mouth locked on to her and he lashed her clit vigorously with his hot, cruel tongue; the spot was so sensitive, so unused to this direct, intimate touch, that it struck her as painful. She cried out and squirmed. He slid his hands up and clamped down on the spread flesh of her hips, squeezing her, even as he nuzzled into her fur, squeezing like he was trying to get juice from an orange to drink. The pain ripened then into a deep, nearly unbearable pleasure. Somehow his tongue could be even more punishing than his hand on her ass had been, merciless as she begged him to slow down, to ease up.

He did neither. At his insistence, she came with an angry wail, like a warrior struck down. The orgasm burnt through her like an exploding star, the most intense she'd ever had; the room darkened before her eyes. She lay back limp on the bed, a defeated thing. He leapt up, away from her, and tossed the blankets back onto the bed from the floor. He lifted his hand to his face and massaged his jaw. "Stay there," he ordered. "Your arm's hurt, and you've been through a lot. I want you to rest today."

At the moment, she couldn't seem to move at all.

"Everyone's going to shit their pants to see me walking around, I expect," he said with a chuckle. "There'll be hell to pay, for putting me under like that."

His eyes had a wicked gleam to them. What would he do? Couldn't be anything worse than what he did to her when she crossed him. But the stoicism she'd come to expect from him had melted away, and something else showed, something ruthless and fierce. Momentarily stripped of all energy and feeling, she could see everything he was, and it was as painful and brilliant as staring into the sun. It left a black spot in her vision when she tried to look anywhere else.

This is him, she thought. *This is the man who was a slaver. This man was Parsons' brother.* He'd told her, but she hadn't seen it. Not *really* seen it. Not until now. That sense of being crushed returned, but it was too late; she'd passed the point of no return and she was his, to be bent as he willed. But where could it lead?

An unpleasant knowledge, her eyelids grew heavy with it, and she was still vaguely aware of him moving about the room as she fell into a dark, dead sleep.

Part II

EUROPA

Chapter 13

S he kept close to the visiglass as they landed, standing up on the bed, hoping to see the surface of Europa, or its sister moon Io, or the city beneath. But an icy cloud cover left an impenetrable blue mist around every window.

She'd not left the loft since the day he'd carried her up to it, as he'd put the entire ship on lockdown. Everyone had been required to stay in their cabins, Rhys excluded, of course, and with a few exceptions for absolute necessity. Now that the ship had landed at the dock, Rhys came into the loft and hurried her along. "You don't need much from here. We'll buy things for you in the city. Come on."

She left with nothing beyond her jumpsuit, jacket, and boots, and followed him out the airlock to the docks. She craned her neck high to the ceiling as it narrowed above her, three levels of hangar space, with each hangar opening to a walkway that led to a central hub. Long windows flanked the hangar doors, but the view out them was as cloudy as the ship's had been. Once outside their hangar, the crewmen Rhys had hired all stalked away without a backward glance, except for the tech, who shook his hand before he left.

"What's wrong with them?" she asked.

"I've flagged them all for surveillance. And they won't be getting the second half of their payment until I've cleared them."

Well, she certainly wasn't the only one he was so autocratic with, at least. "Jesus. But weren't they going back to Earth?"

He shrugged. "I don't know. They pick up work where they can. This possibility was mentioned in their contract."

"Really? You wrote in the possibility that they'd be flagged and not paid if anything goes wrong on the ship?" Her pitch rose as she finished speaking, and the words echoed sharply in the empty space.

He narrowed his eyes at her, but his gaze was vague, as though he had something else on his mind. "It's not unheard of. Besides, any one of them could be the person who tried to kill us."

"Really? What about Walt?"

Rhys shook his head. "He found the hack."

"What about me?"

Rhys laughed. "You?" he said, in a tone that made her wish from the base of her heels that she was the traitor, just so he'd be wrong. He tugged the waist of her pants at the small of her back, hiking them up her bottom lightly while she snarled. He peered down into her face, his hazel eyes gleaming. "I don't need to put a tail on you, because you're with me, and I'm keeping a close eye on you."

She yanked her suit back into place as he released her and glowered at him, but said nothing. Her belly fluttered at his attentions, but she'd be dead rather than to have him know it. She pretended to ignore him as they headed for the central hub, staying several feet behind and gazing up to the ceiling. The walls almost seemed to glow, with a grayed purple light. Was that the only light in here? It seemed to be. No tech she'd heard of or understood. Because, yes, *they* had built this place. It was Io City now, but the base structure had belonged to the beings who had once lived here, on the moon, and had disappeared so long ago.

Rhys had gone much farther ahead and spoke with someone at the center of the docks.

"Sy!" Walt called from behind her. She stopped, to let him catch up.

"We're parting ways, now," he said and scratched the back of his hair, which had grown shaggy over the trip. "I'm taking a shuttle from here out to the academy."

"I'm so glad for you," she said stupidly. Surely, there had to be something better she could say? She stared at her toes for a moment, but he said nothing more. At last, she blurted, "I'm so sorry, Walt. I kept you with me far too long, because I wanted to keep flying. You deserved better."

He closed his eyes, his lashes fluttering. "Sy. Don't think for a moment that I was anywhere I didn't want to be. My place was with you." He opened his eyes and looked right at her, flushing slightly. She was speechless.

"But it's time to move on, isn't it?" he said with a self-effacing grin. "I think he's good for you. Just don't lose your nerve, you'll need it with him."

Nerve? Yes, Walt probably thought she had nerve, when all she had was recklessness. Rash to act, rash to speak… and it would only keep getting her into trouble with Rhys if anything. God, what was Walt trying to tell her, though, saying he wasn't anywhere he didn't want to be? Had he had feelings for her that whole time? And she hadn't seen it, hadn't seen his devotion, she'd just gone on using him, using the old ties to keep her moving, keep her free. But now she was caught, and he was the one going, moving on. "Come visit," she said, nearly pleading.

"Of course, I will. Everything will be fine, Sy. You're safer now than you ever were running a ferry with me."

She forced a smile. Safe, yes. But also uneasy, in a way she couldn't fathom and couldn't express. She had to face her challenges just as he would have to face his at the academy. No sense burdening him further. She gave him a quick, fierce hug. Then he'd gone, heading out to whatever docking bay would take him to the Pilot's Academy. Rhys returned and led her to the central hub, where a huge dais of an elevator took up the center of the dock offices. When the floor of it dropped in descent, she yelped and clutched at him. He laughed but held her close for the ride down. At the bottom, they were met with a long oval of a speed craft.

"Best way to take the tour," he said, folding himself into the speeder and pulling her in after him. It was an auto-nav, with a transparent top half; it launched away from the docks at a clip that made her grasp at the seat, hesitant to cling to Rhys yet again. They shifted into a long, narrow passage, in which other speeders whizzed by and over them. At the sides, people raced by on bright blue streams, hovering over the ground; behind them, a panel of visiglass showed a blur of snowdrifts.

Then the space opened up again, and they had entered the city. The enclosure over the common ground ended at about thirty meters up, but the surrounding buildings reached much higher, stretching vertically past the barrier and into the snowdrifts of the atmosphere. As they drove on, the enclosure grew larger and larger, until they were in some kind of a grand open space, where all the speeders circled through at the center and all around, buildings rose in those otherworldly blues and purples.

"This is the heart of it," said Rhys. "The Promenade, it's called."

People crowded the ample streets, and not people like you saw on Earth. These were stylized versions of people, long and lean and in dramatic cuts of clothing like she'd never seen before, in colors and combinations of colors, unashamed to grab attention. She had the flash of a thought; I don't belong here. She glanced at Rhys, to find him watching her. "I don't spend much time in this district," he admitted. "But we can go shopping here and get you some clothes and whatever else you need."

"Where do you live?"

"Near the City Center, back closer to the docks. But I'm going to take you somewhere first."

"What? Where?"

"We're going out to the caverns."

The caverns. He'd talked to her of them during their time up in the loft—and talked so much. A giant cavern beneath Io City, spanning for miles under and around it.

The speeder whizzed out of the promenade and into another corridor, this one darker and without anyone walking along the sides or other speeders around or above them. Where they were going, no one else seemed to be, at least not right now. At last, they stopped, in a small hangar lit by infinity light and with walls of concrete; it couldn't have been part of the original construct. This hangar had no ships, only large land rovers, some with wheels as tall as she. Rhys pulled her out of the speeder and led her to one of the smaller ones.

"We're going outside?" she asked, a pinch of fear in her belly. Of course, they were, how could she be so slow to only just realize it?

He grinned. "Yep." He clicked a button on his watch and the rover door opened. The windows of it were thick and tinted.

"But I thought the ruins were under the city?" She wrapped her arms around herself.

"They are. But you can't access them from inside it. Io Council closed up most of the entries."

"Why?"

"They'd say they aren't safe. But they really just don't want anyone nosing around in them. Trust me, where I'm taking you is perfectly safe. Now come on." He lifted her into the rover; she scrambled in awkwardly and glared back at him. Before she could say anything, he closed the door. He came around the other side and climbed in, then started the engine. A wave of heated air emanated from the console in front of her. The hangar door opened directly out onto the surface. "There's no airlock?" she asked.

"No. Europa's been atmosphered. The air's very thin, but it's still made pressurizing the city easier. And they want to terraform."

"They never could do it on Mars."

"No, Parsons wouldn't have stood for it," he said with a bitter smile.

A strong wind shook the rover. It also cleared away the snow drifts somewhat, and for a time, the surfaces around her showed as deep violet shadows. Edges of snowy rock crowned just to the left of them; she inched away from it instinctively. In front of them, some kind of a butte protruded, which Rhys drove the rover straight for. As they neared it, it loomed over them; the top of it pointed into the sky, almost like a radio tower, but sloped gracefully. Rhys handed her a breather; the silicon mouthpiece attached to a compression tank the size of a tube of lipstick.

"Throw on one of the coats from the back," he said. He reached to the backseat as he said it and tossed a puffy blue jacket at her. "Tuck your face down into the coat, onto your breather. You won't be able to see too well, but I'll lead us there. Don't let go of my hand until we're in the cave. We won't be able to talk when we're out in the open."

He shut off the rover. Her heart raced and a tremor of nausea caught at her throat. Rhys helped her do up the plackets on her coat, then gave her a vigorous rub on one shoulder, nearly a shake. "Ready?" he asked and smiled, as if trying to remind her this was an adventure.

She swallowed and then nodded. He took her hand in his own tightly, wrapping his thumb and two fingers around her wrist. Silly that he'd told her not to let go; she doubted she even could. The cold blasted her in the face the instant he opened the door, and snow filled the front of the rover, dusting the seats. She tucked her head away from it.

"Come on, hurry!" he shouted over the roaring wind. He pulled her down from the rover, pressing her against him and swinging her to her feet in the soft, piled snow. Her face burned with the cold; she brought the breather to her face and tucked her head down into the hood of the jacket, as deep as possible. Rhys pulled her along by her wrist and she stumbled after him blindly. So cold, colder than she'd ever been! It assaulted her on all sides; some patch of exposed skin on her forehead ached as the wind blasted it. How he was able to guide them, she could not fathom.

Within about a minute, he'd led her into a tall, narrow opening in the side of the butte. She peeped up out of the jacket, now that they were out of the wind. Utter darkness prevailed. The passage dropped; she stumbled into Rhys, but he held her upright, then kept on leading her down. Her feet scrambled for traction on the floor beneath. Was it ice? Or just frozen ground? They walked for an immeasurably long time, into the depths.

The passage ended and light teased her eyes. A huge chamber, and glowing? Softly, with no tenable light source. Rather, the walls themselves, or the depths of them, seemed to be the source. They were lit dimly in an eerie blue.

"What the hell?" she breathed, moving the rubber away from her face for a moment.

"It's called lyndasaline. Sort of like phosphorous," he said, watching her face with a small grin. "It's the same that's in the city walls, in much higher concentration. They probably mined it."

"I've never heard about this," she said. "Why isn't it in the travel reams?"

"The caves aren't open to tourists," he said, nearly sounding possessive. "Especially not these. They're mine."

"And they let you just… own this?"

"I do, legally, at least 'til the Council changes the laws, which they're trying to. They want to control everything on the moons, and they will eventually." He sighed and shook his head. "But they won't have these. Not yet."

Not yet. What did he have planned? As her eyes adjusted to the light, the size of the cavern became apparent, taller than the interior of the domes of the city. Long strips of rock ran down from the ceiling like narrow teeth. She tripped over and over, gawking at the great luminous chasm.

"Try to watch your step," Rhys chided, but he smiled, as though proud of the effect the cave had on her.

"This place is more than a tourist trap, and the Council

knows it," he said. "They just don't want anyone else to know it."

"Oh, right, the mysterious alien caves," she laughed. "I wouldn't have taken you for a conspiracy theorist."

He chuckled, the sound warping and echoing eerily in the huge chamber. "You say that with contempt," he said, "but you have no idea what you're talking about."

His tone was light but had its own sting of contempt. She peeked up at him, but his face stayed unreadable. They entered a small passage, which led into yet another massive cave, this one lighter somehow, with icy white walls reflecting the faint glow on the rocks. As they moved closer to the opposite wall, she squinted, confused. The texture of it was odd. What was that?

They drew closer to the wall; he led them to it. But what was she looking at? Small slashes peppered every surface, whether rock or ledge or overhang. Even the larger of the icy stalagmites had slashes carved into them, giving them the texture of a tree. But, no, it had a sort of evenness to it that one would never see on a tree, not on Earth anyway. Almost unnatural.

She looked to Rhys, to find him already staring at her, his eyes narrowed.

"This is very odd, isn't it?" she said, unsure of what to say about it.

"You can't guess what you're seeing?"

"You want me to guess? Any guess I made would be stupid, since I don't know anything about this place."

"Very modest of you," he said dryly. "But I can do more than guess. They left this here, as some kind of… history. Like a message. And I'm going to find out what it says before the Council can take it away."

A message? All that… *scratching* on the rocks and ice? "Has the Council seen it?" she asked.

"These caves have been privately owned for a long time. So, officially, no. But their people get around. They know something's going on down here. They just have to find some legal method to take it back."

"How do you know for sure it's a message? It looks so random."

"I've scanned all of it. The program I uploaded it onto can't crack it, but it isn't random."

"Are you the only one trying to figure it out?"

"Me, and Corey. My partner. No one else knows. It's too sensitive. I've had the place monitored for a while."

"Should you really keep something like this to yourself?"

He sighed. "It's either that, or Parsons gets hold of it. Anything that goes through the Council goes to him."

Her jaw dropped, though she kept her mouth closed. Parsons had people in the Europa government? But of course, why wouldn't he? All her life, she'd heard of the distant Council colonies as being something of a utopia, free from corporate corruption. It stung, to learn otherwise.

"It's a shame, too," he went on, "because I need help figuring it out. Code breakers, people good with math. I'm doing my best but… well, it's an arcane pattern. Not human."

Yet he had told her. He trusted her? Yes, just as he had laughed when she'd asked if he suspected her, back on the docks. Not trust so much as disregard.

"Well, you wasted a tell on a very *non* mathematician," she said. "You might have told Walt. He's brilliant."

His eyes caught at her, searching for a moment. Then he said, "I didn't tell you because I wanted you to crack it. I told you because you're mine and there's no point keeping it a secret. Figuring this out has been my life for the past year and I can't hide it, you'll be too close to me."

He cleared his throat, ran a finger over the grooves on the nearest wall. "And I'm going to have you help me with the data. There are still mountains of photographs to be transmitted into the program."

Her cheek twitched involuntarily. "Aargh, that sounds awful."

He smiled, his eyes glittering slightly. Fucking sadist. "It'll be good for you," he said, the smile growing affectionate. "And it will be something you can do at the office."

She tilted her head and said archly, "Here I thought I'd just be bringing you coffee and getting bent over your desk." She smiled and broke eye contact at the end of it.

He reached over and scratched her head, tugging gently at her hair. "Of course, you'll be bent over my desk. Coffee sounds nice, too."

She sighed. Annoying, but almost comforting, compared to… well, to all this. Markings in a giant cave, alien markings. A history, a message. Really, though? They had built the city, even if it was a far cry from what it had become now. They had only left a shell. But why shouldn't they have left a message of some kind? Humans would have.

His contention with the Council made her tense, too. If he were at odds with them, how could such contention end? Parsons had won out over the law, but could Rhys? Should he, even?

He stepped closer and curled an arm around her shoulders, pulling her in snugly. He leant and kissed her at the crown of her head, his hot breath making her vision go light and her heart race. "You need to relax. This is a lot to take in, I know. We can talk more about it later. Right now, I'm going to take you home."

Chapter 14

"Canton Excavations," said Rhys, with a careless wave out the speeder window. Here, the enclosure rose no taller than the long stretches of single story buildings alongside them. Canton Ex blurred by as a few windows, nothing more. Not as she had been expecting. Rhys had his eyes on her as they passed it. "It serves its purpose. My father didn't care for much beyond functionality. In our business, there isn't the need to impress anyone."

The speeder stopped after only a few minutes more, at a tall, wide cylinder of a building, reaching up far past the enclosure. Windows wrapped around it like belts. Was this where he lived, then? He kept hold of her hand as they stepped through the broad main entrance, the door spreading open at a diagonal. Inside, a central lift took them up to Floor 16, where a spacious, well-lit hall formed a circle around the structure from which to reach the apartment.

"Does everyone live here?" she asked. She hadn't seen any other residential buildings.

"No. Just people who can't pay the luxury price for a private residence. Or who don't want to." He stopped and swiped his hand in front of a door; it slid open from the left. It was a modest place, but still twice the size of her own family's apartment on Earth. The open floor plan showed nearly all of it in one glance—living room at one end and up next to a wall of windows, the bed, on a small elevation. Only the kitchen and bathroom were unseen.

"Sorry for the mess," he said. "To be honest, this is usually how things are. Please, sit down."

She blinked in surprise at the politeness and sat on one of the two dark gray sofas, set in a semi-circle around a low table. Formed into the wood-paneled walls, gold bulbs glowed softly in sconces, making for a cozy effect, and she even relaxed. After the cold of the surface, the apartment was almost roasting. The mess he'd described proved no more than a litter of papers and books on the coffee table; honestly, she was grateful to find the place felt lived in.

She stripped off her silicon jacket and laid it next to her. Rhys had gone back into a room off behind the wall where she sat; clattering sounds followed shortly, along with the odd clash of metal. Then a thud, followed by a grunt.

He muttered, "If there's one thing I hate about this place, it's this kitchen. Much too narrow."

She tried to picture his tall form in a narrow kitchen, and it made her smile. What was he doing in there anyway? Was he going to cook? While she waited, she peeked curiously at everything laid out on the table. The print on the papers was too small to read without picking it up first, and she didn't want Rhys to think she was snooping. She noted some of the papers were handwritten, with notes accrued randomly in a tight, linear scrawl. His writing? And there were a few printed photographs of those marks, from the cave.

He reappeared about ten minutes later, holding two deep ceramic bowls of steaming food, which he set on the coffee table after clearing some space, piling notes up onto themselves. "I don't have a proper table, so I always eat here. We can get one if you like."

"No. This is fine," she said, imagining sitting across from him at a dining table. Much too strained. He'd made rice, green vegetables of some kind, and white blobs of mimicmeat. It tasted delicious, especially after a month of dried noodles. She held up one of the long, funny vegetables in her sticks.

"It's good. What is it?" she asked.

"My mom called it a gooseneck. It's a hybrid of rabe and squash. They gave out seeds for the farmers in Shenzen district, after the bombs. I'm glad you like it. I hated it when I was a kid, but now…" He shrugged.

"Did you live in Shenzen?"

"No, my mom moved to the States before I was born."

His mouth flattened slightly, as though it were a subject he did not wish to pursue. She motioned to the table. "Have you figured *any* of it out?"

He chewed and swallowed before answering. "No. Not a damn thing." He set his bowl down on a small clear space of table. "But the pattern's there. You'll see it for yourself when you look."

"Are you sure?" she asked, before she could stop herself. "I mean, people love to find patterns."

He smiled scornfully. "They do. But computers are less biased. This isn't random; it's code, and they left it for a reason. They left this city behind, and for years we haven't understood why. I'm going to find out."

The finality of his determination left her with nothing to say, and they finished eating in silence, though it wasn't exactly unpleasant. After, he gathered up the dishes and went into the kitchen. "We'll head into the office tomorrow and start work. And I'll make you an appointment for shunting. I'm not sure how soon I can get you in—"

"No!" It tore out of her before she could think better on it.

From the kitchen, he said, "Excuse me?" with a withering politeness that made her cringe.

"Please," she whined, "I don't want to."

He poked his head around the wall. He frowned, but his eyes were gentler than she'd expected. "Sydell, there isn't a female over the age of fourteen who isn't shunted if she has access to it. It's hard on your body to keep having a period if you aren't getting pregnant."

She flushed hot to hear him talk about it so candidly. But then, of course, he'd been a medic. "You're afraid," he went on. "And that's all right, but it isn't good to let fear rule you."

"There, but you're always saying I shouldn't endanger myself! And you use fear to rule me." This last came out sounding petulant, though she had felt herself very smart saying it.

"Shunting is perfectly safe or else I wouldn't want you do to it," he said. "And fear is only one tactic up my sleeve, I assure you."

What the hell did he mean by that? "Please," she insisted, with an almost hysterical note in her voice which she hated to hear. "Please don't make me."

"Fine," he said and went back into the kitchen, leaving her in shock. A moment later, the dishes clattered about into the washer. Had he truly relented? She could hardly believe it. He came back out, having peeled off his shirt. She stared at his shoulders, at the rusty brown hair peppering his broad chest.

"Time for bed. We go to work early in the morning."

He tossed the shirt toward a little crevice in the floor. "That's the laundry chute," he said. "Better keep your jumpsuit for now, and we'll get you more things tomorrow."

She stood and followed him to the bed hesitantly. Alone with him now in his apartment, a nervous tension sprang up in her, an almost virginal anticipation. He pulled up the coverlet from the bed, tossing it in a folded mound. She stood immobile, transfixed by him.

He reached for her, grabbing not her body but her jumpsuit and, with a swift motion, had pulled down the zipper, his hand pausing just above her thighs where it ended, and her blood ran hot. In the next instant, he ripped it apart at the waist snaps, so that the garment hung uselessly at her legs and shoulders. Then he bent down and kissed her, pulled her up to him with his hands spread along her back, and moved them down, squeezing her ass. She growled, biting at his lips hungrily. He pulled back and stared down at her, his eyes bright.

"Get to bed," he ordered, a curve of a smile on his lips, and as she stepped toward it, he slapped her rear, so that she jumped in quickly. He fell in heavily behind her, swept her down onto her back, and she curled her legs around him. He fucked her without preliminaries, which she did not mind, but as he gave her no special attention, she did not come, and after he finished, he gathered her into his arms possessively and in a few minutes breathed in the slow, rhythmic breaths of one sleeping.

She pushed her back into him and let the residual lust spread out pleasantly throughout her body as she relaxed. Drifting off to sleep, her fantasies wandered no further than the man beside her, in whose arms she lay wrapped. Strange, to have someone hold you captive and still so captivate you. She smiled at the notion as she fell asleep.

He woke Sydell early, gently shaking her by the shoulder, and when she gazed up at him sleepily, he pointed out the window. "You can see Io right now," he said. A draft had pushed out the snow drifts so that only a faint purple haze remained in the height of the atmosphere; through it, the volcanic sister-moon showed, blurred and looking like a squashed maroon eyeball. On seeing it, she sucked in her breath and went tense beside him.

"Our atmosphere has a thick ice layer," he reminded her. "Very few eruptions make it to the surface. None have ever hit the city."

She went on staring up at the moon, agitated, and he snatched her ankles and swept her down flat onto her belly. "Mm, I think you need a distraction." He pinched at her thighs, tickling them as she lay sprawled, until she giggled wildly. From there, he worked his attentions up the insides of her legs; nothing so gratified him as seeing her squirm as he teased her cunt, grown slippery already. Likely, she was still horny from the night before; she hadn't come, and he was well aware of it.

Once he had her quivering, he snatched a new shroud off the bedside table, formed it onto his cock, and plunged it into her as she lay prone. Her cries came out muffled into the pillows around her face, and he took a handful of hair at the base of her head and pulled it, so as to hear her. He planted his other hand firmly on the center of her shoulders and then pumped her thoroughly, slowing down as her cries became louder, then picking up the pace again until he came, shuddering. She yelped excitedly as he did but did not reach orgasm herself; he made sure of it.

"All right, get up. Time to get dressed for work," he said cheerfully, landing a light slap on her rear and rising up to his knees on the bed. She bent around snakelike, on her belly, and whined, "But, Rhys…" She dropped her face under her tousled hair. "I want to come."

The desire to make her come hit him stronger than he'd expected, but he resisted it. "You can come," he said, slowly, gravely, "just as soon as you're shunted."

Her face met his again, her eyes huge and the dark irises liquid. Would she cry? He braced himself to withstand it if she did. She flushed. "That's not fair." Her voice cracked when she said it.

"It's perfectly fair if you think on it," he said. "Now get your clothes on so we have time to eat. And don't let me catch you touching yourself." He reached out to where her legs were still spread and gave a soft pinch to the fuzz between her thighs. She squealed. Too cruel, was it? No, he'd not let himself feel guilty; it would work, and it needed to work.

She sat up, squirming as she did, gazing at him with lust and hostility, which he only returned with a smile. He reached to the floor and scooped up her jumpsuit, then tossed it to her.

"Come on, you can help me make breakfast."

Canton Excavations had the look of a business on its last legs these days. Built into an old parking garage, it had an unusually low ceiling lined with infinity light and desks scattered about without any seeming sense. Most of the desks were empty. His own desk, over by the long stretch of occluded window paneling, lay as cluttered with books and papers as his tables at home did.

Sydell trailed behind him and he mostly ignored her as he searched around for someone. Corey was out today, but he wanted to see Amala. A young man at a corner desk stood and, upon recognizing him, promptly dropped his holotablet onto the floor. Then he scooped it up and rushed over. Rhys knew the kid but, for the life of him, couldn't remember his name. He wore good slacks, a dress shirt, and a tie, none of which Rhys had on himself at the moment.

"Sir, it's good to have you back," the kid said, his esteem genuine.

"Thank you. Do you know where Amala is?"

"I think she's taken the morning off. Maybe the afternoon too."

Rhys sighed. But then, it wasn't unusual. She was Amala, after all, and had become so necessary to him that she took many liberties. "Well, then, would you mind getting a new desk panel set up near mine? This is Sydell; she'll be working with us now."

"Of course! Welcome aboard, Sydell, I'm Fritz. Would you like a cubicle?" On asking, he glanced up at Rhys for the answer, as Rhys expected.

"No. Open desk." He stopped his gaze on her, and she turned pink. Her dark eyes had a hazy gleam in them, the eyes of a bitch in heat.

Fritz stepped over to the window and got to work setting up a new desk panel. He wheeled over a swivel stool as the final touch. Sydell sat, as awkwardly as she could. "I don't think I'm a desk job person," she said moodily when Fritz had gone away.

"No one is an anything person. I don't love working at a desk, but sometimes it's how I need to get things done." He took up a thick handful of files from his desk, knowing instantly what it was. Despite the mess, he was never at a loss to find exactly what he needed. He set it down in front of her.

"I have a system set up for you to try at this like it's a code. It's tedious, and if you get tired of it, you can tell me, and I'll let you do some of the books I had for Amala today." But really, he wished Amala were here. He'd counted on her helping get Sydell set up with some clothes. In the office, her jumpsuit looked like pajamas, and she seemed no more comfortable with herself for it.

"Just ask if you need me to show you anything," he said.

When he left her, she looked lost, as though she'd gotten into the wrong building by mistake. She stared down at the papers he'd given her with something like horror. Well, she had to have something to do, and since she knew about his secret, she might as well help him work on it. At this rate, it would take years. He sat down at his own desk, about five yards away, and started cracking away at it once more. Every time he thought he had his head around a pattern, he tested it and failed. Quite like binary in some ways, those grooves of varying length, but of course, it wasn't. If only there had been symbols.

Hours flew by for him, unchecked, until a gnawing hunger dragged at his gut. He peered around his cubicle divider at Sydell. Hunched over her work, she'd rather created her own cubicle with the long sections of her messy hair blocking her face from his view. His eyes moved automatically to her hips as she rotated them restlessly in the swivel stool. At the seat of her pants, where her bottom met the chair, the fabric of her jumpsuit was a shade darker, almost as though she'd wet it. He frowned. She was still wet from this morning, he realized.

He got up and walked over to her. "Sydell," he said in a low voice, "are you wearing underwear?"

Her eyes darted around furtively. "No," she hissed, "it's

all in the laundry. You said they'd send it back up to the apartment."

"Yes, when it's cleaned. Why didn't you ask to wear mine? You've positively soaked yourself."

She blushed deeply and growled, "Well, whose fucking fault is that?"

"Yours, of course," he said lightly, refusing to lose his temper. "We're going to take a lunch and get you some new clothes. Don't pretend you feel comfortable walking around here in long johns."

"It's a jumpsuit. And I'd rather stay here right now if you don't mind."

"No one can tell once you're standing. Probably. Now get up."

"No!" she whispered fiercely. "It's embarrassing. Leave me alone."

"I told you to get up. I can embarrass you much worse, you know."

She glared up at him, her eyes bright. "If you're going to threaten me, you can at least elaborate." Her tone was steady.

He chuckled. Perhaps she wasn't sure what he would do to her here, out in the open. Was she testing him?

"Certainly," he said and leant himself on her desk, putting his face near hers. "First of all, no one would do a damned thing if I gave you a good spanking right here at your desk. Other than watch, of course. And second, I'd do it with your pants down, so all your worry for hiding how wet you are would be for nothing."

She let out a rapid breath, hot on his cheek. Her lips trembled. With fear? Or the briefest contraction of a smile? Was she starting to enjoy the game at last?

"Good enough," she said, her tone clipped, and she stood, her body unnaturally still.

"Then let's go."

———

They wandered the wide walkways of the Promenade, along tall visiglass windows displaying the latest fashions. "How 'bout that?" She pointed at a dress composed of geometrical layers slashing in fuchsia and lime green down the holographic model. "Perfect for the office, I'd say."

"Amala would think so," he sighed. "I know, none of this works. Let's keep going. I think down at the end of the strip here, there's a more casual store. Hurry up."

She kept on stopping to stare at things and laugh, or make quips.

"I want to have time to get something to eat," he said.

"Canton Ex is pretty strict with you, huh? *One hour for lunch, Mr. Canton.*"

He pressed his lips together, trying not to laugh. "I like to set an example, I guess."

"How noble."

He eyed her pointedly, squinting just enough to make her speed up slightly. "And I don't do absentee management."

"Rather controlling."

"Well, I guess we've met."

She tittered at this and seemed about to retort, when out of the closest shop, stepped a white pillar of a woman. As she sidled up to him, he knew it was Amala. She'd wrapped her long black hair intricately behind her head, her cream colored gown circled her body like a column, and the fabric of it looked just like marble.

"Mr. Canton," she said with regal cheerfulness, "You're back already. How was your vacation?"

"Amala," he said with a nod. Of course, she'd be here,

shopping. "To be honest, it was tedious, and I'm glad to be back."

"I hope you've found everything in order?"

"Everything, except for my bookkeeper," he said with a smile, and as he said it, he suddenly became very aware of Sydell next to him, as though she had moved closer, or stepped away.

Amala shrugged. "I'm too ahead on everything. I'd be happy to come in this afternoon if you'd like, though." At this point, her eyes rested behind him, on Sydell.

"No, of course not. Enjoy the day. This is Sydell." He gestured back to her, in introduction, "She's a new recruit at Canton. Helping out with paperwork and such."

Amala smiled, her usual cold but unpretentious one. "Hello, Sydell, I'm Amala."

Sydell murmured something and Amala looked back to Rhys, her eyes shining amusedly. "I hope my job isn't in jeopardy."

He laughed. For the first time in their long acquaintance, however, he felt an awkwardness. He said, "You're irreplaceable and you know it. Sydell's helping on a side project, something I'm researching. Not exactly business."

"How fun. Let me know if I can accommodate her in any way." Then she smiled again at Sydell, asked politely, "Are you settled in the barracks?"

Sydell stayed silent, and Rhys said abruptly, "She's staying at my apartment." From the corner of his eye, Sydell shrank back as he said it.

Amala blinked for a split second before she smiled pleasantly. "Please let me know if I can help you settle in, in any way." Her tone was impeccably gracious.

Rhys said, "Actually, we're looking to get her some clothes. Crew wear just doesn't suit an office, or this city at all, really. But we were hoping to find someplace maybe a bit less, well, fashionably *haute* than these stores."

"Of course. I think I know the place, exactly. Shall I take you there?"

And so Amala led the way. Sydell stayed quiet now and tried to be on her best around Amala, who tended to have that effect, as he knew well. So, she was much easier to manage. Amala took them into a little classical shop, with re-prints and factory salvage, and Sydell gathered up a wardrobe with fair speed; they could even still have time to get some lunch.

"Thank God you showed up when you did," he said as they parted. "She almost went into the office dressed like you."

Amala's eyes closed when she laughed at this, good-naturedly. Then she left them to go on with her day.

Chapter 15

No, Rhys hadn't engineered the entire afternoon to make her uncomfortable; it would be crazy to think that. All the same, she resented him as though he had. Being dragged about through stores in what felt like pajamas, still wet between the legs and tense as fuck, and then to be joined by that... that goddess of a bookkeeper. A bookkeeper, really? A woman like Amala was never a bookkeeper. That much was clear. But what was she? More important, what was she to Rhys?

She paced about the apartment as he cooked, and when he spread the meal out and started in, she found herself barely able to eat. He took up a book, casually, something on ancient languages, and the peacefulness of his manner made her go hot with inexplicable fury.

"If those marks in the cave are a language, you'll never figure it out," she said, barely able to conceal it. Indeed, the nastiness of her tone surprised her. He glanced over at her, his eyes still and watchful, the color of a murky river she could not plumb the depths of.

"Oh, no?" His brows raised, and his tone was light, almost playful. Or taunting.

"Language is personal. You need context to understand it. You don't know anything about the people who wrote it; you don't know how their minds worked."

"That's occurred to me."

His lack of reaction maddened her. She pressed on. "But maybe it's numbers. Like binary. Some of the lines are shorter than others, so that would make sense. But maybe that wasn't even deliberate. How would you even know?"

"I wouldn't."

"Why would a species advanced enough to build a structure like this even resort to using marks in a cave, like primitives? It doesn't make any sense."

"Again, these are all things I've wondered about."

"Maybe the depth of the grooves is something to account for. Have you thought of that?"

"I hadn't." He blinked. "But actually, that's interesting." He frowned, as though thinking on it.

"It's not interesting. It complicates things to infinity!" she all but shouted.

"I think," he said softly, his eyes meeting hers, "you should go to bed."

"What use is it trying to figure it out when it could be anything, literally? Some kind of deposit of nesting cave worms or something?"

"I see no reason not to try. You may stop if you like. I have plenty of other things you can do."

"It's just stupid. I don't know why you'd waste time on it. Doesn't Canton Ex have any real work to do?"

"Is that what you really think, or are you just taking out your petty frustration?"

She glowered down at her food. If anything, her frustration was his fault. Her first day here had been terrible. Well, not all of it. She'd liked being with him at his office and going out into the city. She'd actually had a good time with him, for a hot minute until Amala showed up.

"You can't win this, Sydell. I know how ludicrous it is, trying to solve this. A shot in the dark, really. You can't convince me of what I already know. You can irritate me, like you're trying to do. You can keep at it, until I paddle you, and if that's what you need, you'll get it. But you aren't getting what you want."

What you want. Her heart raced and she looked stubbornly away from him.

"I'm going to bed," she said dully. The raging snow outside the window was not cozy as it had been the night before; now it suffocated her. She plunged face down onto the bed angrily and fell, after a while, into a fitful sleep. She woke to Rhys settling in next to her, kissing her tenderly on the ear. A chill ran down her neck to her toes. Of course, she knew, as her eyes opened, exactly what he was doing. He built her desire to torment her, and he tormented her so that she would submit to his will and be shunted. She stiffened in his arms.

"You're being a baby," he said.

"I don't want things just done to my body. I don't like people inspecting me, putting things in me."

"You seem to enjoy when I do those things," he teased, tracing a finger over her tense brow. She snorted.

"I'm trying to give you the motivation to overcome your fear," he said. "This isn't about trying to torture you."

"I think you love to torture me," she replied, muffled by the pillows.

He laughed softly. "I do, in a way. I want to hear you beg me to come." He spoke just next to her ear, and she gasped. "I also love to make you come. But." He kissed her ear, and she whined. He went on, "We're waiting on you for that. The only way you'll get over this fear is if you move through it."

He kissed her neck and down along her shoulders. He ran his hand down the length of her back, until it rested on the groove where her bottom met her thigh. He caressed her there in a soft, maddening tickle. A rush of heat flowed down to her groin, and she trembled, in awe of her body's power over her, and of his power over her body. She craned her neck up and kissed him hard on the lips, aggressively, as though delivering the first blow in some kind of battle between them. To her shock, his response was tender; he took her chin in his hand and kissed her face around her mouth, soft and slow. For the first time, she noticed that he was completely naked.

The night had ended madly for her, but now he slept.

She'd sobbed, she'd pleaded, she'd even scratched him along the back of his shoulders. His motions had been slow, controlled, always watching her lest she got too excited. What was that, if not torture? She'd murmured curses lying in his arms, but he remained calm through it all and now breathed the serene and deep breaths of a satisfied sleep.

He had reduced her to an animal mind, to being nothing beyond the thought of release. She lay still beside him, in a dark, wordless hate. After a while, his arms felt much heavier. Before she could think on what she did, she lowered herself from under his grasp, sliding down his chest on the bed until his arms slipped over her head. She tensed. He rolled onto his back with a deep breath, not quite a snore. She slunk back and stood, watching him. In his relaxation, his face had an innocence at odds with her knowledge of him, while the beauty of his muscular, bare body held her fascinated for a moment. Then she crept into the bathroom.

A rebellious thrill tinged with guilt accosted her when she realized what she would do. But what right did he have to tell her not to do it? None. Even if sneaking behind his back to do it gave him a certain superiority. She pushed that thought away. She would get what she wanted, now, albeit without him, and so she would win.

She climbed into the shallow glass bathtub, its surface chilly on her skin as she leaned back into it, and drew the silisilk curtain around its sides. She'd not brought her pillow, which had been her way of pleasuring herself since she was young, and for a moment this put her at a loss. Old habits really did die hard. Hell, she was so pent up, she probably didn't need it. She leaned back her head as best she could against the hard edge of the tub and reached down to touch herself in a way she never had.

It felt so good, she gasped. She pushed beyond, down past her muff to where her nether lips began and parted. She was so wet, her fingers slid about clumsily, and she knew it would not be easy to bring herself to release. She pulled Rhys to her mind, the night they'd just spent. Yes, Rhys fucking her slowly, and then, after she'd scratched him so viciously, taking her hands calmly in his own and holding them at her sides. His body shuddering over her in a climax she could only experience sympathetically, and she'd howled in both ecstasy and frustration. It lit her up to just think on it, and she bit her lips as she rubbed herself harder. Hot, she was hot; she no longer noticed the cool of the glass pressing on her naked shoulders.

And then he pulled the curtain open. Light flooded through the bathroom door from the other room.

She sucked in her breath violently and curled up, as though she could hide what she did. Holy fuck, he saw everything! He reached out and she shifted away, but his reach was above her, leaving her a split second to be puzzled before the tap blasted a deluge of cold water down her bare back. She reared up and flopped out of the tub onto the floor, refusing to scream. He tossed a towel over her, and she wrapped it around herself, wanting to crawl into some space in the bathroom and hide from him. But there was nowhere to go; she knelt before him, mortified, and could only be glad that he hadn't turned on the overhead light.

"Dry up and get to bed," he said sternly. "You have one minute."

"But…" She glared up at him. "I need to, I have to…"

In the near dark, the shadowed oval of his face peered down at her. "In fact, you do not. You are mine and right now, I forbid it. I will see through having you shunted. And you will be, soon. You clearly can't hold out with this singular obsession."

"Obsession?"

"Indeed. In the future, I may choose to show you why your obsession with orgasm is clouding your ability to feel how great pleasure can be. But you don't know that yet, so for now it's a good tool to get you to do as I see fit."

"So, even if I get shunted, you'd still do this to me?"

"Maybe at some point you will only come as I command, and you will love it. But for now, all you need to do is let go of one stubborn fear and have a minor procedure. Now get to bed before I whip your wet butt 'til you're too sore to sleep. Go on."

She stood, her legs shaky, her head and shoulders wrapped in the towel so that her face stayed hidden. Did he really mean to keep doing this to her? Even if she were shunted? But of course, why wouldn't he? Just another tool to train her, as he said. Her pussy throbbed, despite the cold of the rest of her body. His self-assurance as he'd spoken, the way he seemed prepared to deal with whatever way she'd rail against him and would prevail over her, made her want to give up. Give up, admit defeat and be the animal, begging him to fuck her to orgasm.

And he'd love to do it. It was this thought that stopped her. She dropped into bed next to him, armored in her towel, still red hot with shame at being caught and not wanting to see or be seen. If he loved to make her come, as he said, then going on like this would frustrate him too. Wouldn't it?

He'd win out eventually, of course, but she would make him wait.

***

They settled into a sort of a tolerable rhythm over the passing weeks. She wasn't sure if it was the fourteenth or fifteenth day of the Europa cycle when they went into the office and a man she hadn't seen before stood at Rhys' desk. She'd worn her silisilk red blouse and flared skirt, and she'd clipped her hair behind her head so that the tail of it flounced as it doubled over. In the mirror of this man's eyes, she knew she looked good and was glad of it.

"Corey, this is Sydell," said Rhys. Corey seemed to know of her already and spared her the awkwardness that had passed with Amala. "This is my business partner, Corey Hale."

"Good to meet you, Mr. Hale," she said, businesslike. Rhys gave her a small, approving grin, with a touch of irony in the gleaming of his eyes. Something about it made her glow warm inside, but then, these days she lit up any time he spoke to her or looked her way. And she knew why.

"I'm going to lunch with Corey," he said. "I'll be back in a few hours. Be good."

She wrinkled her nose at him for speaking with her in front of his partner as though she were a house cat. He just raised his eyebrows as if to emphasize his point. He left her, and she shuffled to her desk and sat quietly for a moment doing nothing. The code sat locked in the top drawer, and she had no desire to even look at it. At last, she got up, went to Rhys' cubicle and sat down heavily in his well broken-in chair. His desk remained cluttered with papers, as always. But now she noticed a picture tacked onto the cubicle divider, among many other little jotted notes. The photograph showed a young man, not over twenty, she guessed. His eyelashes were deep in contrast to his dewy skin, his eyes a sparkling blue like sun on water. He stood in front of a frigate class planet cruiser and wore the colors of the Jupiter Alliance Navy. Could it be his younger brother? No, he'd said it had been just him and Callie. Could it be an old picture of Parsons? Surely, she would have heard if he'd been in JAN, and anyway, Rhys wouldn't keep a picture of him up.

"*Do you know who that is?*"

She flinched. She knew instantly it was Amala, from the cool poise of the tone, but also from the striking intimacy it managed to convey. She'd kept away from Amala, mostly, and thankfully the woman hadn't been in the office much. But now, finally. she would have to face her, and alone.

"No," she said. She made herself look up at the woman. Today, she wore a seafoam green Grecian gown, at once making Sydell forget her earlier confidence in her own appearance.

"Well," Amala reached up to the edge of the cubicle, her fingers touching near the picture almost affectionately. "This was sent in a few months ago. It's from Jason. He sends pictures every few years, letters too, sometimes."

She peered down at Sydell's confusion and smiled, as though expecting the ignorance. Sydell's face grew warm, and she looked out the window into the snow gales.

"Jason is the child Rhys saved. On the Pylons," Amala said. "He won a medal over it."

"I don't know anything about it, actually," Sydell admitted, not wanting to have Amala drag it out.

"Oh. I'm sorry. I thought he might have told you the story. It's how he lost his leg."

"Oh," said Sydell. It was all she could say.

"It's certainly not a secret. He probably just doesn't like to brag. Rhys saved a boy on Mars during the Mutiny. An entire Pylon had been rigged with explosives, and the kid was looking for his mom, who worked in one of the lower offices. Rhys went after him and thankfully no one was killed. He never talks about it. But…" She touched the picture again.

Yes, of course, it meant something to him. And he hadn't told her about it. Sydell moved uneasily in the chair.

"I think we should go have lunch," said Amala.

"Um." Have lunch? Where had that come from? It so startled her, she couldn't think of how to say no. There were sandwiches in the cooler, which is what she and Rhys usually had, but of course, that wasn't an excuse.

"Come on," Amala insisted cheerfully. Despite the cheer, Sydell knew her suddenly to be as irresistible as Rhys. She shoved her hands down in the pockets of her skirt and stood, trying to hide how unwilling she felt.

Amala did not have to call for a taxi, as she already had a car waiting. "What do you like to eat?" Amala asked, smoothly settling into the seat. Sydell sat on the bench opposite her, noting the luxurious style of the interior, like a small version of a limousine. Little rows of lights lined the windows and tops of the seats.

"I'm not picky," Sydell said, dreading to go someplace fancy.

Her eyes paused on Sydell for a moment, narrowed and scrutinizing, and then she smiled. "I know. Take us to the Blue Cafe."

The car started off. Amala spread her gloved hands out over the supra-leather seats. "I have to admit, I'm extremely curious about you. I've never seen Rhys with a girlfriend."

Girlfriend? She wasn't his girlfriend, was she? She'd not thought of herself in that way, but, yes, it was the best word that fit the situation. She didn't know how to respond to Amala, and so she just shrugged, with a quick smile so as not to seem rude.

"May I ask how the two of you met?" Amala asked. The wings of her finely groomed black brows twitched. To Sydell, this had begun to feel like the time they'd taken her to the state clinic as a child, and the nurse had asked all the prying questions. *What did her dad do for work? Why didn't her mom live with them? Would she like a free training bra?* That sort of bullshit.

Sydell told haltingly of being hired to transport Rhys, keeping out all the details of Callie and Parsons that were probably private. She told of her ship being repossessed, and Rhys buying it, glossing over most of how things had gone down after. But she could not skip over the fact that she'd stolen the jammer. "I was being sent out to a field prison," she stammered on, feeling her own face burn. "And Rhys came back and recruited me. To Canton Excavations."

Amala lowered her head. "Well, I'd be lying if I told you I didn't know all of that. I maintain the books and I have to keep up with everything."

"If you knew, then why—" Sydell blustered.

"I'm sorry, I thought you might have a story, something more personal. Who doesn't like talking about how they fell in love?"

Love? Sydell glared down at her own knees. "I'm sorry, I'm not good at this."

"No. No one's good at being pried away at. I'm terribly sorry. My curiosity gets the better of me. Look, here we are." They'd reached the Promenade. Amala flounced out of the car with an energy that surprised her and led the way at a good pace, toward one of the taller buildings.

"None of these are marked," Sydell remarked softly. "I don't know how you'd tell your way around."

"Things are more subtle here," Amala agreed. "Signs the way they do them on Earth are seen as garish. Look at the shift in colors between the floors."

Sydell squinted. The colors of the building material between floors looked similar, rich, undulating blues and purples. But as she looked, she could see some difference.

"Most things are color coded," said Amala. "The Blue Cafe is blue, of course. It takes up the central floor. Above that, is a library."

"Did *they* make the buildings like this?"

"No, Io City was empty when it was found. I think some of their tech was used, though."

They took the lift up to the central floor. It was little like cafes she'd seen, except perhaps that people sat along the outer edges of a balcony at long lengths of table, and some of them had small plates. Amala approached a wall; as she did, several soft-toned pictures lit up, pictures of cake? Yes, all cake.

"These are all designed to be full meals. They only taste like dessert." She made her selection and Sydell approached, waving her hand over the screen as Amala had, over the cake that looked the most like chocolate. A small slot in the wall appeared and pushed their plates out onto a newly materialized shelf. She took up the piece of plastoid china with her cake on it and followed Amala out to the table at the balcony.

It overlooked the street below which, from up there, looked like an enormous catwalk, people parading their elaborate styles down between the weaving of the speeders.

"Mr. Canton worked on a lot of the newer architecture here. Like these buildings."

"Mr. Canton? You mean Rhys?"

"No, no. Anjel, his father. That was many years ago."

She sipped at a ridiculously small cup of espresso. Sydell cut down into her cake with her fork; it was thick, marbled, and rich looking. She took a bite. Full meal or not, it tasted like a delicious chocolate torte. Amala watched her, her dark eyes luminous as if she enjoyed her reaction to the food. Then she started in gracefully on her own berry covered slice.

"Did you know Mr. Canton?" asked Sydell, trying to sound light, as if it were just conversation and she wasn't desperate to know how connected she was to Rhys.

"I worked for his business here," said Amala, her lashes dropping for just one flutter of an instant. "But not long. Rhys took over five years ago. I also knew Mr. Canton when he lived on Mars."

She stopped, as if this had some meaning. Canton, on Mars? Wait. He'd done trafficking on Mars, with Parsons. And with Rhys, too. Amala had been part of it?

"I think we should take a little walk," Amala said, standing rapidly, leaving half of her tart unfinished. "I walk up to my flat most days on my lunch, keeps me fit. Shall we?"

Sydell could not find a way to say no, and so off they went. Her flat was in one of the spire shaped buildings just a few blocks down the Promenade. They walked without speaking, and quickly, while Amala kept glancing back at her as if to see if she were keeping up. At the stairs, she lagged behind, panting up the steep seven floors in the little enclosed staircase. The building was much nicer than the one Rhys lived in. Each flat had been built on a dais flaring out from the central structure, so that each had one wall of all windows which encircled most of the room. The flat felt as if it floated over the city. Amala watched her as they stepped in, perhaps looking for her reaction to the luxury? Had she brought her here just to show off?

"You're wondering how I afford it," she said, cracking a good-humored grin. The grin surprised Sydell, seeming at odds with the rest of her. She went on, "I'm paid well, of course, but the truth is I couldn't, not on what I make. Mr. Canton left me the flat when he died. It used to be his, at least when he was on Europa. He designed the building, actually."

She stepped up to the window. "He didn't like this place much, which is strange, because he made so much of it. But he was almost always at one of the mines, or on Earth." She shrugged. Her voice had grown heavier, almost sad.

"It's a beautiful city," said Sydell, crossing her arms as she looked out over the Promenade. What was Amala saying? That she'd been Canton's mistress?

"It is. I've done my best to live up to it, and to him. I've tried to do things the way he would have wanted. We disagreed on many things. Now Rhys is in charge, and things are easier for me in a way. We agree on most things, and when we don't, it doesn't matter to me."

She held Sydell's eyes for a moment with her own. Then she said, "Would you like a drink?"

Sydell was still doing her best to breathe regularly after the climb. She nodded; water sounded amazing. Amala walked to the icebox and took out a bottle, then poured out two slender glasses of champagne. She handed one to Sydell, who had the absurd desire to laugh at it.

Amala spoke down into her glass. "Mr. Canton would have hated this… *war* that's sprung up between his sons."

"War?"

"Yes. Rhys has spent a fortune fighting Parsons, keeping him from getting too big. And he's right, of course. Parsons is a dark force in this little system of ours. God help us if he really got a firm hold in it. But Mr. Canton would've preferred that Rhys had worked with Parsons and tried to change things from within. And I can't say that I don't see the point he tried to make."

"I'm sure you know that Parsons is a slaver?"

"Yes."

"So, Rhys should have tried to make human trafficking, what, better?"

"Yes." Here, Amala met her eyes. "Sometimes you have to keep your enemies close. Rhys can't do much out here but be a hindrance to him, all at cost to himself. If he had stayed a part of things on Mars, he might have put a stop to some of the more inhumane things Parsons does and had a better knowing of his weaknesses, too."

Sydell saw in her mind that massive demonic doorway carved into the side of the mountain, and Amala's words struck her as insane. "From what I can tell, Rhys was pretty young when he started working for Parsons," was all she could think to say.

"Yes, Anjel had him shipped to Mars when his mother died, I think he would have been fifteen," said Amala distantly.

"He was just a kid. Pulling him into that was criminal. Did you know him then?"

Amala's eyes were vague. "I came into the operation a few years later."

"Of course, he made the right choice to leave. I'm sure he would have left earlier if he hadn't been so young."

Amala said nothing. Sydell went on, emboldened by the champagne. "I'm sure he hated it there."

"It's hard not to like what you're good at. Or so I hear."

"If he liked it so much, he would have stayed." She suddenly hated Amala, hated the intimate way she spoke about Rhys.

"That's true," said Amala, with a detached smile. The words were merely polite, Sydell knew. The woman set her empty glass next to the dish depository. Her eyes were almost sad. Could she really be this sad over the family's estrangement, when one of those brothers was Parsons?

Amala continued with small, pleasant talk, which Sydell mostly ignored, and then they made their way back down to the speeder to return to the offices.

Chapter 16

Corey tossed the holopad down on his desk with annoyance. He glared up at Rhys, his pale, freckled face looking more pinched than ever. "A new algorithm? Really?" He almost shouted it.

"Yes. We never accounted for the depth of those lines. It complicates things, but if we ignore it, we could end up completely wasting all our time."

"We couldn't figure it out before, Rhys. How does adding more complexity make you think we can figure it out now?"

"We have to try."

"Rhys. This can't be solved by one or two people. And it can't be solved with our systems. We need to turn this over to Io City Council."

"Which is all but turning it over to Parsons. Besides, the second I do, they confiscate the whole site." He turned, as if to walk somewhere, but found himself nearly facing a wall. Corey's little offices on the ninth floor were obscure, to say the least. He let out his breath in a huff.

Corey sighed, just after he did. "All right, but if

Parsons gets it through Io City, we still have it figured out. If it's tech, then the Council will have whatever Parsons has, and it will be a standoff."

"The Council won't let *us* have it if it's tech. And what about twenty years from now, when everyone on the Council is in his pocket?" Rhys set a hand flat on the desk. "Hell no."

"If it's tech, and it's the kind of tech that can make a weapon, which, by the way, all of it can… then you know the Council *could* decide to see you withholding it as tantamount to treason."

"You've given me that bit of lawyerly advice before. I won't bother to thank you again." It came out sourer than he intended.

"They still shoot people for treason, at least on Europa."

"They shoot people everywhere, for whatever reason, if it suits them." Rhys took his jacket up from the hook on the door. "I'm going back to Canton Ex. Can you get that up and running?"

"I can. But I think we'll need to re-scan the caves."

"Yes, I'm going to do that myself. It may take a few weeks." He turned back to his partner, wanting to end things pleasantly. It certainly wasn't the first time they'd disagreed, and Rhys knew it was mostly his own fault. The last thing he wanted was for Corey to lose his patience and pull out his investments. Rhys said, "This is my project. No one will ever know that your assistance was anything but ignorant."

"I'm not worried about that."

Rhys shrugged, not sure what else to say. He knew when he left that things had changed with Corey, that some kind of a timeframe had appeared, that his assistance would not last beyond it. But it didn't matter. It only meant he had to work harder, solve it faster. He called a speed craft and went back to Canton Ex.

The day had passed quickly, and it was much later than he thought when he returned to his offices. Sydell was the only one there, sitting at her desk beneath the snowy darkness of the visiglass. He had the urge to rush over to her and scoop her up, pull her away from the wild, roaring background, as if she needed protection from it. She looked tired, lost. He approached her slowly, almost casually. "Did you have lunch with Amala?" he asked as she glanced up from her seat.

She frowned. "Did you tell her to take me to lunch?"

"I suggested it, so you wouldn't have to be alone all day."

"I can be alone, you know. I actually don't like people much."

"True, but we can't have you going off and being naughty in the bathroom." He smiled as he spoke, hoping she would know he was teasing her, at least in part.

"I'm not an animal, Rhys," she snapped. "I can control myself. Jesus, if you're that worried then you should get me a chastity belt."

He scratched her head. "You are *my* animal, and if I catch you rubbing yourself again when I've told you not to, I *will* get you a chastity belt, and believe me, you will hate it. Now get up, we're going home."

She scowled, her face screwing up in that resentful expression he knew so well. A small yawn broke it as she gathered up her sweater and the funny basketweave purse she'd insisted on buying. He pinched at the side of her waist affectionately, and she leaned her body into him. He wrapped his arm around her as he led her out to the speed craft. She fit so perfectly there, tucked into him. The sweetness of it nearly made him silent. "Did you have a good lunch?" he asked swiftly, leading her out to the speed craft.

"No. Who eats cake for lunch? And Amala's nosy." Her eyes jumped to his, as if trying to gauge his reaction.

He chuckled. "She's gotta be damned curious about you. She's always been a bit too involved with our family. She doesn't mean any harm."

She shrugged and looked out the window, clearly troubled by something. Who the hell knew what Amala had said to her?

"What's the matter, baby?" he asked softly. Her eyes snapped up at the affection, and that helpless look came over her, the one she'd had after he'd come out of the coma. Then her eyes dropped to the side, and she closed to him.

"If you were in my place, you'd be troubled," she said, mysteriously.

"Well, I would never be in your place," he said matter-of-factly. Not a kind thing to say, but he wasn't about to tolerate her cryptic games. If she had a problem, she would tell him directly.

"I don't know anything about you," she said, her voice dull.

"You know almost everything about me. I've hidden nothing from you. I don't talk about myself much. But you may ask me anything you want." He meant it. And he would tell her anything, except for the very few things he could not. That was out of security. But, of course, she said nothing, went on staring out the window morosely. Part of him wanted to drag her across the seat and spank her, but something stopped him.

"I've told you the very worst thing about me," he said,

coaxing her. She peeked at him, nervous, and he was suddenly glad he'd been gentle.

"You never told me how you lost your leg," she said in a breath.

He sighed. That, really? "Amala told you, right? She loves to tell people about it, for some reason."

"She's proud of you, probably."

"It's part of a larger story that I'm not proud of at all, so I don't really care what she thinks."

Her mouth parted in surprise. The speed craft had stopped outside their building but he made no move to get out, not yet.

He sighed. "The people who worked on the Pylons were as good as slaves. The market crash pushed them to the bottom, and they had the choice between being sent there for work or going to prison. If you'd been convicted a few years back, you might have ended up there instead of a field prison."

"So, what is it you aren't proud of? I don't understand."

"When the Mutiny happened, I fought on the Corporate side. I was a medic, of course, so I didn't fight much, but at the time it was the only way to get away from what Parsons was doing and still stay in my father's graces. I was eighteen. I didn't know what else to do. Most of the people Parsons bought and sold came from the Pylons, and most of them were glad to get away from it. It was a death sentence. Working for us was safer, much less brutal."

"That's how you justify it."

"None of it can be justified. I'm only trying to tell you how awful the Pylons were. Those people *had* to mutiny. And I was part of the force that crushed it. Because, at the time, they were burning all the soy fields and bombing the Pylons, and it looked like madness. Jason was an overseer's kid. The Mars Tribune ran a story about us after, just to show how vicious the Mutiny was."

"But they won, right?"

"The soy fields were destroyed. But most of the rebels died out on Mars. They had nowhere to go. A few made it back to Earth, I think. The Pylons were left abandoned. So, in a way, yeah, they won." He fell silent for a moment. Then he went on. "My brother's wife actually helped plan the Mutiny."

"What!"

"Yep. No one knows how long she was involved, whether her marriage to Parsons was a total sham or not. He thought it was. He had a lot of stock in the Pylons. Either way, he'd been betrayed, and you don't betray a man like that." He shook his head. "You've probably heard this story."

"I think… I think I heard he sold his wife to slavers."

"He sent her down to his worst men, as a gift. But before that," he swallowed, but it still came out, by a dark compulsion, "before that, he blinded her. So he'd be the last thing she ever saw."

He leant back against the seat, not taking his eyes off her. She blanched and averted her face; he'd terrified her. Which wasn't what he wanted at all. It was why he didn't want to tell her things like this. But it would be worse, he knew, if she found it out from someone else.

"Sydell," he said, his voice stark. She peered at him, her dark eyes enormous.

"I'm not my brother," he said. "I'll see him destroyed if it takes everything I have."

She sighed. "I know," she said quietly and looked at her knees. His heart stung for her, for the trust of her words, for the way she sat with her knees drawn close, demurely, while they stuck out, knobby from under her skirt, like a tomboy. He climbed out of the speeder and helped her out, staying close to her as they made their way up to the apartment.

Once inside, she pulled off her wedge sandals, yanking them off at the ankle so that he almost scolded her for being hard on her new shoes. But he liked the motion of it, found something sweet in her desperation to be comfortable. She collapsed in a heap on one of the sofas. He pulled off his pants and flung them in the general direction of the laundry chute. Then he trod over to her, scooped her up from her spot, and sat himself right where she'd been, holding her on his lap. He put his legs up on the coffee table, crossing his ankles over a pile of his notes.

"So," she said, pushing her face into his shoulder so that it muffled her, "what am I to you? Am I like a pet or something?"

Ah. The "what am I to you" question, which he'd not had the occasion to hear for a long time. His relationships had been less than traditional. Amala's queries had likely made her anxious about her role with him. Too bad women always had to put a title to everything and limit it. But he could understand.

"Yes, you're my pet," he said and gently lifted her chin up to face him. "You're the first pet I've really had." He kissed her forehead lightly. "But I'll tell people who ask that you're my girlfriend if you'd like."

"But which am I? I don't understand."

"A pet is more precious than a girlfriend," he said, more stoically than he should have, perhaps. But she trembled a little on him, and he knew she liked what he'd said, and he held her tighter. She rested her head on him and stared down at the table, at his legs, for a few moments.

"Did it hurt?" she asked, querulous.

Did what hurt... oh. She was staring down at his leg.

"No, not at all, when it first happened. Just the explosion, and then shock. Probably a lot of adrenaline too. I put on the tourniquet myself. But later, yes. It hurt."

"And now?"

"No. I have a nerve blocking implant." He flexed the leg. As always, the perfection of its movement entranced him; the cool, matte titanium so unlike his flesh, but moving exactly as his brain remembered his flesh leg to have moved. They sat quietly like this for a while more. A warmth spread through his chest, and he exhaled onto her hair, as if he needed to release it. He was about to ask if she was ready to eat, when she said in a rush, "Okay. I'll be shunted."

He grew totally still, to hide his shock. This was not the circumstance under which he had predicted she would give in. He thought one more week of her pleading might have done it, really. Though her face had such a lovely glow to it that he wondered if she was already beginning to appreciate some of the ecstasy of denial, if only unconsciously. He'd even worried he might have to change his tactics.

No, this was something else entirely. Something like trust, or… His heart contracted, almost painfully, that she would give him this, and in this way. He cleared his throat. "All right. I'll make the appointment right now. Are you ready for dinner?" He stood up, moving her onto the couch.

"Yes, please," she said. He kissed her tenderly at the top of her head. He would still make her wait, until it had been done. He would be sure the surgeon made an immediate opening for her, however. He had the sudden urge to fuck her silly, to overwhelm her sweet, soft body with all the orgasms she'd missed.

It took two days to get the appointment. The surgeon had been off world, otherwise nothing would have deterred Rhys from having his way. They sat now in the waiting room, on the third floor next to a window overlooking the outside. For once, it was not snowing. The dark fields of ice glowed a deep, hollow violet under an inky sky, reflecting nothing but the light from the city itself.

"We ought to have a trip off world ourselves," he murmured, stroking Sydell's hair as she sat curled in the chair next to him. She'd not stopped visibly shaking, and he planned on asking the nurse for a tranquilizer if they had to wait much longer.

"Where?" she asked, her voice distant. He grasped her hand; it was freezing.

"Where would you like to go, pet? I wouldn't mind somewhere we could see the sky, myself." Not that they could go anywhere until he'd finished scanning that cave.

The nurse showed up before she could answer. The woman led them into a small room and sat Sydell down on the table and, after taking her vitals, put the breather mask to her face. It reminded him of that day on her ship, when he'd strapped her to the bunk. She'd looked just about as terrified.

"It'll be over before you know it. And then we go right home." He squeezed her hand and smiled. "I'll be right outside that door the whole time." He pointed. Her hand, in his own, grew limp as she inhaled the gas. She didn't answer him, only went on counting as the nurse had directed, but her eyes stayed on his, right up until they rolled back into her head, and she was out. He didn't want to leave the room at all, now; he wanted irrationally to stay right by her side and protect her. But he nodded politely and stood, as the surgeon entered, and stepped out, taking a seat at one of the empty chairs just outside the room. It would be good for her to go through it and wake up safe.

After an indiscernible amount of time, his holowrist pulsed. He glanced down. It was Corey. He answered, a bit reluctantly. "What's going on?"

"We're supposed to go out to the caves and start today. Right? Where are you?"

Fuck. Yes, that's what they'd finally agreed on. Then she'd agreed to the surgery and somehow it had slipped his mind. "I'll be down in a couple of hours. I need to take Sydell home; she's having a medical procedure."

"I'm sure Amala would be happy to do that for you," said Corey coldly. Onscreen, he had that look to him, that he had when Rhys had first suggested that they re-scan everything. He would not be easy to appease. "Amala's not available," Rhys said. No, she was out at his undisclosed office, for reasons only he knew about. "I'll see you in two hours." He tapped the screen off. He leaned his head back again. God, how long would this take? The specs had said no more than thirty minutes. It was a simple procedure. He closed his eyes.

He must have dozed in the chair, because suddenly the nurse was next to him, shaking his shoulder.

"Sir. Your friend is awake now."

He thanked her, then stood and stretched, his legs stiff. Even the metal one registered in his mind as achy. He stepped back into the surgery room.

"We'd like to keep her under observation for a few hours," said the nurse, in a lowered voice, "Her blood pressure is running a little low, and Doctor just wants to be on the safe side."

A few hours? He couldn't leave Corey to do the scanning alone. Not the way things stood right now. He moved over to Sydell and stood at the bedside. Her brown eyes moved up to meet his dreamily. "Morning, baby," he said. "How does my pet feel?"

She nodded sleepily. "Fine." She seemed very relaxed, from the drugs, of course. Well, it would be easier to tell her now. "Sydell, they want you to rest here for a bit longer. Everything's fine, and your procedure is all done. I need to go to the office for a little while and then I'll be right back again to take you home. Okay?"

She looked like she was about to fall back asleep. Her eyes crossed. But she nodded. He bent over her and kissed her on the cheek, and her head rolled to the side as she passed out.

He stopped at the nurse's station as he left. "I need to go for a bit. If she wakes up and gets upset, give her something to relax her."

"Of course. It's unlikely, though. She's pretty sedated already."

He nodded. He stood a moment longer in the waiting room, not wanting to leave at all. Then he stepped out and hailed a speeder.

Chapter 17

S he just wanted to sleep, why did they keep shaking her? She moaned in complaint, trying to wave them away, but her hand wouldn't raise. Where was Rhys, surely, he would tell them to let her sleep? She opened her eyes. "Rhys?"

The nurse stood over her.

"Miss Rivas. Miss Rivas, you've slept for four hours. Someone else is scheduled for surgery here now and you need to get up."

She sat up. "Where's… where's Mr. Canton?"

"He said he was going to his offices. You can wait for him in the lobby, but you can't use this bed anymore. I'm sorry."

Sydell crawled out of the hospital bed shakily. The nurse pointed to where her clothes had been left folded on a chair. She dressed silently after the nurse left, leaving the hospital gown where the clothes had been. She approached the reception desk, where the same nurse now stood, working at the terminal. "How close are we to the Apartment Spirals?" she asked. She wished she'd been paying better attention when they'd made the drive out.

"You could walk from here. The lift sidewalk is right out front."

Her abdomen felt oddly stiff. She told the nurse.

"That's perfectly normal. And having a light walk will be good for you." She handed Sydell a post-op pamphlet and went back to what she was doing. Sydell wandered out to the corridor of the street and looked down at the pamphlet. On page one, the first bullet point read, *No sexual intercourse for forty-eight hours.* Her heart sunk. Hopefully, it would disappoint Rhys, too. She couldn't believe he wasn't here.

Well, she certainly wasn't going to wait here at the hospital, where he'd left her. He'd gone to the office, and she would go home. He could find her there. Picturing the apartment, it felt finally to be her own home, a place she could go be safe, her den.

She found her way to the lift that ran along the edge of the street. The soft blue glow of the stream ran along the long stretch of visiglass. She stepped into it tentatively and gasped as her feet lifted off the ground and it pulled her into its trajectory. Except for the occasional speed craft running down the center, she was alone, floating along, and she giggled, feeling faintly ridiculous. But it was sort of fun. Why hadn't she tried it before? Rhys was so busy; all they did was go to work and eat. He'd been talking about taking them off world. Did he mean it? Where could they go? Earth? Did she even want to go back there?

Her thoughts halted abruptly, with the strange prickle of realization that she was no longer alone in the stream. She caught his form from the corner of her eye, about two hundred feet or so behind her. Traveling along at the same speed, his distance from her stayed the same. Her brief glance back gave her little of his appearance. She had no reason to be afraid of him. None. But when the lift ended, she leapt rapidly into the next one, her heart racing. She didn't want him to get any closer.

It took about ten more minutes to reach the spirals; that's what the holowrist told her, but it felt much longer. When the last stretch ended, she sped along to her building, glancing back as discreetly as she could over her shoulder. He'd stopped just after the lift ended and stood still, as though he waited. He was tall, his hair pale and thin, balding even. He wore a jumpsuit not unlike the one she owned. She kept up her pace. She almost ran into the building and dove into the first elevator going up.

Once inside the elevator, she forced herself to laugh. She was being silly, paranoid. She wasn't used to being alone, especially out in Io City, which was still strange to her. She certainly wouldn't tell Rhys about it. When Rhys came home, she'd be mad at him for leaving her alone, but right now she just wanted him to come back. Even the thought of fighting with him about it felt safe, cozy even. The elevator bobbed as it arrived at her floor, the weight shifting through her in that strange way she could never get used to. She walked out into the hall and peered down it.

The strange man stood at the third elevator away from hers, looking down at his holowrist. She froze, a mad tension rising up from where her feet bolted to the floor, making its way into her belly. He lived here; he had to. She'd not seen him before but that didn't mean anything. She never went out this time of day; they were usually still at the office. But why was he just standing there? As if he were waiting for her? What if he actually had followed her?

Then she shouldn't go home. Right? That would lead him right to her if he didn't already know where she lived.

But why would he be following her? And where else could she go right now? The blood pounded in her ears, and she felt lightheaded, certain that in a moment she would faint. The outer edges of her vision were dark, pulsing. She had no choice. She had to get to the apartment.

She walked as steadily as she could down the hall until she reached the flat and ran her holowrist over the door with a quick glance behind her. He'd moved along the hall toward her but kept his face down at his holowrist casually. No, it didn't seem natural at all. She held her breath as she pushed the door open and shut it behind her.

Her breath rushed out in relief, and a sudden warmth of embarrassment overcame her at her silliness. She felt like a little kid running spooked back home, after dark. But a tunnel of darkness persisted in her vision, and she plopped down heavily on the sofa and began to drift into a strange sleep. *The drugs,* she thought, *it must be the drugs.*

She vaguely heard herself saying, "Rhys, is that you?" to someone in the room, but no one answered, and so she fell back asleep.

"Sydell." Fingers brushed against her forehead, pushing her hair away from her face. "Sydell. Wake up. You need to drink something." Rhys sat her up and moved in beside her on the sofa. His body felt warm and strong next to her, his presence making her feel safe, as she had known it would. He pressed a cool glass to her lips, and a few droplets of water splashed along her chin. She opened her mouth slightly and took a small sip, then pulled the water in faster, relishing the feel of it in her parched throat.

"Those drugs must have hit you really hard. I can't believe they just released you," he said. He sounded stern, angry even, and she peered into his face. The corners of his mouth turned down, but otherwise it was inscrutable.

"Where were you?" she asked weakly.

"I'm sorry, baby. I got caught up with Corey in the caves."

"You went to the caverns?" Her voice was thick with hurt. In her weariness, she couldn't hide it.

"A blizzard came through and we had to drive back at a crawl. If I'd any idea, I would never have gone. I'm sorry. But when you're better, we're going to have words about you leaving the hospital without me."

Hot irritation flashed through her, and she sat up. "Really? You expect me to have just waited where I was, like a dog?"

"Shh. Calm down, pet. It's time to rest now and get better. I'm going to take you to bed." Then he had her in his arms and carried her to the bed. She thought to tell him about the person who had followed her, but had they really? He'd be angry, to have thought she'd left the hospital and put herself in danger. No, no, she wouldn't say anything. Maybe later, when the drugs wore off and she could think clearly. But even now, her memory of the whole encounter had blurred, faded into the distance. Just like when she'd thought back over the things that had happened before she'd had that null crown on. Within seconds of closing her eyes, she was asleep.

When she woke, it was dark. She turned to the clock face; it was early morning. Too early to be awake. But she did not feel sleepy anymore, not at all. Her mind had awakened, alert, trying to recall something. She'd walked home, and then what? Yes, someone had spooked her. Now she lay here in bed with Rhys. She'd been shunted, and everything had been fine. She scooted over, hoping she could cuddle in close without disturbing him.

He brushed her face. "You awake, baby?"

"Yes," she said, her mind brilliantly clear, her body alive with a ringing expectation. He held her close against him, and she felt his hard cock press solidly into her hipbone. "Rhys, we can't—"

"Shh, I know." He kissed her on her lips. "I'll bet you're really pent up, aren't you?"

She wriggled her legs. "Don't toy with me, I can't—"

"I'll toy with you when I please, pet. You're mine."

He slipped her panties down her thighs, the only article of clothing she'd been wearing. She sighed as a warm tingle charged deep within her, from her belly button down to her bared crotch. He pulled the blankets off her, and she found the room to be warm, as though he'd switched the heat on. Had he been waiting for her to wake up? He leaned back and turned on the table light, a low, soft glow. He was naked, his form silhouetted against the light attractively.

"You're so beautiful," he whispered, as the outlines of her body showed up in the dimness. He ran his fingers along the side of her waist and her skin suffused instantly in gooseflesh. He sat up next to her and pulled her onto his lap, his legs straddling her waist. His hardness pushed into the small of her back as she leaned into his warm torso.

He spoke low in her ear, nuzzling into her hair. "I want to see you, like you were when I caught you in the bathtub." He reached down and held her breasts in his hands, caressing each of her nipples with the lightest of touches. Every tiny hair on her body flared up and her pussy tingled again as if with electricity.

"Wh-what?"

"I want you to touch that sweet cunny for me. I want to see you make yourself come." He pulled at her hard nipples, and she squirmed in his arms.

"I can't do that in front of you!"

"You will do as I say," he said silkily, but with a firmness that made her go liquid inside. The depth of her throbbed. She whined and found that her hand had slipped down along her belly, then come to rest over her furred mound, as though it had a mind of its own.

"Good girl," he whispered, and like clockwork, she began to tremble. The achy feeling in her middle had gone; she couldn't tell she'd had the surgery at all. And it certainly hadn't curbed her desire; it flooded back now with all the verve of being denied for so long.

"Look at my sexy pet touching herself," said Rhys, his voice gone flinty with lust. A fear nibbled at her that the lust would overwhelm him and he would fuck her, that it would hurt her somehow… but no. Rhys knew that it could hurt her, and he would never do it. She knew that in her bones. The thought thrilled her, of being with this man who cared so much for her in his unusual way. He strummed now at her nipples, and her pussy ached with a pulsating heat from within.

"I think you want to come," he encouraged, kissing her on her ear, sending a cascade of chills down her neck. She stroked at herself now in earnest, rubbing in circles around her near painfully sensitive clit. He kissed along the sides of her face, with a passion she'd not felt from him before. The passion crept into her by sympathy and her hips began to gyrate against her hand, almost of their own volition.

"Yes, naughty girl," he whispered. His breaths came hot, his hands on her breasts almost scorching. He ground his cock against her tailbone. She cried out excitedly, thrashing her whole body around. She was just at the precipice, but it eluded her. Her hand slipped helplessly over her wet folds, unable to get the friction she needed.

"I can't, I can't!" she nearly sobbed.

"Shh. It's all right. I just want to see you touch it. Doesn't it feel so good? *Good girl.*"

She whinnied at his words, twisting in his grasp. He stroked her neck with one hand and held her throat firmly.

"Now," he said with a strange, gently insistent tone, "you are mine, and I want to see you rub that hot pussy of yours until you howl with pleasure…"

His words! Hypnotic, demanding, they commanded all her attention, they drove her mad, how could she come with him talking to her like that? Yet her body writhed about; her hips plunged against her hand like stormy waves breaking over a rock. His words possessed her, as though he controlled her body even as her mind tried to push the words away. "You can't stop it, you're going to come for me, you're going to—"

When the wail escaped her throat, he sank his mouth down over hers, so that it muffled her cry but not her climax, which surged so fiercely through her that she kicked her legs and flailed around on him like she'd purged a demon. He shook a little as he held her, and she knew he laughed, but she did not care. The muscles in his arms grew hard as he held her tighter. On the crest of the surging wave of it, she spoke into his mouth, glad that the words were incomprehensible. As she came down from it, she thought she might have said, *I love you.*

He shifted around on the bed to face her, his eyes hot with passion. She closed her eyes, lay still, panting, for what felt like several minutes. He moved down toward the end of the bed, and for a moment she didn't care. Her body twitched.

"I'm proud of you, pet," he said. "For having the shunt put in, even though you were scared. You were a brave girl. You deserve a reward."

"Huh?" she breathed, barely sensible. At the edge of her awareness, she thought she heard a strange, distant buzzing sound.

"We're going to make up for lost time," he said. She raised her head up and peeked down at him. He sat doubled on the end of the bed, and he held something, no, he had something on the tip of his finger, something black? Is that what was buzzing?

"You've got a lot of coming to do, pet," he said and broke into a laugh, and then he touched her with it, right on the soft petals of her pussy, and some insane sensation jolted her clit. She shrieked and orgasmed, reflexively, with a piercing intensity that left her ears ringing. What the fuck? She felt wetness flooding out of her, drooling around his warm hand as he stroked her puffy cleft.

"Oh, please," she whimpered, not sure what she begged for, for the sensations to stop or for more, oh god, more. Then he ran his finger over her again, and the singing vibration pulsed through her clit and just as if he'd pushed a button, she came again, pounding her fists against the quilt and screaming... It was too intense, pressed on her sensitive clit; it was too much, it nearly hurt. She flopped onto her stomach and dragged her way up the bed, sluglike, and heard him laughing delightedly behind her. There was no escape if she even wished to escape; as he climbed over her, she felt a strange delight as he pulled at one cheek of her bottom and she yelped with a thrilled terror.

He slid the horrid thing between the deep flesh of her buttocks and pressed it against the ring of her asshole. She yowled like a cat, squirming, writhing under the unnerving pleasure of having that place so ferociously stimulated. That way took longer, but eventually, she was squalling into the pillows, her asshole spasming around the vibrator as she came yet again, so shamefully, so shamelessly.

After that, he let her lie still a moment, and she tried to catch her breath.

"There are so many ways to train you, pet," he said reflectively. His words caught at her, rousing her mind for a moment; was she being rewarded now or punished? Was he still angry that she'd left the hospital alone? Maybe… maybe there was no difference between reward and punishment now, not in a situation such as this. Didn't her body respond the same, either way? Were right and wrong an illusion too? The intensity had flipped the world upside down, and right and wrong were just poles to be switched out at will. And with Rhys, these poles had no meaning.

She gazed helpless out the window as he secured her thighs and the buzzer neared her. Was it night or morning? Dark out, but the timelessness of the flipped world bewildered her. He skimmed the buzzer over the tender creases of her flesh. She bit at the sheets, which had gathered into a nest around her during her struggles. Usually, the pleasure ended with an orgasm, but there seemed to be no end now to the sensations he could make her feel. It made her think of torture, that no matter how much a person was tortured, they could always be made to feel more, and then more.

She came again and again, no longer even aware of the vibrations, only of the fact that Rhys could just make her body react now as it pleased him. And wasn't that the point? Not any right or wrong, just her bending around his will. Around this dark, crushing force… as her mind went dim, she cast about for its antithesis, which must exist, which had to exist. There had to be some light at the end of it, some clarity to be found. But there was just darkness. And in the darkness, only Rhys.

Chapter 18

Amala cocked up a single brow, that expression of hers ever preemptive of some kind of scolding. But for the moment, she stayed silent, finishing her cake. She had something to say, and it wasn't to do with what she'd finished doing out on the asteroid. Or was it?

"Clearly, you want to tell me something," he growled, pushing his own cake away. Who ate cake for lunch, anyway? "Just say it already."

"I want to talk with you about Miss Rivas."

"I thought as much. Parsons knows about her?" His tone went hard. This conversation was long overdue, but he hated needing to have it.

"I think he knew already, before I told him. And I told him straight away, of course."

Rhys nodded. Of course, she'd had to. If Parsons learned of anything that Amala should have told him, then her loyalty as his agent in Canton Ex would become suspect. Which, of course, it was. But she hadn't told him about the code.

She entwined her graceful, spidery hands underneath her chin. "I just want to know you understand that as long as you're with her, she's a weapon for him. I don't think he'll make any moves just now. He likes to strike when it can do the most damage. But when he finds that opening, he'll absolutely strike."

"Don't patronize me; of course, I know that." He sounded hollow to himself, mechanical. "Is there a reason to think he's going to take her?"

"It's a question of *when*. And you need to ask yourself whether you will do what he wants, to get her back."

"He doesn't know what I've got. Not specifically. Hell, I don't even know what it is."

"I'm worried for you, Rhys. I've seen you care about two things for the last decade of your life. Stopping Parsons and figuring out what made this city. I'm worried you could be letting your emotions blind you to seeing those through."

"I know," Rhys said quietly. Amala was only parroting his own thoughts now.

"I guess I can't hope that you'll take the higher road and extricate yourself? I can put her somewhere comfortable. But she won't be safe as long as Parsons knows the attachment is real."

"The attachment would still be real. I'm sorry, Amala. We just have to deal with things as they are. She won't be allowed anywhere alone. And I have to finish what I'm doing."

Amala sighed. "You were never cold enough. I think if you hadn't run away, you might have learned to make the tough calls."

Run away. Like he was a child, like he was a captive. He had no reply to make.

"Just promise me," Amala said, "promise, that if she *is* taken, you won't give up what you have. Please."

"I expect you to be able to convince Parsons of that right now."

"I've done my best. I've downplayed your relationship all I can. But I want to know it, for my own well-being. Don't let this whole thing be for nothing."

"You want me to say that I will let him keep her if he takes her?" Not just say it, *mean it*. She wanted him to choose his discovery over Sydell. And he could not blame her.

"If he takes her and demands your work on the code, yes. You need to be firm on that right now. If you're not, then you've opened a chasm of doubt for me." She spread her hands apart on the table, as though to emphasize *chasm*.

Rhys watched her for another moment. Since they'd left Mars together ten years ago, they'd had their disagreements. She tended to take his father's side of things, that pushing back against Parsons would make things worse. But she'd supported him. All the way to becoming a double agent for him. But right now, they were at the edge of a rift between them, and if he did not speak and immediately find a way to bridge it, the rift could be critical. The only thing he had to do was lie. But he had never lied to Amala. He stood up. "As always, I'm grateful for your advice," he said coldly. "Thank you. But I'd like to consider this topic finished. You will never bring that question up to me again."

Her face stayed smooth, but he knew what had cracked underneath. Her faith in him must have been shattered. "Of course, Rhys," she said. Unbelievably, she went on eating her cake.

They stayed quiet in the speed craft back to the offices.

Then all at once she said, "Do you trust her? It's clear she's subordinate to you."

"I have no reason not to trust her."

"She stole from you once. And not petty theft."

"Foolishly, impulsively. She won't do it again."

"You know she's probably getting right into that head-space in her training where her sense of morals is breaking down?"

Amala was unnervingly good. Could she tell that just from watching Sydell at the office?

"It's a dangerous time," she went on. "A trainee almost killed me once, going through it."

"Trainee," he scoffed. "Why do you call them that when they were slaves?"

"Is Sydell your slave?" Amala kept her head facing forward as she spoke, neither looking at him or away.

"Legally, she's indentured by Canton Ex. Our relationship is voluntary."

"I won't try to dissect it, it's beside the point. I just want you to be careful. You've been spending a lot more time working, and she's alone more, and if she's in an amoral headspace, then that's hardly helpful."

Amala, always excellent at her cool, sage advice that made him want to throw her out of the speeder. He laughed to himself. She was right, of course. That's why he never failed to ask her opinion on anything, as much as it might piss him off. "Thank you, Amala. You're probably right." He paused, then gave her a small, sardonic grin. "Anything else?"

She returned the grin. Maybe things weren't as bad as he'd thought. At the very least, she ought to be glad he'd been honest with her.

"No," she said, "not for now."

When they returned to the offices, Sydell was there. "I

thought you were staying home today?" he asked, gruffer than he intended. He certainly didn't want her moving around on her own right now.

"I was sick of being there," she grumbled.

"Yesterday, you were sick of being here," he said with a sigh. She'd grown weary of working on the code. She had cabin fever, not uncommon among people new to Io City, and even longer residents. Something about the constant dusk, the swirling snow outside… probably why they spent so much time at their cafes, obsessed over their fashion. And he'd done nothing but push her to do more work.

"We're going to get some shore leave soon, baby, I promise. I just need to finish all the re-scans." He rumpled her hair, tugged gently at that silly green strand of it. "Now, listen. I want you to call me up the next time you're going to come out to the office. I'll send one of my speeders out. Did you take a taxi?"

"I took the walkway."

"Don't do that again." When he said it, her mouth flattened, like she wanted to argue with him. He narrowed his eyes and waited. But she said nothing.

"You call me next time. I want to know when you're out. Is that understood?"

"I'm a prisoner. Understood."

He stepped behind her, sweeping an arm around her shoulders. "Technically, yes. You are."

She huffed. A shitty card to play, but no way was she going out alone anymore. Amala had wind of something, or she wouldn't have brought it up to him. At least, an intuition, but he trusted that too. And he wasn't about to have Sydell in morbid dread over things. If she thought he was just being restrictive, it was a small price to pay.

"Let's go home." He took her hand, pulling her in close as they went out to the speeder.

Rhys' dark murmured tones sounded again early the next morning, in the kitchen. She stood, crept to the bedroom door, and peeped through the crack of it. He was on his earpiece, and she knew he was speaking with Amala.

Yesterday, she'd become so sick of being in the apartment, with the raging of violet and lavender flurries swirling manically outside the window, that she headed for the offices. She called no speeder, because she wanted to run. On arriving, she'd felt better. At first. And then, sitting at the desk, he'd arrived with Amala, and she had that strange, intimate smile, and his eyes shone. Then he saw Sydell, and he'd been angry. And now she wasn't allowed to go up to the office without calling.

She was here, trapped in a dome, no, trapped in an apartment in a dome, like a fish in a bowl. She was Rhys' prisoner. Because she was a criminal, and he had mastered her. He owned her legally and completely and she'd accepted it. But now, with Amala? Could she face that? That something was going on with them, probably always had been? And why should it ever have stopped, just for someone like her? He'd never assured her of any such thing. She'd never asked.

No down or up, right or wrong. Perhaps then, it was just one more thing that, on closer inspection, could have no meaning? But when he left the next morning, kissing her on the head, she cried senselessly and did not say good-bye. He stared long at her, concern on his face, and then he left.

No, of course, there wasn't anything going on with Amala. Nothing he would care to hide, anyway.

He hopped up from his chair at the office, the next day. "I'm having lunch with Amala. Take a break from that shit, baby. You'll get another headache. I'll bring you something to eat."

On the days they ate together, they ate at the office, usually going on with their work.

That night, she turned away from him, onto her side.

"What's wrong, Sydell?"

It shook her, to hear her own name. He didn't use it much. "I hate this place," she said and cringed at how her words came out sulky, like a child's.

"You have cabin fever," he said. "We're going to take some leave as soon as these last scans are finished. That's part of the reason I'm out there so much. But I can't leave until its done."

"I want to go see Walt," she said. It came out of nowhere; it hadn't been something she wanted at all, it just felt like something to say. Something to put a wedge in, so that he had to feel something of what she felt. Maybe it would make him wonder… at the very least, he'd know that she had something extending beyond him.

"Okay," he said after a perplexed silence. "Have you messaged him? I'm not sure how often they get leave at the Academy."

Now he'd shown her up, that her desire was fabricated, even without intending to. She said nothing, could say nothing. Finally, she said, "Why can't I go out there?"

"You'd have to check the visitation policies. They have sensitive tech, and they don't just let people tour the place. You'd have better luck having him come out here. Besides, I don't want you traveling right now, not without me."

She broke into a quiet sobbing, burying her face in the pillows. He touched her face, and his voice softened, concerned. "Hey! Hey, baby, if you want to see Walt, I will look into making that happen, all right? I promise. I'm sorry if you feel like you're on lockdown, but it's only for a little while."

She wept helplessly, as one does who has no under-standing of the cause. How could he be so kind, as to her seeing Walt? She'd only been trying to make him jealous. Maybe he didn't have the sense to be jealous. His kindness, in response to her bad motivation, shamed her, and she cried harder.

"Of course, you want to see someone, go somewhere, sweetheart. I realize it's been months. I'm going to send a message out to the Academy right away." He kissed her forehead.

Her weeping subsided, comforted even by his misguided caring for her. But she didn't say anything else and, after a few minutes, pretended to be asleep.

───

Time flew by these days for Rhys. So much work to be done. Maybe he should have taken her out to the caverns more, but having her scrambling around the caves always managed to distract him, slow his work down. He'd rather that she was safe at home, or at Canton Ex. The day after her tearful request, he'd been sure to write Walter immedi-ately, though, honestly, he'd rather she was the one to do it. He wasn't sure as to her intent in telling him that, whether she truly wanted to see Walt at all. Anyway, he'd not heard back yet, and it had been three days.

Corey was off today, and so he would make the trip out to the caves alone. As much as he told Sydell they'd be done soon, he knew that was optimistic. Even if he went out every day, with Corey's help, it could be weeks yet. He rather hoped Walt would visit, hoped it would cheer her up some.

And yet… her sulkiness also rang a bell for him, as to what she needed. She was so sweet, and he'd grown soft with her. Hard not to be. Maybe she needed something else from him, which he'd been too occupied to give her, which he had thought to back off from, now that she hadn't been so reckless. But he also knew that once initiated to physical discipline, some people grew to crave it, grew unbalanced when they weren't handled firmly on the regular. It might be that Sydell was just one of those people.

When he returned from having brunch with Amala, she was at Canton Ex, and she greeted him with a hostile expression.

"I hope you didn't walk here," he snapped.

"No, I called the car," she returned, peering at him, then at Amala. Amala excused herself and went out to her offices.

"I thought you weren't coming in today," he said.

"I wasn't, but I'm sick of being at the apartment. I'm sick of being here, too."

"What is it that you want, Sydell?" he asked slowly, to keep his patience in check.

"I want to go to the caves, but you won't let me."

"No, I told you that after last time, you'd lost that privilege for a while. And you know why."

She'd tried jumping across a scaffolding. He ought to have paddled her then, maybe she wouldn't be so moody now. He could see he'd neglected her; it was obvious. "Okay. You can come with me to the caves. But you're going to stay where I tell you."

"How can I scan things, then?"

"You're more useful to me working on the code here, but you want to come along. So."

"Not if I won't be useful." Her words stretched out snidely.

"Too late now. Meet me out at the car and bring a helmet. I'll be there in a minute." He had something he needed to get.

Chapter 19

I t was late; time had flown by at the caves, and he still needed to scan more, always more. But he was exhausted. Sydell, of course, had kept on doing everything she could to prove to him that it was just as he thought, that she needed him to come down much harder on her. But even as she'd climbed around the caves, ignored his requests, and generally just been as difficult as she could, he had not allowed himself to react at all. No, that had waited. Until now.

They made their way out of the cavern and across the snow back to the rover. Io hung close in the sky, a huge red blur behind the violet cloud, and she stopped to stare up at it apprehensively. He hiked her up into the rover, gave her bottom a light push and settled in next to her. The heat of the vehicle overwhelmed him after the caves, and he cranked it down. Sydell wriggled out of her suit and smoothed out her skirt, which she had bunched up into it.

Rhys pulled off his helmet and rubbed a hand over his hot scalp. "I'm going to talk to Amala about finding you something else to do that's more interesting than working on code. If anyone can come up with something, it's her."

She turned her head to the window with a jerk.

"Is something the matter?" he asked, taking a deep breath.

"Nope."

He pulled the rover into park. They'd left the buttes behind but were still too far from the city to even glimpse its outline; only a halo of lavender light echoed up to the cloud cover. They were, for the moment, adrift in a sea of snow. "Can't we just go home?" she asked with her face leaning on her hand and the words muffled.

"We can, when you've told me what your problem is."

She sighed. "Every time I go into the office, you aren't there." Her words ran together a bit, as though her jaw was tense.

"I don't have to be," he said, trying to guess where this was heading. He hoped it wasn't just another misdirect, like bringing up Walt.

"No, but it sucks to just be someone's pet while they go out all the time."

He started to speak, to remind her that she had been wanting to stay behind, of late. He waited, however, letting the silence overcome her.

"You don't go out to lunch with me," she went on. "Is it because I'm a pet? Something that's not your equal? But with someone you admire, like Amala, you'll go."

There. The other shoe always dropped when you stayed quiet. "It's not something I normally do," he answered calmly. "Amala likes to do it, and it's a good way for us to catch things up. If you'd like to go out, I need you to tell me that."

She said nothing, just pushed her head against the window morosely.

"That's not what this is about, though, is it?" he asked.

"She's possessive of you. What is she to you? Something real, something that's not a pet? Why do you even have me around?"

Christ, it was worse than he thought. She'd grown that insecure. "You're the one being possessive right now," he said mildly, much more mildly than he felt.

"You literally say that you own me," she snapped. "*That's* possessive."

"I literally *do* own you. You're property of Canton Ex. Is that what you're upset about, or are you jealous of me and a co-worker?" His voice stayed calm, but it had gone a bit scolding; he couldn't help it. "Amala is my bookkeeper, and she practically holds my business together." And so much more that he couldn't say, for Amala's protection. He added, "She was my father's mistress, which is no secret. And so she acts like part of my family, butts in."

When she did not reply, he grew quiet. Jealous of Amala, insecure… well, of course, she felt out of place here, and Amala could be intimidating. Maybe they had a chemistry there, between them, albeit one that had spent itself long ago. He'd disappointed her, leaving Parsons, refusing to compromise. She saw him as childish. But thinking on it, he could see why Sydell felt how she did. Add to that all the contact he'd had to make with her, of late. But, of course, Amala wasn't the point, not really.

"Sydell, why do you assume that because you're my pet, you aren't very real to me?" His tone was rough when he said it, but he didn't know how else to get it across. Part of him needed to launch his love at her like a grenade; it had to startle her.

"Everything is a secret; you tell me nothing!"

"You ask me nothing."

"How am I supposed to ask you, when you act like

231

you're a god who's not to be questioned? Who settles everything we argue about, himself?"

"It's true I'll have the final say in things. But if any other part of that were true, we'd not be having this talk right now. No one else gets to talk to me this closely. Not Amala, not even my sister."

She fell silent.

"I've been busy of late, and I've neglected you. It's not fair to you at all, and I'm sorry. I've ignored things from you that I shouldn't have let pass, and you think I'm not in control now."

"What?" The word tore out of her like an expletive, like she couldn't comprehend him or wasn't willing to.

"For weeks, you've been testing how long your leash is, and you're at the end of it, pet."

"This is how you respond when I'm jealous?"

"You're insecure and stressed, and you're going to feel a lot better after I spank you. It'll go easier if you don't fight me but—" He took her sleeve, at her elbow, and she tore it away. "But I know you will," he sighed, mostly to himself. She had that wild look in her eyes, and he knew she'd try something stupid. She pulled the handle at the rover door, as if to jump out into the snow, but the doors were auto locked.

"What are you even spanking me for?" she yelled.

No need to overcomplicate it. "You've been a brat all day. Go on and deny it."

She screwed up her mouth, as if to confirm his accusation as best she could by expression. In the next instant, she'd launched herself over the seats, to the back of the rover, as if that could deter him. Good. He didn't want her kicking at any of the equipment up front; it was expensive. He followed her to the backseats in one smooth motion, legs first, and swept her under one arm as he landed. She raked her nails across his arm, but for the moment he felt nothing. "You can't just do this out of nowhere!" she cried.

"I can't?" He laughed. He bent her over his lap and pinned her wrist to the small of her back. "I think you know I can do anything I'd like."

He swiped her skirt up over her hips, and she cursed with rage and kicked at the rear door with her heels, a drumming of protest. She wore a pair of panties he'd not seen before, sheer black mesh, very sophisticated; something she'd gotten with Amala perhaps? They irked him, and he yanked them down her hips hard enough that they tore down the side and through the crotch, apparently as flimsy as they looked.

"What's wrong with you? Those are mine!" she shouted. "You haven't even got a reason to punish me. You're a bully and a fucking sadist."

"Keep taunting. Let me know just how hard you need it to be." He kept calm; he felt calm, much calmer now he had her in place over his lap. Dimly, it rose in his awareness that the need for punishing her was also his own. The elation crept into him like a sunrise but he stifled a smile.

She roared, trying to break free. On utterly failing, she huffed out, "You said you did this to train me, to make me stop doing things that could get me hurt. But this is just about power, about breaking me."

"I thought you grasped that a while ago," he said, and whatever she'd started to say next—he guessed it was something along the lines of a "Fuck you"—the first slap he landed stole it right out of her mouth.

She still couldn't believe it, as she lay crying on his lap. Yet she'd known it would happen, somehow. Had been waiting for it to happen. And now that it had, something which had been hounding her, some weird, mounting fear, had dissolved the instant he'd had her on his thighs. Then the only thing to fear had been the sting of it, which had been considerable. But it came as a relief. It relieved her, like some heavy object had been pressing down on her and now it had lifted, and she was light again. Goddammit, was he right? What he'd said about her feeling better after she was punished? It was like she'd been asking him a question, over and over, finally screaming it, and at last he had answered.

She had yelled at the top of her lungs, kicked, even bit at him, and, in giving him her all, had been met with his. Her whole body trembled to remember the terrible rapture of it, even as her tears still soaked her cheeks. The dark cloud which had pitched over her these last few weeks had vanished.

He'd stopped spanking her and now rubbed his hand over her bottom, both soothing and stimulating her seared nerves. Humiliating, for him to do these things, things she would have done for herself and which made her feel better. She sniffled, quite unable to stop him, and so she relaxed, enjoyed the sensation. Her entire body tingled, her nerves sensitive with expectation.

"Now that that's straightened out," he said lightly, "you should know that though I call you my pet, and you *are* my pet, this hardly excludes that you mean everything to me."

She caught her breath. He pinched at her cheek, then slid his hand down the split of her, to the tenderness between her legs. She felt his fingers glide along her sensitive folds, felt how wet she'd become, and she moaned and pushed her mouth shut to hide the sound.

"My whole life the last two years has been focused on the cave ruins, on solving a code. Besides that, you are the only thing I care about. You're the only person I call my own; it's more than I would say if you were my wife." As the last word aired, he landed another slap, sharp but lighter than the others. Her rear blazed with warmth, deep and radiating all along the hidden parts of her. She sighed and laid her head on the seat. He petted her hair for a moment. "I hope you take what I give you as love. It's how it's meant," he said simply, and her whole core throbbed.

"Now," and she heard him smile as he spoke, "we're going to spank you to an orgasm. How does that sound?"

"What?" she spluttered, but he'd already begun to rub sensuously once again down between her legs, so she forgot to protest his suggestion. But it wasn't a suggestion, was it? He was going to do it, the horrid sounding thing, whether or not she wanted to, and she would probably enjoy it, whether or not she wanted to. She blazed hot all over.

She yelped when he went on spanking her, lighter but still with the crisp, smarting sting; he kept his right hand grazing her soft mound, while he did the more arduous work with his left, inflaming her with every slap. Her butt had been so sore, she didn't think she could stand another, but as he went on, the sting spread through her as a lustful warmth. Again, the poles had flipped, the boundaries between pleasure and pain blurred. Her little yips of discomfort were overtaken by throatier cries of desire, loud and feeling as though they came distantly and from someone else.

He rubbed at her pussy in earnest now, expertly; the flood of sensation was unbelievable. The sting of his hand on her ass built her fury, which built her lust; she could not escape it, both the pain and the pleasure were a given, inevitable. She was his, to do with as he liked. The shame that she could be brought to this so quickly, after such a harsh punishment, clung to her, but if anything, it only made her burn hotter.

She came loudly, violently, held down on his lap, kicking her legs to the sharp slaps even as he slowed them, as he caressed her soothingly.

"That's a good pet," he said, stroking her tender back-side and quietly laughing as she whimpered. He tickled at the insides of her thighs, as she lay limp and quivering, her face and ass still burning as the last of the glow pulsed within her, ringing through her whole body. She became aware, just barely, of his erection pressing through his jeans, jutting against the softness of her belly. He petted her for a few minutes, until she grew still, and her body felt light.

He sat her up slowly, moving her onto his lap. She peered up at him and he kissed her square on the mouth, so that something in her started to wake again, the first flush of lust dawning on the horizon. How he could do it, she did not know, making her passion rise again from ash; she gazed at him in a sort of wonder at it. He peeled away his own suit now, and her dawning desire flushed brighter to see his body. The smooth, strong lines of his abdomen, the rusty bristles of hair at his naval trailing down to… he wore his boxers still, but just the same, her face and neck warmed. As if knowing her anticipation, he slid the boxers off, a casual motion, and his cock slipped free, bobbing in deceptive friendliness.

"I'm going to fuck you, pet," he said, and she yelped and spread her legs around him eagerly.

"Hang on, we're gonna try it like this," he breathed, and plucking her from his lap, he bent her over the back of the bench seat, so that she dangled into the storage space. It felt strange, to be displayed like this, to feel like she was two halves, one utterly available to him, the other separate, powerless to affect what went on with the other. Panting excitedly, she planted her forearms on a flexicrate to prop herself up, but doubled as she was, she could see nothing behind her. He rustled around for a moment, then presented her with some object, which he dangled in front of her face, some black, obscene thing, a rubber cock? But small, maybe only three inches long, and certainly not as wide.

"Put it in your mouth. Get it nice and wet."

"Why the hell—"

"Trust me when I say you want it wet." Then without further ado, he plopped it into her mouth, and she grunted with annoyance. Not rubber, silicone maybe, with a flared base. When he pulled it out, she said nastily, "If you want me to suck, just say so."

"When I want you to suck me, you will," he said pleasantly, and in the next instant, she knew his plans for the thing as he prodded the tip of it at the opening of her asshole.

"Ah! Don't!" she cried.

"Relax. It's much easier if you relax. I promise it will feel good."

"Why the fuck would it feel good?"

"Sweetheart, you came like a rocket the first time I touched your asshole," he said, and she cried out, flushing hot as he spoke, as he went on to remind her of the night with the little vibrator.

"Just get on with it then!" she growled, sick of him talking about it, embarrassing her.

"That would just be cruel," he said, and then he slipped it in with an awful slowness, so that she had all the time in the world to imagine what she must look like to him back there.

"I hate you," she said. All the heat flared again, the

tension growing down between her legs, prickling around her crotch, even as it had just been eased.

"No," he said softly, impossible to anger now. He was just impossible.

"Why do you want to make me look ridiculous?"

"You look adorable," he said and pinched affectionately at her cheek, making the awful toy move around. It had burnt going in, but now that it had stilled, it made her even more aware of the sensation as he ran his fingers down to her over-pleasured clit. Without anything more, he settled behind her, and taking her at her hips, he buried himself inside. She gasped and yipped as he slid his full length in and hit the end of her. He moved in forceful thrusts, ardent as his hands gripped her hips, his fingers pushing hard into her flesh. She was spread out absurdly, his thick cock and the phallus both filling her to the brim, making her feel as if she would burst. She moaned deep in her throat, as he pushed in and out of her, each time pressing the little cock around in her ass. The pressure there linked, somehow, with her pussy, and as he thrust into her, he ground her pussy into the scratchy fibers of the seat.

"Oh, god," she cried, and he pumped harder, faster, switching his grip to her shoulders to better hold her in place. She felt herself dripping wet around him, both holes spread helplessly.

"Rhys, Rhys, oh, please, please!" And then she came again, screaming hoarsely, while he wiggled the phallus around in her, and she pounded her fists on the flexicrate. She went on hollering as it reverberated through her, as he pounded her rowdily to his own climax and surged up inside of her. There, that strange sense of heat as he came, as warm liquid inundated her insides; she mewled, weakly, as she felt fuller than ever. He gave her a light smack on the side of her hip and slumped over her, laughing tiredly. He pulled out of her, and she felt the warmth of his seed dribble out over her labia.

"I think you're gonna love getting fucked up the ass," he said, almost offhandedly.

"Jesus, Rhys." She closed her eyes. What else could she say?

"We'll get you nice and trained for it," he said and scratched her head. "You sure went crazy for this thing." And then he ripped it out of her, and she yelped, not in pain so much as at the weirdness of the sensation. He moved over on the bench, pausing to kiss her tenderly on one sore butt cheek.

"My pretty pet," he whispered, sounding almost euphoric. He pulled her skirt down over all of it, even as she felt more of his cum sliding out of her. He lifted her up from the bench and dragged her onto his lap, hugging her close. She heard sounds, like soft crying, coming from somewhere. Like a whimpering animal. Oh. It was coming from her.

How long he held her like that, she could not say. She did not sleep, but she did not think herself conscious, either. The molecules of her body felt to have spread out, so that she grew light, like air, a tingling cloud. A tingling that drifted through her limbs, exiting through her fingers and toes, an ecstasy of levity. Were it not for the slight sense of Rhys, warm beneath her, she should have taken herself to be floating.

This is it, then, she thought. The other side of the dark crushing well she had found in encountering Rhys, as he was. The other side of darkness, which she had crossed. And right now, the other side was bliss.

Chapter 20

The next few weeks, though dull, passed by with a new satisfaction for her. She would sit quietly at the window, curled up on the bed and reading, while Rhys worked on the code. He would look up and smile at her, and she would smile back.

When it was her night to do the dishes, she did them; if she complained, he told her he could spank her first if she liked. And so, she did them. Sometimes he did spank her first, just as he had in their days on the ship, and she'd cry just like she had back then, and she would feel strangely better.

He started taking her out to dinner some nights. She argued, reminding him that he didn't like to do it; he told her he could spank her first if she liked. And so, they would go out. She didn't quite understand how she had come to be more content, but here it was, and she had no need to question it.

He still went out with Amala for lunch, sometimes, and she didn't really care anymore.

One evening, after he'd been out in the caves all day, he

returned, changed into his tailored coat and told her to put on a dress. They would go out again, to the old Euro Cafe she liked. She didn't argue but scurried into the closet and put on her shirtwaist silk dress, an emerald green, which she liked because of its exact match to the streak in her hair, even though that had started to fade some.

They took a taxi speeder; as he opened her door, his holowrist flashed, and he checked it before crowding in beside her. "Corey wants to see me," he said, voice flat with annoyance. "We're going to stop at Canton Ex for a minute. Really, he could just message me."

She leaned against him, and he kissed her forehead. She sighed, closing her eyes as the car zoomed through the speedway. What ought she get for dinner? The creamy pasta with the prawns? Or that filet steak in the mustard sauce with little potatoes? God, she was famished.

The speeder slowed to a stop. "I'll be right out, pet," he said.

"I want to come in with you."

"All right then. Come on."

Sydell sat down at her desk, while Rhys went into the enclosed office with Corey, who she'd only seen through the window. As Rhys entered, the tint went up on the glass, fully to black.

She spun her chair, back and forth, the way she did when she wanted Rhys' attention. Twenty minutes passed, and she groaned. But she wasn't going to interrupt. Probably something had come up, and dinner would be canceled. She couldn't hear them speaking, recalling vaguely that the offices were soundproofed. Wouldn't he at least come out and send her home? What the hell?

Even more time passed, and as her stomach grew heavy with worry, her hunger vanished. Rhys wouldn't have left her so long, not unless something were really the matter. Her anger melted away. Should she go in, see what was wrong? Surely, he'd come out and tell her where she needed to go? What could be wrong, anyway?

At last, Corey came out. Rhys did not follow. Corey had dark circles under his eyes; they fixed to her as he approached and came to stand next to her chair. His face was haggard, his expression blank.

"Miss Rivas," he said, "I'm going to need you to come with me."

"What? Where's Rhys? What's wrong?"

"You will need to come with me," he repeated, in a clipped, almost dead, tone, "to the car outside."

What the hell was going on? Why wouldn't Rhys come out? "Where's Rhys?" she repeated, a strange fear crawling in her guts.

"He won't see you. You will come with me at once."

"Are you kidnapping me? You don't have a weapon."

"Don't escalate things."

"You're the one escalating things! Rhys and I are going to dinner, what's the matter with him?" All kinds of things filled her head now; Corey was betraying them in some way, Rhys lay dead in the office and now she would be killed too. Part of her didn't believe that at all, but something was terribly wrong, and her breaths started coming in fast. She had to move; she stood, starting for the office. Corey moved and blocked her path.

"Why can't I see him? What did you do? Rhys!" The last, a shout, panicked.

And then Rhys burst out of the room. Corey stepped back and held a hand up to stop him. "We agreed you should not talk with her."

"Not talk with me?" she shrilled. "What the hell, Rhys? Why—"

"Do as he says," said Rhys, his face stony. His eyes

bored into her with a rage that left her stunned, that made her fall utterly silent and look away from him. For a moment, she could not even think. Then she peeked back at him and found his face as telling as a mannequin's. Her heart contracted painfully. A sharp, deep pain. She chased it off, summoning her anger.

"No!" She scowled at him, daring him to react to her. He would react! "I will not! Not until you tell me what's going on."

"I'm taking you somewhere to be held, for the time being," said Corey.

She did not even look his way when he spoke; her eyes stayed only on Rhys. "Held. Why am I to be held?"

"We found the uplink," said Rhys, and she stared at him stupidly, failing to comprehend.

"The data transfer to Parsons." His eyes stayed on her, with cold fury.

"Don't tell her anything!" Corey snapped.

"Why not? She'll confess." He spoke with such withering contempt that her blood went cold.

"What are you talking about?" she cried, the pitch of her voice rising at the end, a doglike whine she despised. "Transfer to Parsons? Of what?"

"All of it. Everything that's been my life for two years, for longer even. And now he'll have the power to control what he wants and destroy the rest. Did you think about that?"

"The code?"

He smirked, a forced effort. *Yes.*

Oh, my god! The code, all transferred to Parsons? For a second, she forgot he accused her of doing it, it so horrified her. Then she said, "Just how am I supposed to have done it?"

"We know you uploaded it through your holopad."

When he said it, Corey stepped forward and pulled the holopad from her wrist.

"It wasn't on my holopad, how would it be?"

Rhys took the holopad from Corey. "We'll figure it out. Corey, get her out of here."

Corey, now directly beside her, took her arm. This couldn't be happening. Rhys had turned, walking back into the office. "Rhys!" she screamed, "I didn't! I didn't do this, I wouldn't—"

Corey pulled her with an iron grip on each of her arms, which hurt enough to make her cease her appeals. Besides, Rhys had gone, had shut the door to the sound-proofed room and would not hear her. He thought... he thought she'd given the code to Parsons, worked with Parsons! It made no sense; how could she convince him?

This couldn't be happening. No, Rhys would come back out, and they'd go to dinner, and then they'd go home together to the apartment. Home. She would read herself to sleep and he would work on... on the code... *Oh, God.*

She broke into a frenzied sobbing as Corey led her out onto the speedway, where the car waited. He opened the door to the backseat. "Lie down," he commanded. She stood still for a moment, rocking in hesitation... could she break free and make a run for it?

Corey sat her down roughly in the backseat. "Lie *down!*"

She lay down, her heart pounding. She'd never seen him show a single emotion before, but now she knew; Corey was pissed. He tossed a blanket over her; God only knew where from. She pulled her breath in and out; the blanket impeded her not at all, but she could not seem to get enough air.

"Do not take that off. You aren't to see where we're going. Stay down until I tell you otherwise."

The dark panic pressed down on her, and for a moment, she thought she would suffocate.

"Don't go see her," said Corey. He opened the cooler and pulled out something cold and caffeinated and handed it to Rhys, who took it absently. He stayed as he had been for the last few hours, hunched over his desk, poring over all her holologs. Every uplink, the timing of each one; what had been going on during that uplink, and that one, or that one? Each one, he'd been at the offices, she at home. The last had taken place on the day they'd gone out to the caves together, just before she'd joined him at the offices. No more after that.

"Did she talk to you?" Rhys glanced up to ask.

"No. She was hysterical."

Rhys tensed. "There's nothing in that room she can hurt herself with?"

"No. I don't think so. I mean, there's a bathroom. Has a shower, no tub but—"

"I want to go over there and see for myself. We need to get a camera in too."

"I don't think you should see her—"

"You couldn't get her to talk. She'll talk to me."

"Why would she? She's a fucking spy!"

Rhys paused. He'd forgotten how angry his partner was, and justifiably so. He chose his words carefully. "She did upload the data. But I don't think she was planted."

"Of course, she was."

"She can't have been," he said. Amala would have known; something that deep-rooted couldn't have escaped her. But Corey didn't know about Amala. So, Rhys said, "There's no way Parsons knew whom I hired to transport me to Callie. But he got to her at some point. Obviously. I just need to know when, and how." His voice was calm; it reverberated through his aching chest, reminding him he wasn't dead.

"Rhys. Listen. If Parsons was going to hire someone to gain your trust, wouldn't someone like Sydell be the exact person to do it? And wouldn't he know you well enough to know that?"

Some pressure in his chest was normal, probably nothing serious. He cleared his throat. Corey must have known to change that subject. "Jesus, Rhys. We have to go to Io Council now."

No, no, that couldn't happen. They'd have everything, the code, the ruin, all his work. *No.*

"Parsons has it now," Corey pressed. "He *will* figure it out. You want him to figure it out before us and use it whatever way he wants, with no one to stop him?"

"I'll…" *I'll stop him.* He could not say it; it was stupid at this point. He had failed. He stood and, in one smooth motion, shoved the divider surrounding his desk, toppling it. The picture of Jason fluttered to the floor. The pressure relented slightly. Corey watched him, eyes gray and empty, though a bit red at the whites.

"She will talk to me," Rhys said, his voice distant.

"Do not try to handle this yourself," Corey warned. But he made no move to stop him.

He took an express car out to the warehouses and then dropped it, walking the rest of the way. He couldn't risk anyone tracking him there. He'd had Corey take her to an old storage unit they'd turned into a shelter a few years back, intended for if they ever needed to go into hiding.

Maybe he would still need to, maybe Io City would charge him with treason. But those thoughts, he put out of his head swiftly. Sydell would tell him everything; who'd linked her to Parsons and why she'd… But he knew why, didn't he? All those uplinks had been made during that time, that few weeks between her shunting and the day they went to the caves together. She'd been angry, emotional. He'd ignored her, and she'd been more upset than he'd guessed. Upset enough to… but for all her crazy actions in the past, this, he had not expected. He had been utterly blind, stupid. Even Amala had warned him.

All right, so he'd get her to confess. And once she confessed, what to do with her then? Turn her over to the city? Then she'd go back into the system, and Europa was no kinder to felons than they were back on Earth. No, she remained his responsibility.

The old warehouses were deserted these days, giant steel bunkers under a great translucent dome. God knew what else was kept down here. He waved his card over the lock. He entered as slowly and quietly as he could. A small space, a single room and a bathroom, the rest of the place he owned actually serving as storage. The main room, with its double-sized bed, made exactly as he'd made it years ago, was empty. The starkness of the room shocked him for a moment, sink and mirror gleaming cold under the lights, bed angular with its precisely tucked blankets. The tiled floor slanted slightly, to a drain in one corner that made him think it had once been used as a butchery.

The bathroom door had been closed, and light glowed from under the crack of it. He had a gnaw of dread, then, as to what might be behind the door. Could she have hurt herself, tried to? She hadn't been alone too long. Corey had been here, questioning her. He approached the door, his throat tight. He flung it open in a swift motion.

She stood, wrapped in a towel, the room still steamy with her shower. Her eyes lit up when she saw him, and it took every ounce of will he had to harden himself to her.

"Come out of there," he ordered.

"Rhys!" she cried, holding the towel around herself. "You can't believe I did it, can you? I don't even—"

"Come. Out."

She walked out, her eyes wide, pleading. He closed the door behind her and locked it with the keycard. "What the hell, Rhys? My dress is in there."

"You don't need it. This place is temperature controlled." He pulled the towel from around her, a cruel motion. She stood as she had when he'd first seen her, trying to cover herself with her arms, her hair hanging modestly over her breasts. A mermaid, he had thought. Naked, vulnerable, helpless, and it excited him, even in all his cold fury. Perhaps because of his fury. The pain melted some, into an exhilaration. Her skin flushed pink all over as he stared, her breath quickening audibly. Despite everything, because of everything, an electricity surged between them.

"Rhys…" she whimpered. He crossed the space and curved an arm around her, gripping the fullness of her ass hard in his hand. She moaned, she pressed into him, grinding herself on his thigh. He smelled her desire, musky and strong. He ran his hand up to her left breast; her nipple hard in his fingertips, he pinched it, and she cried out, the tail end of the cry stretching out lustfully.

He forgot everything in that moment, everything but her naked helplessness and her lusty sounds. She pushed her cunt into him shamelessly and moaned, "Please, Rhys."

"Please what?" Was she going to try to explain herself again?

"Please… fuck me." The last two words were small.

He pulled her up in his arms and then he had tossed her onto the bed and fallen on top of her. Her legs curled around him, clinging to him. He shifted about, unfastening his pants, while she whined impatiently, biting at his shoulders and neck. The last bite piercing skin, and he grunted and snatched her ear. "Do that again, I'll spank you with my belt."

She gasped almost joyfully and planted her mouth on his shoulder, but did not bite him again, only sucked at his skin. He plunged into her, and she howled, her cunt clenching him at once, desperate with desire. Her arms and legs stiffened under him, trembling as he drew himself out and thrust back in. Her cries grew sharper, running together with words he could make no sense of. He fucked her roughly, fairly slamming her into the bed, grabbing at her breasts in his hands and pulling her nipples in his fingers.

"You're mine," he growled right into her ear. She squealed, her legs quivering under his; she snatched at the blanket beneath them. He heard a little tearing sound as she rent a handful of it. Then she came with a series of howls, her pussy spasming wildly as he pounded her. Her cries drew long in ecstasy, and he fucked her in a frenzy of his own excitement until at last, he reached the peak, coming and coming, groaning as the pleasure hit a new high. Awareness left for a moment, or became distant, and then he returned, and her warm, soft body twitched under him, her exhausted panting steadily waking him. He pulled out of her, rolling over on the bed. They lay for a while in that strange silence, the only sound, their heavy and erratic breathing, nearly indistinguishable from one another's.

She spoke first. "Rhys. Tell me. How am I even supposed to have done this to you?"

A little shock of pride went through him, that she

would face it, that she knew the situation could not be changed, even after what had just happened. But it seemed, she still wanted to lie to him. "I told you. We found the uplinks in your holopad." His voice was flat, and for the moment, the surges of furious emotion he'd been feeling had evaporated.

"How would I even know where to send them? And why in hell would I do such a thing?" Her voice cracked a little at the end.

He said, "Really, those are things I'd like you to tell me."

She stared at him, her face cradled in the crook of her arm, stretched over her head where she lay. She spoke quietly. "I can't tell you, because I didn't do it. This is insane."

"Then give me some explanation of how else it could have happened." His voice sounded reasonable in his ears, but also sad. Because there could be no explanation.

"I can't," she breathed, "I don't know how they could have… they linked it from my holopad, so it must have been hacked or something."

"Convenient, wouldn't you say?" he asked bitterly. A twitch of the pain had returned, clawing at his chest from the inside. He forced a smile, mocking, showing an amusement he could not feel.

"Oh my god!" she gasped, her eyes growing wide. "Rhys! I think I know when they hacked it! Someone followed me home the night I was shunted! They followed me up to our apartment. But how…" She frowned. He waited, watching her. What else would she come up with?

"I think they used something on me, Rhys," she said. "Remember how I slept, how you said I had a bad reaction to the drugs? That can't have been it, because I walked home just fine. Then I got in the house and felt… it felt the way I did after I had the null crown on."

A null pulse? He stiffened. "Why did you never mention any of this to me?" he demanded.

"I didn't know. I didn't know why I felt so weird. But then, after I got inside, I fell asleep, and I thought maybe someone was in the apartment with me. He could have hacked me then."

"You never told me you were followed."

"No," she said, her eyes vacant, lost in whatever dream she'd conjured. "I knew you'd be angry. You were already angry I walked myself home. And besides, after I slept, it didn't seem like… it seemed unreal. I felt like I'd imagined it."

He waited a moment, after she fell silent. He could grasp at it, a straw of hope, if only to delay the inevitable. But he was not that weak. He said, "Who asked you to do this?"

Her eyes snapped to his. "You won't even consider what I said?"

"No, because I know you've just pulled it out of your ass. We are going to start talking about *what happened*. I will know how you got in touch with Parsons' people, and when. You can tell me why if you like, too, though it's starting to matter to me less and less every minute. I will not be lied to." He cringed as he said it and sat up quickly, to hide it, and also to avoid seeing her reaction.

"You're a stupid bastard," she said, her voice husky and strange.

"Careful. Your situation depends entirely on me and Corey now. A little respect would be in your self-interest."

"Why? Because you're going to kill me, Rhys? Is that what you mean? Now, if I piss you off, you just kill me?"

He laughed. "Hell no. I need to know how you got in with Parsons, and I need you alive for that."

"Then torture me. I'm sure I'll confess to something. Torture tends to do that. Then you can kill me. But get it the fuck over with."

He glanced back at her, before he could think better of it. As he'd expected, she had that gleam in her eye, that pulling-the pin-on-the-grenade crazy gleam. Had she been like that when she'd decided to upload everything to Parsons? But why then, would she go on lying about it? Did she regret it, want to keep up their life together? Or was she actually in fear for her life?

"You're always trying to rush the consequences," he said smoothly. "Because consequences are too unpleasant for you, aren't they, pet?"

"Don't call me that," she snapped, her tone brittle.

He went on as though he'd never said it. "Well, you're going to face the consequences this time. And it won't be an easy escape, like death. You're always ready to jump right to that because you haven't the spine to face reality. So. You needn't fear any such thing. You're going to live on to see all the misery your decision is going to cause. Every hardship, starting with what happens to me and Canton Ex, and spiraling out through the whole system, when Parsons has God tech and can control us all. You will live and you will face it."

He heard her breathing, behind him, rapidly. He turned and forced himself to watch her. She'd gone pale.

"And, of course, you'll tell me everything I want to know. You're right, you'd confess to anything under torture. Torture is overrated. But I've plenty of other tools. You'll get tired of living here with nothing to do. You can regain some privileges as you start to cooperate."

"Privileges?" she asked vaguely.

"Yes. Hot water, clothes. A toilet. For now, you may use the drain," he said cruelly; he only knew just how cruelly when she winced. "Perhaps we can even get you books, or a screen to watch. The sky's the limit," he said and then added sourly, "*pet*."

She shuddered. A pain darted through his chest, the worst yet, and he swallowed thickly. He had expected to enjoy seeing her hurt, but he did not. Perhaps Corey had been right, it had been a horrible mistake for him to come here.

He had to leave. She did not cry, but she'd sort of crumpled up on the bed. He mumbled something, about Corey being in shortly with food, and told her there were cameras in the room—there were not; he intended to rectify this swiftly. Then he left and locked the door behind himself with the card. His heart stabbed in his chest. He started off at a clip, jogging down the warehouse paths. He ordered a taxi to meet him at the edge of the city. He needed to see Amala.

Chapter 21

Amala's apartment was empty when he showed up there. He paced about like a caged animal. He searched the kitchen, rifling through the liquor cabinet. Inside, a bottle of whiskey, which had likely been around since Canton had been alive. Amala didn't touch the stuff. He poured himself three fingers of it in one of her ridiculous champagne cylinders.

Amala returned after about half an hour. Her face glowed, as though she'd been exercising. Morning walk? What time was it? He thought vaguely it must be early still. By this time, he had poured his third glass of whiskey, and while his troubles still existed, they'd been rendered smaller now, and distant.

"Rhys," she said, immediately alert. She slipped off her long-draped shawl and gloves and asked, "What's wrong?"

Now the time had come to explain, and he felt stupid for coming there. But he'd had a reason for doing it, beyond just the need to talk. "We've been compromised," he said flatly, "and we need to get you someplace safe."

She took in a deep breath. "All right," she said steadily. "What's happened?"

"Company data has been leaked to Parsons' people. Including the code. He knows you're ours now, since it didn't come from you."

She shrugged. "He probably knew anyway."

Right. Well, he must have had his suspicious, or else Amala would have gotten wind that they were going to get to Sydell.

Amala stepped to the icebox and took out a bottle of her champagne. "It was Sydell?" she asked.

"Why would you say that? Were you suspicious?"

"No. Not at all. But you're in my apartment and you seem to have been drinking for some time, so."

He snorted and set the glass down on the counter. Was he always such an open book to her?

"Are you certain it was her?" she asked.

"Yes. Absolutely. The uplinks came from her holopad, all at times when she was alone and had the opportunity to do it. The only question is who got to her, and when."

"You don't think she was sent to you, as a spy?"

"No. I mean, I guess it's possible, but I don't want to think it." There it was. The weakness. He closed his eyes.

"You don't want to face that possibility," said Amala, with her odd brand of cool sympathy. She sighed. "I can't blame you. Going off my own feeling, I'd say it's unlikely."

"Don't tell me what I want to hear."

"When have I ever?"

He smiled, or tried to. It hurt to try. His face had gone stiff, numb.

"Has she confessed?" Amala asked.

"No. And that's what gets me." He cleared his throat. "If she did this because she was angry at me, then she ought to have thrown it in my face. That's what she'd do, even if she were scared. Especially if she were scared. She runs from her problems by tackling them as blindly as possible."

"Maybe she was angry, and she fucked up, but she's changed her mind?"

"Yes, that's what I think it might be. Last month, last month, it was just like you said. She was passing through that phase. And I neglected her, and she was miserable. I think that's when it happened."

"And you still love her."

He could not respond, so he shrugged and knew the shrug looked helpless.

"She's emotionally unstable," Amala went on. "You felt she could benefit from your domination, no?"

He nodded slowly. "I wanted to straighten her out. But I wanted her for myself too."

"You accepted her volatility. We both know people are capable of insanities when they're being trained."

"I thought we were past that. I thought I had control."

"You're not objective. You never could be. That's why I was better at breaking people than you. I never really enjoyed it."

He swallowed. It hurt, hearing her say it. She was right, of course. He had enjoyed it, that's why he'd never been clean of it, while she'd walked away and never looked back. He could never be free of what he'd done, as she could. But he was not Parsons, either.

"Rhys," she said, "what happens now?"

"I find out what happened. Who compromised her."

"And then?"

"We find that person, or people, and clean this all up. Canton Ex is going in a box."

Amala nodded. He knew it hurt her, just like it did him,

and there was consolation in that, but also guilt. She said, "And Sydell?"

"If she's no longer a recruit for Canton Ex, then she goes back into the system." He closed his eyes and found his whiskey glass blind. "Out here, she'll end up on a mining colony. A death sentence."

Sending people down into asteroid mines was criminal, in his opinion, but the Council still did it to criminals. Amala said nothing, but stepped over to the window, tall and slender against the soft blue light of the Promenade. Businesses were opening up as usual, patrons rushing to cafes for coffee and pastry, running the boulevard for morning exercise. Life went on.

"Can you do that?" Amala asked finally.

"No." He put a hand to his temples; his fingers were cool, cold even, in contrast. "As long as she wasn't a plant from Parsons, she's still my responsibility. I didn't expect it, but it's an outcome I helped create."

"That may have wisdom to it, but perhaps you aren't the best person to deal with her, at least for the time being?"

He didn't answer. Having said that Sydell was his responsibility, meant Sydell was still his. He'd told her so, not too long ago, as he fucked her, he'd said, "You're mine," and it had just burst out, but now it repeated in his head. They were connected and it could not be broken.

Parsons blinded his own wife, so he'd be the last thing she ever saw.

He slammed his mind shut to the thought. He wasn't Parsons, could never be Parsons. Even if he enjoyed some things Parsons did, enjoyed power. It wasn't the same. He didn't have the ruthlessness, the ability to cast someone aside and shut off from them forever, destroy them. But then, why had Parsons blinded her?

Because she'd betrayed him. It was pride, wasn't it? Arrogance over an injury. Was it, though? Or had he missed something vital in his assessment of his own brother? Had Parsons only wanted to make sure she belonged to him, in some sick way, forever?

"Rhys?" Amala stepped in closer, nearing the kitchen.

"Thanks for the drink," he said and set the glass in the sink clumsily. He tensed and redoubled his efforts to control his movements.

"I'll have a taxi here for you in a few hours, so get packed," he said steadily. "You're going to need to get off world for a bit."

"Of course. Be careful, Rhys."

"You be careful."

Lying on the bed, with nothing to do but stare up at the ceiling and around at the four walls, she realized that the building had been constructed about the same time as her ship had. Same style of steel paneling, each panel meeting the next in a lip running floor to ceiling.

Rhys was right that she didn't want to face conse-quences, that she leapt immediately to something as easy as her death. Even now, when she didn't deserve what was happening to her, she imagined Rhys coming back and finding her dead. She didn't know how else she could go on, without being restored to him. What would happen to her? Would she go back to the field prison?

No. No, she couldn't die, having him believe she'd done this to him. She had to show him he was wrong. But she would have to get out of here first.

She started first at the paneling next to the sink. The plumbing had to go somewhere. She unscrewed the steel faucet from the metal bowl and used it to wear away at the seal between the panels, slamming it over and over. Once she had an inch of space, she used it as a pry bar. Not so unlike some of her methods of repair on the ship, whenever she'd gotten to something before Walt did. At last, the panel swung free, but revealed that the pipe behind spanned straight down into the floor, with no space she might crawl into. Behind the panel, another solid wall. She threw the freed panel aside angrily.

She tried the door next. It had an energy seal, she guessed, which meant there had to be a panel somewhere near it to access the conductor. She made a guess based on the layout of her own ship and went to work with her improvised pry tool.

She'd guessed right, and now made a mad job of all the wiring, trying to rip away at it. Several times, the flow through the wires burnt her, but her arms were a mess before she had the passing thought that this tactic might be dangerous. She stopped; she couldn't tear the wires by hand, or even with the metal handle; likely, their material was superior to what her own ship used. She cursed, and even cried, and finally felt the pain of her arms, which were already blistering. She sat back against the bed, furious. After a while, she leaned her head on a pillow and dozed.

Rhys let himself in at some point; she opened her eyes to find him looming over her. Her heart raced and she started to smile. Then she remembered it all. His expression was angry, anxious, his scowl almost haggard looking. "What have you been doing?" he growled.

She ignored him coldly. He knelt and took up her wrists in his hands, and she could not stop herself from yelping as he did. He scrutinized the room, shaking his head slowly.

"This is unacceptable," he said. She laughed and did not know why. Was he hungover? He certainly looked it. He left again, and she cried softly, the tears flowing down her cheeks, her face relaxed. She stared up at the ceiling. The panels up there had seals too and might have a crawl-space. But how would she get up to them?

Rhys returned about half an hour later. "Sit up," he said.

She knelt beside him, keeping her face averted. Why couldn't she at least have her clothes? She glanced over when she heard him spray something, which misted cool on her arms, and then the burns went numb. But as he bandaged her, she could not bear to see his hands, and so she looked away again. When he'd finished, he said, "Stand up."

She did, and he slipped something over her arms and wrists, which looked like long leather gloves but without fingers. Gloves, which reached her elbows and had straps and buckles. He had already started buckling them when she understood he was binding her. "No," she whispered.

"You aren't going to hurt yourself anymore," he said stoically. Then he spun her around by the shoulders and moved her toward the bed. "Bend down, over the bed."

"Why?" she piped.

He did not wait for her to obey but forced her to her knees and loomed next to her. "Don't move," he said. "You know my rules for you, and they've not changed."

"No!" she cried and craned her head back just in time to see him swing the paddle. She shouted abruptly, as it hit her ass.

"You knew what to expect," he said and landed another.

This time, she smothered her cry, though the sting hurt

worse. After the third, she growled, "I'm not yours and you can't do this anymore."

"You've been mine since you left the field prison with me," he said smoothly, then swung again, and again, until she howled.

"If not as my pet, then as my recruit," he went on in that cold, clipped tone, which she could not bear, which hurt worse than the paddle. "And you knew the terms." He paddled steadily, almost mechanically, and at last she sobbed, falling forward onto the bed, and wailed, "I don't want to be your recruit! Send me back to the field prison. Send—"

Interrupted by the harsh swing of the horrid paddle, adding more to the roaring pain on her cheeks, she buried her face into the blankets, so he wouldn't hear her cry out.

"You made your bed. Now lie in it," he said. "And don't feel sorry for yourself."

She screamed then, more in rage than anything else. Rage, and a burning in her chest, her heart breaking perhaps. "Parsons has the code," she sobbed. "He's won. The end."

The paddle flew; she flinched, but it clattered somewhere in the room. He'd thrown it. "You're a fool," he said quietly. "You can't bait me. You can't self-destruct. I told you, your penance is to continue on. Right here."

"Don't do this to me," she pleaded.

"You're fine. You've always known to expect punishment when you do this sort of thing. And you can continue to expect it. Nothing's changed."

"Everything has changed!" she screamed. She rolled onto her back and glared up at him. He had a stupid, angry look on his face. "Everything has changed," she repeated. Then, in a venomous whisper, "And you know, I really wish Parsons had sent me to you. Then it all would have meant something."

He stood in place, eyes dull, but his hand twitched slightly. Having said it, regret pained her, but she would not take it back. "Goodbye," he said suddenly, a bit vaguely, and then he rushed out the door.

Corey waited now in the dimly lit office, his face tense and, in the light reflected off his screen, looking to have aged about ten years. Rhys had slipped in quietly, and when Corey saw him, he jumped. "God, Rhys. You fucking scared me. I haven't slept in, well, not since—"

"Nor I," said Rhys. "And you were right."

Corey followed him with his eyes but moved not a muscle. "I've been right about a lot of things."

Rhys snorted, sitting at his desk. Corey did not spare him. He went on, "You ought to have given this all up to Io City Council long ago. Why the hell hold onto it, when it's been at risk the whole time?"

"It was in just as much danger with Io City."

"They would have cracked it first. Now Parsons already has."

"What? How—"

"I have my own people on the inside, too. Or did you think I left the whole of the game to you? This was my investment, Rhys. Canton Ex was everything. My whole future." He did not shout, but his whisper had an edge to it that cracked like a whip just the same. Rhys could only stare at him.

"Are you so surprised?" Corey asked bitterly. "He's got every mind on his payroll working on it."

"What is it?"

"From what I could tell, it's what you thought. Access to some type of particle that could allow FTL. And infinite energy to boot. He's won the arms race, for now. That's all I know for sure; my people aren't that close to the inside."

Rhys shook his head. "We'll have everything he does. I'm going to turn it in."

"Good."

"And I'm going to need you to take care of *her*, for a while. I need to step back."

"Good."

Rhys nodded and took up his holopad. Then he made his way to Io City Center. Seemed like the sort of thing to be done in person.

It went worse than he expected. They accused him of keeping secrets which belonged to humanity in general. They would shut down Canton Ex, though he was already in the process of doing so. The results of the code belonged to the Council now, and he wouldn't even be privy to learning what they found.

"Son, be glad you ain't facing a firing squad right now," said the official who met with him, "And I can guarantee you haven't heard the last from us. What you've done is nearly treason, would be seen as such by some of my colleagues."

By the time they were through, he was surprised they let him leave at all.

He headed back to Amala's, because he didn't want to go back to his apartment, didn't even want to think about why that was. Amala had gone for good, her closets left gaping and emptied. She loved this city, and now she would be exiled from it, forced to live in hiding because of him.

Because he had to keep his precious code to himself, because he'd been so stupid as to think he had Sydell fully under his thumb. He opened the kitchen cabinet and found she had left the whiskey. He set about finishing it off.

"Everything has changed." He shuddered. She was volatile. She'd pulled a gun on him. And yet, he'd given her the power, not just to hurt him, but to destroy him, and everyone around him. Parsons could become a god now, all because he had been so arrogant as to think he could take Sydell in hand and succeed. He'd not thought her capable of betraying him. He'd scoffed at the very idea.

He saw her arms in his mind, suddenly, and felt as he had when he'd taken them up in his hands and bandaged them. How could he still care? Did she even comprehend what she'd done to him? Could she? And what was he doing to her now? Deep down, he knew it would break her, to go on as they were. He would have to step back. Perhaps she deserved to be broken, but he would not do it. He was not his brother.

The whiskey didn't help now; it only made things worse. Thoughts raced through his head without his control. He crashed down on Amala's silly circular bed and tried willing himself to sleep. Or, at the very least, to pass out.

Chapter 22

The next time the door opened, she did not look, but she knew that it would not be Rhys. Some part of her did not expect that she would ever see Rhys again. She thought it would be Corey, and she kept her head to the opposite wall.

"Sy?" She snapped her head up, to hear Walt.

"Sy," he cried and turned away with a blush. Oh, yeah. She didn't have any clothes on. With the stupid gloves strapped to her hands, she couldn't really cover herself with a blanket, either.

"How did you find me?" she asked, while he kept his eyes locked on the ground.

"I got an anonymous message that you were being held here. Sy, what the hell happened?"

An anonymous message? Who would have done that? Who even knew she was here, besides Rhys and Corey? "Rhys thinks I betrayed him," she said. "He thinks I leaked data of his to Parsons, and it looks like I did because someone hacked my holopad. I have to get out of here. I have to find out what happened."

"All right. I can get you out. But where should I take you?"

"I need a taxi and some clothes. I've been thinking about it, and I think Parsons did have a plant, like Rhys thinks. I think I might know who it was."

"Sydell, we need to just forget it right now. We need to get you off Europa." He went to work on the straps at her arms, all the while keeping his head turned away from her.

"No. I'm going to show him I had nothing to do with it. Besides, I don't want you involved. How did you even get in here, anyway?"

He smiled and held up a little black sphere. "It's cutting edge stuff. Sends out a pulse and overrides the energy signature on the door."

"Would it work on other doors in the city?"

"If they're energetically sealed, yes."

Did Amala's flat have that type of seal? She couldn't remember. Probably.

"Where are you planning to go? I'm not letting you do it alone." He crossed his arms, almost reminding her of Rhys when he said it. She knew well that to argue would be pointless. She'd have to figure out a way to ditch him.

"I'm going to investigate the person I think helped leak this," she said and then gave him the lie, "Alan Corey."

Walter nodded. "All right, then are we going to his apartment?"

"Yep," she said. She took the little black sphere from Walt and opened the bathroom door. Her dress lay on the floor, now as wrinkled as a rag. So much for the superiority of vintage silk. The heeled shoes, she left; she'd travel faster barefoot. Hell, why did they have to have been going out to a nice dinner before all this happened?

She crossed the room to the door, buttoning up her dress as she did.

"You don't have shoes," said Walt. She glanced down at her feet and had an idea.

"Shit, I left them."

"You can't go without shoes," he said and headed right for the bathroom. He could not have cooperated more perfectly. She rushed out and shut the door behind herself, and as she'd expected, it locked automatically behind her.

"I'm so sorry, Walt," she called, but she didn't think he could hear her, because she heard nothing in response. The storage room had been soundproofed.

She didn't dare use a taxi, so she rushed through the streets with a paranoid haste, taking the streamways wherever she could. There would be cameras all over the city, and even if the police weren't looking for her, Rhys would be, as soon as he knew she'd escaped, and he could probably hack the city cameras.

Once she reached the Promenade, she regretted leaving her shoes behind. She moved faster, yes, but the people out on their fashion strolls stared at her in horror. Likely, they would have anyway; she was a wreck. She ignored the stares; she needed to focus. Someone had hacked her, but that someone also knew when she had been alone, knew she had access to all of Rhys' scans of the code. It could only have been Corey or Amala.

She didn't think it was Corey. He seemed too genuinely angry over what had happened. Her instinct fixed on Amala. Her constant communication with Rhys, her extreme curiosity about herself. It all fit together when she connected her to Parsons.

She hitched the elevator up to Amala's floor. Her heart pounded as the lift accelerated. What if Amala was home? She probably wouldn't be, but Rhys said Canton Ex was through, so she might not be at the offices. But she had to try.

She walked quietly through the hall to her door and stood for a moment just outside it, listening closely. Dead silence. She waved the module over the panel next to the door and it clicked. Her heart leaped and she opened the door slowly.

Rhys… The whole room smelled of Rhys. She scrunched back in the doorway, scanning the room. Empty. But he had been here, and not long ago. The smell of alcohol pervaded as well, and she remembered that she'd thought he had been hungover when she'd seen him last. So he had been drinking here, with Amala. The room blurred as her eyes filled with hot tears, and her throat hurt. Of course, he'd gone right to Amala for comfort.

She took in a breath. It did not matter. All that mattered was that she found a way to prove to Rhys that she had not betrayed him. Throw it in his face even. And then what? What would she do after that? Would he let her go? She had no idea.

She started first with Amala's holoscreen, which had been left on. She'd expected to find all sorts of security, but instead, the whole thing had been wiped to factory settings. The desk terminal beneath it had been emptied. She dashed around the apartment. Closets, emptied. The cupboard above the bathroom sink, empty too. A lone champagne glass sat on the kitchen counter, mocking her.

She'd fled. She had fled, which meant she had guessed right, and Amala had been working for Parsons. Would this clear her? Would it be enough for Rhys to believe her about the hack?

The sound of the hail made her jump. She snapped her head to the little desk terminal at the wall. Someone was calling. She crept up to the console on the desk. "Unknown caller" flashed across the screen. Probably not Rhys, then.

What if it was one of Parsons' people? She ducked down, under the desk, so the camera wouldn't detect her. Then she reached up and swiped the receiver on the screen.

"Sydell?" An anxious voice, a woman's voice, one she did not know. How did they know it was her? Were there other cameras in the room? Fuck, probably.

"*Sydell Rivas?* This is Callie. Please talk to me. You're in danger!"

Callie? Rhys' sister? Why would she be calling? And how would she know it was Sydell here, in Amala's apartment? She sat up, too curious to hide any longer. "How did you know I was here?"

"I'm the one who sent Walt the message! I saw you on the warehouse camera and followed the feed to the Promenade. I guessed you were headed to my dad's place. Amala's place."

On the screen, Callie's girlish face shone angelic, illuminated in green; she was calling from somewhere dark, somewhere Sydell could have no clue of. The pupils of her eyes lit up like a cat's under headlights.

"How did you know Rhys was holding me? Wait, where are you? Aren't you on Earth?"

"I arrived on Europa two days ago. I've just seen Rhys. I can't understand why he doesn't believe you. This was obviously Amala."

"Obviously?" Her heart soared to be right, but had it been so clear?

"Yes. She worked for Parsons, on Mars. Back when Rhys did. They left him together, but I never believed she just switched loyalties like that."

"I came here to search her things but… but it's all gone."

"Gone? Then she's escaped. Rhys will believe me now.

Father was always unsure about Amala, too. But Rhys wouldn't listen."

Mr. Canton, suspicious about Amala? But wasn't she his mistress? Hadn't he left her this flat?

"When Father died, I always thought something wasn't right," said Callie. "I've been trying to tell Rhys that it can't have been you. Then I saw on his screen where you were being held. So, I messaged Walt, to try to help you. We need to get you off Europa until we can find Amala."

"What? Why?"

"Because she's still going to try to pin this on you. No one else knows she's gone. If something happens to you, you'll still look guilty. We have to get you out of the city, somewhere safe."

"How?"

"I have a way. You'll need to make it to the docking bay. Get out of Amala's place quickly. It's not safe there at all. Even if she's gone, I'm sure she has people in the city working for her."

"Jesus. All right. I'll be there as soon as I can." She ended the call. Holy shit. Callie, of all people, had stuck up for her, if only because of her own suspicions. And Rhys still wouldn't listen. Was he that blind when it came to Amala?

Her stomach hurt, a deep ache just under her ribs. Something felt wrong. She wanted to stay here, maybe Rhys would come back... she just wanted to see Rhys. That was stupid, of course. Rhys hated her. He wouldn't listen; he would put her back in storage. She had to get out of the city, off Europa, like Callie said. Maybe then she could prove him wrong.

"Look," said Walt, now seated in the dark, emptied offices of the Canton Excavations building, "I heard she was being kept in inhumane conditions. She's my friend. What would you have done?"

"Inhumane conditions," Rhys scoffed. "And having been locked in those conditions yourself, by your friend, is that your conclusion as well?"

"She had no clothes. Her arms were bound. What was your end game?"

"It was a temporary set up," said Rhys. He could barely stand to look at Walt. Sydell was out on her own now, and who knew what she would do, what could happen to her, all because he had interfered.

"She passed weapons grade tech to Parsons. You know of Parsons, I'm sure," Rhys said, mockingly sweet. "Some people call him the Devil. Infinite energy tech. He has that now, because of your friend."

"I didn't know any of that. Just that she was being held against her will."

Seated in the corner, Corey rubbed his eyes. "And you've no idea who sent you the message?"

"No. I didn't take the time to trace it. I just wanted to get to Sy."

"Well, my trace is almost done now. We'll know where it came from at least, if not who," said Corey.

Rhys racked his brain, again. Only he and Corey knew where she'd been. They hadn't used a single device to communicate the location, or even that she was being held. Too risky. Yet someone had known, so they had to have been followed by someone locally. Maybe it was the agent who'd compromised Sydell. Who else could it have been, even?

"I'm putting a tail on you now, too," said Rhys. It felt stupid, pointless, but he was still angry.

"Fine," Walt snapped. "Whatever. Look, what are you going to do with Sy when you find her? You ought to turn her over to the authorities. It's wrong to keep her like you were doing."

"Wrong?" Rhys said with a dry, tired laugh. "All right, Walt. What happens when I turn her over to the authorities?"

Walt shook his head, hung it, said nothing.

"She goes to a mining colony. She's a felon. Felons get life sentences out here."

"It's fucked," said Walt.

"Maybe." Rhys shrugged. "But my point is she was better off where I had her then anywhere else, at least right now."

Corey glanced up from the screen. "The trace is done." He frowned. "What the fuck? The message came in from the docks. Here, on Europa. From a ship, ship one four five seven—"

"Fifty-eight?" Walt piped.

"Yes, how did you know?"

"That's our ship. *Your* ship." Walt stared at Rhys. "Why would someone be on that ship?"

"Corey," said Rhys, "access the camera feed from the ship's interior."

Corey waved a hand across the screen and, after a moment, said, "The feed's been disabled."

"When?" Rhys snapped, "Why weren't we alerted?"

"Let's see… it looks like the ship's systems never synced up here when we arrived two months ago. I'm not sure how it was overridden."

Rhys stood. "I'm going out there."

He dashed to his desk, now empty of everything it had once stored, save for what he took from it now, his ionic charge pistol. Contraband on Europa, of course, but most weapons were.

"Anything you can find, would be great," said Corey, though his tone said he did not really care. For him, Rhys knew, the damage had already been done.

He stuffed the pistol in his jacket pocket and rushed out to the street, hailing the first speed craft he could see.

It didn't move fast enough for his liking, but then, they never did.

It was just as he'd thought all along; someone had been on board the ship, working for Parsons. Someone who'd hacked the system and tried to kill them when they'd gone outside, or made it look like they were trying to. Could it have been Sydell all along? And had she returned there, now, to hide? It did not bear believing, but it did simplify things. If it had been her, he had no compunctions about turning her over to Europa. If it had been her, then none of it had been real.

But it did not seem possible. More likely, whoever it was on the ship had been the one to turn her against him and convince her to upload what data she could get to Parsons. What had they promised her in return? Freedom, perhaps? A wipe of her record? Certainly, they could do it.

A hail came over the holopad. He swiped it; it was Corey.

"Rhys. I've been looking through the vid logs on the docks. I've got... I've got a picture of your sister in one of them. From three weeks ago."

"Callie?" His brain reeled. Callie? What the fuck?

"Yeah, it's on one of the newer cameras. My guess is she was trying to avoid all the others but didn't know about this one. Got partial feed of her coming and going from the ship."

He swallowed. "Thanks, Corey."

Callie, on the ship. Which meant she would have left Earth with them, would have somehow stowed away. But why?

His mind ceased grasping about for an explanation. He was just starting to fathom what was going on.

———

"Sydell!" Callie called softly, waving her over from where she stood at the ship's egress. She did not move from there but waited for Sydell to approach.

"I can't stay here," Sydell hissed. "He'll search the ship for me, I'm sure of it."

"We aren't going to stay here," Callie soothed. "Come on, we're going to launch."

"What? They'll report the ship as stolen! We'll be tailed before it hits escape velocity."

"Not if we have the launch codes. You have them, right? And I've got a jammer, so we can fly out of here invisible."

A jammer? How had she… well, yes, she *was* rich. She could get anything she liked. Sydell followed her onto the ship. Callie wore a white jumpsuit and had her hair pulled back behind her head; she looked absurdly young, like a teenager even. She moved quickly down the hall to the cockpit and Sydell trailed after her.

"It's funny," Callie said when they'd reached it, "You're still saved on here as a pilot. With the launch codes, we should have no trouble at all. You remember them?"

"Uh, yeah, think so. But I don't know how to pilot it." Walt had let her do it sometimes, but she'd never done a launch.

"I think we can auto-nav to one of the asteroids," said Callie.

Sydell sat in the pilot's chair. Why had she never forced herself to learn it? Rhys was right, of course; she was undisciplined, got tired of things when they grew difficult. She sighed. She opened the Nav screen on the control panel and touched on her signature. The screen flickered, and she imputed the codes. She'd seen Walt do it too many times to forget. The interface came to life, all electric greens and oranges, flashes of words and images she couldn't comprehend. The familiar hum of the engine both thrilled and soothed her. She smiled. "All right, I'm gonna try to set the auto-nav," she said.

"That won't be necessary," said Callie, suddenly sounding much more grown up. "I have my own pilot. Thanks for getting it started, though."

"What?" Sydell spun the chair around. She and Callie were no longer alone in the crowded cockpit; a man had moved into the doorway, and Callie shifted to the side. Sydell gasped. She knew him; she was sure of it. Yes, it was the same man who'd followed her home from the hospital!

She shouted a senseless sound and stood as he rushed her. She tried to move to the side as the blow came, but there was no space to do so. His fist connected with her ear, and she fell with a dizzied thud against the control panel. He grabbed her shoulder and wrenched her toward him, then caught her by the hair. She screamed.

"Time to go down with the ship," said Callie softly.

Sydell stared up at her in horror.

"Guess they'll wonder if you were trying to escape, or just trying to die," she went on, swiping the interface screen. "I doubt either is too out of character for you."

Sydell struggled, trying to tear herself from his grasp, letting strands of her hair rip from her head as she did. Then she shrieked as he slammed her whole body into the bulkhead. She sobbed now, in pain and terror. Callie stood and took something up from the side panel. Sydell couldn't see what it was, but she knew it painfully when the needle jabbed into her thigh.

"Goodnight," said Callie sweetly, and the pain and terror were pulled from her against her will. She would have kept them, had she the choice; she needed them now to try to fight, to save herself, but instead, everything was lost to blackness.

Chapter 23

When Rhys reached the docks, he found his ship was gone.

He ran over to the little docking agency in the hub at the center of the walkways. Thankfully, it had been manned rather than automated. A young man with a pointed beard sat inside, reading on his holoscreen.

"I need to rent a ship," Rhys said. "Immediately. And I need to see your launch records."

"I just let out the last rental I've got," said the man irritably, only just peeking up from the screen. "And I can't give out any launch records if you aren't with the city."

Let out the last ship? "Where is it? Has it left yet?"

"None of your—" the man started.

Rhys tossed out some credit notes, and the man rolled his eyes and said, "It's still in the dock right now. Bay twenty-seven. It's the little schooner."

He raced to Bay 27.

Callie stood in the doorway of the small craft, her back to him, but he'd know her form anywhere. So slight, youthful. It was still unbelievable to him that she could have done anything like this. Or that she would have done it to him. Callie had rented this ship and was boarding, but where had his own gone, and who had taken it?

"Callie!" he shouted, and she turned. On seeing him, her face darkened to fury. For a moment, he did not recognize it. In that moment, he knew it was true, couldn't doubt her betrayal.

"It's too late!" she screamed. "She's dead in the air, Rhys! Forget about her."

"She's on the other ship?"

"It's launched to crash. Fuck, why are you even here?"

"Why are you doing this, Callie?"

"Because he's the only one of you who ever loved me, that's why," she shrilled in a tone he had never known possible to her. "Because I love him, more than Heaven and Earth, and I'd do any goddamn thing for him. Is that too much for your basic porridge brain to comprehend?"

Jesus Christ. What had Parsons done?

"I wanted to spare you, Rhys. You'll blame yourself; you'll think he brainwashed me. What's love but brainwashing, anyway? I wanted you to think it was that crazy bitch. It makes the most sense. But you had to come down here. So." She shrugged, throwing her arms up, her hands bouncing carelessly off her hips at the end of the gesture. "Sorry to disappoint you. She's dead and Parsons loves me, and I'm going home to him."

Rhys couldn't move or speak. Callie whisked into the ship and the door shut behind her. Only then, did he break into action. He rushed back to the docking agency. "Stop launch of Bay 27!" he roared.

The agent stared at him stupidly. "I can't do that, sir."

"Can you not now?" Rhys pulled out his pistol. God, this was going to put him in some real shit.

"Fuck." The man automatically put up his hands, his

screen clattering to the desk. "No, I really can't. It's already launched."

"Then get me a ship. Now. And you're going to fly it."

The man stood, shaking his head in something like disbelief.

Dead in the air, she'd said. So, she'd launched Sydell in the other ship, wanted to make it look like a failed escape, probably. There could be time to get to it before it crashed. Or to get her off the ship once it had. He'd lost Callie. Long ago, perhaps. But he wasn't going to lose Sydell.

She woke to the sickening heave of the very ground beneath her.

Lights flickered. She lay groggy on the floor in the barracks, the skin of her arms imprinted in red with the steel grid of the floor and her body aching brutally. Her muscles screamed in pain as she tried to rise. The ship lurched again, and she fell into it as it flew up to meet her, bashing her on the chin. What the hell had happened?

"Time to go down with the ship." She sucked in her breath, remembering. She must have crashed. Callie must have set the Nav to make her crash somewhere on the surface. As she'd said, it would look like a failed escape attempt, or suicide. And that's what Rhys would believe it had been.

She pushed herself up again, clenching her teeth against the pain. As she moved her left arm, she screamed, froze in place. Fuck! It had to be broken. She couldn't move it and it scared her to even look. What if the bone was sticking out through the skin? She stood up but fell again, sliding toward the door as the ship heaved. Why hadn't it settled yet? The whole of it tilted, as though it had landed at an angle.

She scooted along the floor, using her good arm to balance. How could she get herself out of this? Crashed, somewhere out on Europa, but where, exactly? Could be miles from the city, and who knew how long she'd been out? Unless Callie had been lying about having a jammer, no one would be able to trace the ship. Even so, if the life support was intact, it would be better to stay on the ship and wait. But wait for what? Who would come looking?

She scooted up the hall to the first terminal she found. Still running, thank God. A mass of green text barraged the screen. She propped herself against the wall. The ship swayed, again. Could it have landed on rocks? A cliff perhaps? She swallowed. Maybe staying on the ship wasn't the best call.

She opened up the tabs for the exterior cameras on the screen. A senseless picture flashed up, dark blue and blurred, like the lens was dirty. Then the camera feed switched to the hull. From there, she could see that the ship had indeed landed along its side, on a sheet of icy white. Then another camera view, pitch black. Buried? Or a dead feed? And then another feed of the dark blue, through a different camera from the first.

Her stomach tightened. Water. The blur of the camera being underwater. And the white, the flat white… shit, the ship had landed on ice, and part of it was underwater, enough to make it sway. Sway, as it sunk? Most of the surface of Europa was ice, so of course, that was where she'd landed. But the ice sheets started miles out from the city. No way she could get back on foot.

And then a groaning sounded, deeper than the ship, seeming to have come from the bowels of hell itself. A frozen hell. The ice had groaned. She had to leave. Even if there was no way to get back. The thought of being pulled down into the freezing deep, trapped on the ship, horrified her beyond reason.

She made her way toward the airlock; the path angled downward, she was sure of it. The ship pitched forward, and she stumbled, clinging to her wounded arm to keep it still. The lights flickered. It had grown colder; her breath came out now in a cloud of white. When she reached the airlock, she took up her spacesuit gratefully. No, too small. She took Rhys' instead. That way, she could fit her useless arm in next to her chest, rather than putting it through the sleeve.

The suit smelled of Rhys, and she sobbed softly as she secured the helmet. Suit or no, she would probably die out there. She'd never see him again. And he would probably be glad to never have to see her. But how could she die with him still believing she'd ruined everything that mattered to him? She could not. She had to get herself out of this. Somehow.

She slammed her fist on the button to open the hatch. The door clunked. Nothing else. Jammed. Well, she would try another door then. The main egress, at the other end of the ship. She cranked the heat in the suit all the way up and started back.

The floor angled up, against her now. Had the angle increased, even? Climbing up taxed her; she grew hot, and by the time she made it to the egress, she'd turned the heat down in the suit. She pounded at the button. The door groaned open and snowy air blasted in all around her, almost blinding her. Here it was, then. The exit. Leaving the ship was probably a death sentence, too, but at least she wouldn't be trapped, helpless.

She threw her legs over the side of the ship and slid down. She landed on the ice with a thump and flinched, fearing it would crack beneath her. Behind her, another loud groan. She whirled around to see the ship. It stuck up out of the ice at an angle, a near quarter of it already buried. Jesus! Would it sink? She could hardly tell. Maybe it would stay as it was. But she wasn't about to risk staying onboard.

She ran a distance from the ship and peered out at the flurried horizons, trying to find some way to orient herself. Too far to see the light of the city, probably. She thought, though, that she saw a soft violet, ebbing at the distance behind some of the clouds. Could be it.

As good a direction to try as any.

The docking agent, now compelled pilot, scowled as he shot out another scan, under Rhys' orders. "Nothing," he growled. "Again. I told you, it probably left the surface."

In the cockpit beside him, Rhys shifted, peered out the visiglass. So much fog and snow, like wool, all around the windows.

"You're gonna go to jail," the docking agent muttered.

Rhys glared at him, sidelong. He still held the gun, though he had it lowered, resting on his thigh.

"Keep scanning," he directed. "Search the ground. It's likely a crash site."

"Why would it have crashed?"

"Just do what I say."

After a moment, a mass of something flashed on the screen for a split second, and the scan pulsed. "What's that?" Rhys asked sharply.

"Looks like rocks," the man said.

"Fly out toward it."

"In this fog? What if it's a butte?"

"Be careful and don't hit it."

"Fucking hell."

They had to fly right over it, to see it. It angled up from the broken ice sheet, looking from this height like a discarded toy.

"I'm not landing here," the agent said firmly. "The ice is compromised. That ship's going under any minute, and we'd go with it."

"Then put me low enough that I can jump out. Now."

The man scoffed but complied, circling back around. As he did, a massive cracking sounded from below. The ship beneath them shivered, then, to Rhys' horror, it slid, slowly, into the ice, like a rat being swallowed in the jaws of a snake.

"Jesus," said the man beside him.

Rhys shouted something insensible. His ears roared, filled with some rushing blast that made his head go light. The man said something beside him, but he could not hear it. The man tugged at his arm, yelling. All Rhys could see was the black maw in the ice that had just swallowed her whole.

The man punched him on the shoulder. Rhys stared at him, his jaw so tight, he felt it might break. The man pointed emphatically at the ice next to where the ship had been. "Tracks. Tracks!" he was shouting, now furious with impatience. "You hear me, idiot? There are tracks down there; someone got off the ship."

Sure enough, a thin line of footprints, just a shade darker than the snow, trailed westward from the ship toward the city.

She discovered within the first ten minutes of her walk that the suit had not been charged.

She turned the heat down as low as possible, just above what would trigger the alarm. The hyper-compressed atmosphere wasn't affected by the charge, so she wouldn't suffocate. No, she would just freeze to death. She thought about turning around, getting back on the ship. But the lavender light ahead seemed brighter, somehow. She might be able to make it.

As she trudged on, she wished she'd thought to have left a message back on the ship, however. Something so that, once it was found, Rhys would know about what had happened to her, that it had been Callie who had done it. Of course, he probably wouldn't have believed it. It still seemed unbelievable to her, even now. She'd been stupid to trust Callie, but how could she have suspected? Why would Callie want to do that to her own brother?

Family issues. Something she'd said to Walt, back what felt like a hundred years ago. They weren't like regular people; they were like gods from the Greek myths. What human could understand their motivations?

She hit the hail proximity button over and over, with the hope that maybe some rover out beyond the city would respond. The snowdrifts grew thicker, and she could no longer see her guiding light. The swirling white made her feel that the world had rotated; was she even heading in the same direction she'd started out? She could not be sure. The compass in the helmet had shut off, due to the power save settings.

The pain throbbing madly in her arm had spread through her like a drug, confusing her senses but without relief. Heat flooded her, and she reached for the zipper of her suit. She stopped herself just in time. She glanced at her wrist meter. In low power mode, it warned her it could not compensate for the subzero temperature outside. It directed her to go indoors and charge the suit, at once. She laughed weakly. She stopped for a moment. Everything swirled about her wildly; even standing still disoriented her. Her nose had gone stiff with cold, and her fingers were numb. She heard herself, as though from a distance, crying.

She knelt. In the snow, her feet had gone numb and could not seem to move.

No. She had to get back, had to get to Rhys and tell him about Callie. Had to have him know she had never betrayed him. And then they would go home. But would they? Could they, still?

She stayed where she knelt. She didn't think they could go home anymore. Callie had escaped. Proving her innocence felt distant, suddenly, meaningless. It would only make him unhappy for how he'd treated her. Better if he never knew. The part of her that wanted to throw his wrongness in his face and be vindicated had gone. It no longer mattered. They couldn't piece things back together now anyway. She would have to go back to prison. She was still a felon, after all. So, she stayed there, kneeling in the snow.

As she began to feel warm and sleepy and her arm ceased to hurt, she rose to her feet. She trudged forward without knowing why. What would happen to her? Her life had been an adventure tied madly to a ship, and then an adventure tied less madly—or was it more—to Rhys. What would life on the ground be like? Could she even bear it?

She fell again to her knees. The snowy ground felt soft and cozy. The lights behind her came later and could have been the last lights, the lights of Heaven. Tunnels of light. She laughed at such silliness.

Then something pulled her up to her feet, a warm, strong force that could only belong to reality, to a very physical reality. To the Earth. Earth, of course, was millions of miles away. But the Earth was also right here, its arms tight around her. It lifted her up off the ground. She thought to say that her arm was broken, but the way they cradled her, this seemed to have already been known. Then she had been borne up into a transport ship, where she remained seated on top of her rescuer. When he removed his helmet and she saw it was Rhys, she was not surprised. Somehow, she had already known it.

Rhys kept her held close on his lap. She tried to get her hand up to her helmet, so that she could speak to him.

"Get us to the city center, now," he said to somebody. He peered down at her struggle and helped her to take the helmet off.

"My arm's broken," she croaked.

"Here I thought you just forgot how to put on a suit," he said. The teasing sarcasm shocked her, and she searched his face. At odds with such a remark, he looked more somber than she had ever seen him. Except at that last moment, when he had told her goodbye. New lines cracked the sides of his rusty-stubbled cheeks and over his low-drawn brows. This was Rhys? He did not look like any god of myth. He looked worried, even old, and a trifle lost.

He held her, without touching her arm, yet held her with an implacability she knew she could not break away from. She did not want to; for the moment, it felt good to be held just like this, by this strange new Rhys she'd never really seen before.

"Rhys," she said as she suddenly remembered, "Callie was here. She was on your ship the whole time. She—" Here, she broke off, not sure how to tell him what Callie had done.

"I know it, baby."

She swooned inside when he said it. He must know everything, then. She leaned her head into him. There was nothing else to say. The little ship was so warm, she could just doze right off if she didn't try to stay awake. "Did you catch her?" she murmured. What would Rhys do, with Callie having betrayed him?

"No. It doesn't matter," he said. He held her tighter. But he did not look down at her. He stared straight ahead.

"Rhys?" she asked tentatively. "Can we go home?"

He flinched. His mouth contracted oddly. In pain? And then it vanished, and his face grew expressionless. He leant his head down, pressing his forehead into hers. His cheek rubbed scratchily against her, and she found his mouth with her own. He returned the kiss with an intensity that startled her, made her dizzy. She whimpered and felt the warmth flooding back into her body as she started to tremble.

"God, get a room," the pilot beside them muttered disgustedly.

When Rhys pulled away, and she looked up into his eyes, she knew that they would not be going home. "Everything's gonna be all right now," he said. "I promise."

She stayed as she was for the rest of the flight, pressing her face into his chest, and cried as quietly as possible. Something had gone wrong and could not be fixed, just as she'd feared. She wanted time itself to break so that this flight back could be all of it, everything, just a moment stretched out into eternity. She'd thought Rhys had been a god, thought that he could do anything. He'd been the dark star that had pulled her in and crushed her, warping everything she'd thought was real. But now he was just a man, tired and sad. He couldn't break time, and he couldn't take her home.

The ship landed. They took an emergency shuttle to the city center, and from there, Rhys carried her to the hospital. They sat in the waiting room, and he kept her on his lap the whole time. At one point, he said, "I couldn't let you go. I wouldn't, no matter what you'd done."

"I know," she said. Her voice sounded apathetic, which was not how she felt.

He lowered his head over her. "I'm so sorry."

She did not know what to say. The city police arrived a few minutes later. Rhys set her on a chair, softly murmuring assurances as he did. He looked her in the eyes, and his eyes were sad, weary, and bloodshot.

"Rhys," she whispered, panicked. Peace officers had gathered around.

"Everything's going to be fine," he assured her. They handcuffed him. He was led away.

A nurse sat next to her, pulling at her. "Miss Rivas? The doctor needs to see you now."

Rhys had been arrested, and she was alone.

Chapter 24

She'd cracked three ribs on her left side, and her arm had a clean break, though thankfully the bone had not punctured the skin as she'd feared. She spent several days at the hospital, recovering. During that time, she learned, from Corey no less, that Rhys had taken the ship he'd rescued her in at gunpoint, using the pilot as a hostage. He faced some heavy charges and was still in hot water with the government for concealing what he'd found in the caverns.

"I don't think they'll let him out for a while," said Corey. He acted vaguely guilty toward her, probably for all that had happened. Canton Ex had been dissolved, all its assets taken. Rhys had nothing to hide behind, it seemed. He'd made himself vulnerable and the city council had stripped him.

So much for any help from Corey. What about Amala? Could she do anything? It seemed she'd been faithful all along; she'd fled, because she'd been a double agent and Parsons would probably kill her if he found her. But where had she gone off to?

When the hospital released her, she found a car waiting for her outside. The back door hissed open and a stretch of sky-blue fabric was visible on the seat. "I'm sorry, I can't get out," came Amala's composed tone from within. "I can't be spotted here. Please get in."

Sydell slid into the back next to her. "I thought you were in hiding."

She looked as epic as ever, wrapped in a thick gown which bundled about her throat in a dramatic cowl neck collar. "I am. I'm here for you. I have this for you, from Rhys." She handed her an envelope. "Canton Ex may have been liquidated, but there's still a small outpost on one of the asteroids. That's where I've been. Its Rhys' outpost, but it's not tied to Canton Ex. They didn't even know to look for it."

Of course. Why would Rhys ever put all his eggs in one basket? She held the envelope without looking at it, fearing what it would contain.

Amala went on, "It's a mining operation, fully machine run. A few employees keep the offices. Which is what I do now. So much fun. But I've been sent to bring you back with me."

"With you? Won't I be going back into the system now that Canton Ex is gone?" Surely, she'd have been listed on the Canton Ex assets. She'd been waiting for an agent to come for her.

"Mm, I think that's still on the table. Rhys is trying to reach a deal with them, and you're a piece of that, I'm told."

"A deal?"

"He's cooperating with the Council, helping them with the code. And so, they are more willing to help him with a few things. He's negotiating for your charges to be dropped. Seeing as he was the one you stole from, I think they're inclined to be reasonable."

"But I'm not free?"

"Not yet. But you can wait it out with me. It might be hard for you to find work here, because you'll flag as being recruited already, at least until you get free. Once you are, well, you can do as you will."

Sydell stared at her. She couldn't help but feel as if she were being kidnapped, but considering the whole situation, she knew it was more like Amala offering her a hand. And Rhys, through Amala. "All right," she said. They stopped briefly at a storage bay to get some of her things; Rhys' apartment had been totally cleaned out and searched. And she was glad of it, because she did not want to go there.

They took the speeder from storage to the docks. She caught a glimpse of the docking agent Rhys had kidnapped; he sneered at her. She scowled back; she didn't know why, what had happened was hardly his fault.

They boarded a shuttlecraft and flew out to the asteroid core. When Amala had called the outpost small, she'd not been lying. It was no more than a few domes sidled next to an arch of rocks, the building material matching the surface perfectly for camouflage. Inside, it was one huge room for device storage and records, a room for mess, and a barracks, divided by curtains hung from the ceiling.

She took a bunk in the corner for her own. Besides Amala, there were maybe three or four others, but they ignored her. She curled up on the stiff little mattress and opened the letter from Rhys.

"Miss Rivas, you have to watch these folders closely," Amala said crisply. "Look, you've filed 'zw' behind 'zi'. These need to be precise."

"Mm." She bit back a complaint and walked over to the wall of files to fix her mistake. It still horrified her how much physical paperwork had to be done here. But, as nothing was committed to wireless, nothing could be hacked. If anyone breached the building, orders were to destroy everything in the cabinets; there was a button to do so, even. She wondered how it would work. Often, she wanted to press the button.

Clearly, the outpost was for more than just mining. Something else was going on here, which Amala would not discuss, and which Sydell could no longer really care about. All she knew was that she had to file things; she couldn't type fast enough to please Amala, and there wasn't much else she could do with the cast on her arm. It had been three months since she'd had it on. A doctor had been flown in several times to do scans. Three more weeks, he'd said. It had stopped hurting at least.

Later that afternoon, Amala stopped at her desk. Sydell held her breath in annoyance, waiting for the inevitable correction. Amala never lost her temper, just explained calmly what had been wrong and why it needed to be fixed. But right now, she only set a letter down in front of her. Sydell picked it up. It was from Io City Council. How had they known to send it here?

"They didn't, of course," Amala replied when she asked. "Rhys probably had them give it to Corey, or someone, and they sent it to one of ours, who sent it here."

God, how many people did Rhys have? How did he keep paying them? From the operations here? She opened the letter, deciding it better not to think too much about it.

It was a transmute of her sentence. Her record had

been cleared. Or rather, was listed as "time served". But the felony charge had been cut, the graveness of it marked down to "minor infraction".

Amala glanced at the paper. "Ah. Well, he's really done it, hasn't he? You shouldn't have any trouble finding work, now."

"What about Rhys? Is he going to prison?" Asking it nauseated her, but she had to know.

"Prison? No. He's much too valuable to them. But he's not a free man by any means."

"You keep saying that. What do you mean?"

"The Council wants him to work for them, on whatever they're doing with the tech they got from those caves. For whatever it is they are planning to do about Parsons. Rhys is an asset against fighting their enemy. That's really what's saved his ass."

"So, they don't care that he hijacked that ship?"

Amala laughed. A pretty sound, but one Sydell had grown sick of hearing. "They never cared about that. Treason, on the other hand."

"*What!*"

"Yes. Rhys didn't want me to tell you, until we knew he wouldn't be charged with it. They wanted to, at least some of them did. He hid a discovery that they'd call monumental to humanity. Out here, a company can't do that, and a man can't, either. Not without risking his neck. But it seems there are still some practical members who think he's more useful alive."

She felt sick. All this time, they might have killed him.

"Are you ready to have lunch?" Amala asked.

She shook her head. She didn't know when she could eat again. As Amala stepped away, Sydell asked, "How long will they keep him?"

"Depends on how long they want to use him, I guess. I'd try not to think about it too much if I were you."

She was free now, but she went on working with Amala at the outpost. She didn't like it, but she wasn't sure what else to do. Return to Io City, try to get a job at a dress shop perhaps, or a cafe. Something as meaningless as what she did now. Here, she was still connected, at least by a thread, to Rhys. He knew where she was, where to find her if he wanted to.

Every day since she'd arrived, her eyes would dart to the entrance, as if he were going to walk through it. The thought of it happening got her through the most tedious of days and the loneliest of nights, curled in her bunk in the corner. She took out his letter every night and read it by flashlight. She had the feeling Amala knew, that she thought her silly, but she did not care.

Six months had passed. She hated the outpost. She considered returning to Earth. What would she do there? Her only ties were to criminals, and after what Rhys had done for her, she loathed to fall back into that world. She started scanning for available jobs on her holopad, anywhere. Most were contract recruitment, indentured servitude. Could she really go through that again? Did she have a choice?

Then she got a letter from Walter. Apparently, he'd been alerted that her record had been cleared and he'd been on the lookout for employment for her. A vacancy had just opened in a work program at the Academy; they offered to train students for basic piloting in exchange for doing jobs needed around the facility. Could be anything really, maintenance, cleaning, cafeteria help. But if they accepted her, she could become a pilot.

He'd already entered her name, it seemed. If she was interested, she had only to come in person and meet the director herself. She wanted to do it, so much so that it felt she had no chance and ought to just throw the letter away. She stopped herself from doing something so self-destructive. She went to see Amala about it at the end of the workday.

"You should go. At least try it out. From what I hear, these things don't open up much. If they're giving you an interview, Walt must have really turned their heads for you."

Sydell blushed. Would he really have done that?

"If it doesn't work out, you come back." Amala shrugged. "Nothing to lose."

"Really? I could come back?"

Her manner was cool. "As long as this outpost exists, you're welcome here."

Sydell held her breath. "Thank you."

"Don't thank *me*." Amala took up her things from her desk and headed toward the mess hall, with the poise of someone on their way to the opera.

The Academy director had a dull face and sleepy eyes, and her heart sank when she met him. But she would at least try.

Somehow, the conversation steered to her days with Walt, running transport, and then back even further to when they were kids, doing pickpocket hits for her dad. It seemed that Walt was really liked here, and the director loved to hear about him in this new light. Perhaps she oughtn't have revealed it? But the boring old guy's face lit up, and she rattled on, telling him about the time on Mars with Rhys, about coming over on the ship with a stowaway, then how that stowaway had wrecked her ship, with her inside, and she'd escaped.

God, it all seemed so unbelievable, to tell it. Would he think she was lying? But he could verify all of it. The story of the wreck had certainly been all over Io news, including the part about a ship hijacked at gunpoint. Things like that didn't happen often on Io City, at least not that anyone knew about.

At the end of it, she said, "I'm so sorry. I've just blathered on and on, you've hardly even interviewed me."

He smiled, a dry half-smile. "I think this has been sufficient."

She returned the smile to conceal her disappointment. But she was not surprised she had fucked it up.

They sent her a message that night. She got the position.

Chapter 25

The days blurred together for Rhys.

Mostly, he worked on the engine. It had been up and running within a month of the code being cracked. He'd underestimated the Council in how quick they'd been to figure it out, and how fast they'd been able to put it to use. It wasn't predictable yet; they told him it couldn't be trusted to send out a manned ship. So, they kept him working, with the others, perfecting it.

Often, they questioned him. He would be brought in from his new little apartment, which he called his cell, and interrogated, just as he had been at the start, only with new questions sometimes. The AI voice, neutral but uncanny over the speaker, the infinity light hanging low over his head. They needed more details, always more. Every little thing he knew about Parsons. His friends, the reels he watched in his free time. What shampoo he used, for Christ's sake.

The interrogations broke up an otherwise tedious life. He pushed Sydell out of his mind completely when he worked. But at night, that proved difficult. He tried to picture her, if not happy, at least content, in working with Amala at the outpost. She would be bored, probably, but at least she was safe.

Some nights, he just saw her as she had sat crumpled in the snow where he'd found her, her body broken from the crash. And he wished to tear himself apart for having let it happen to her. She might have died, might have been swallowed in that ice, or frozen out on the surface, surely would have been if they hadn't picked up her stray hail. The fault of it was entirely his, and he lay with it, awake, many nights.

He'd got her sentence scrapped at least, which had been nearly impossible to do. He'd been entirely at their mercy. At one point, he felt sure they'd kill him if he didn't cooperate. But he would not see her sent to a mining colony or back to prison. At last, they relented, if only because they didn't care much about her. They fixed up her record, but in exchange, he was theirs. Completely. And he accepted it.

After, he'd written to Walt, to tell him she was free, to ask that he try to help her find some work to do. What else could he do? He heard back that she'd been accepted into the Academy, under a work plan. It gratified him, but thinking of Sydell as a pilot… shit, she'd get herself into all sorts of trouble. But no worse than what he'd gotten her into. At any rate, he had to let go.

After six months, he was allowed a few privileges. He could go out, a few times a week, to the cafes and the shops. Under guard, of course. It seemed the Council thought such things would benefit his work. He'd never really bothered with doing things like that before; he did them now at every chance he could get. It helped keep his mind from returning to dark places.

There were many of them to return to. He'd been

furious when he'd first learned it had all been Callie, but as time wore on, he only wished he had caught her, to have kept her from returning to Parsons. Surely, they would have ruled her unfit to stand trial for what she'd done. Parsons had held her for a month, and of anyone, Rhys knew the types of mind-breaking the man was capable of. Yet he'd missed it entirely in the short time he'd spent with Callie, because he could only think of getting back to Europa and the code. He had lost his own sister, and she wasn't somewhere safe now like Sydell. No, she was in the mouth of the beast, believing that monster loved her. He tried not to think on it.

It had been close to a year of his involuntary service when he got another letter from Walter. It was an invitation to a wedding. Walter was getting married and had gotten permission to use the Academy grounds, a rare accomplishment. He wished to extend Rhys an invitation, as someone who had given him patronage. The letter was very formal and made no mention of his bride.

Rhys tensed to read it. He had no clue what to expect; he had a strange dread of an idea, however, of what might be happening. Why would Walt not mention who the bride was? The dread, however, compelled him to go. He had to put in several requests and use up two of his rest days, being tossed around the bureaucracy that was Io City Council. But since the Academy was on Europa, they granted it. He was shocked, and some part of him wished they had refused. Now he would have to attend. He would have a Council shuttle, and a guard would be sent along with him.

"Maybe you should send me in handcuffs," he remarked to the official who'd informed him. The woman had given him that dry, bored raising of eyebrows that every other official gave when he made such a comment.

Well, he'd be able to see for himself now that she was all right. Of late, he'd been thinking to volunteer for some of the first manned test runs, as soon as the unmanned shuttles started returning. So far, none of them had. It was a trip out to God knows where, and who knew if a human could survive? He wanted to see her, once, before taking such a leap.

He rented a tuxedo and felt absurd in it. His features had never been right for such attire, not refined enough. He sighed at himself in the full-length mirror. Ridiculous. She would find him ridiculous. But it did not matter. Some bureaucrats would get pissy about the extra expense on his account, so it wasn't all a waste.

On the day of the event, they flew out early. The guard, who was also the pilot, with him was in high spirits. Likely, his own position was boring, and he kept talking about all the women who would be there, how women always gave out their social profiles at weddings, even to strangers. He might even get a date, he said. Rhys tuned him out. A tightness sat in his guts that he knew would be with him until he saw her.

He hadn't seen the Academy in many years. Its architect had been in love with classic old stone, so the building rose at odds with the long stretches of wild violet rock and gleaming snow surrounding it. It had its own transparent dome, so the grounds were open. Inside it, they had grown sprawling green hedges, trimmed into walls and labyrinths all around. Very British, and weird against the bright alien sky. The cloud above was thin now, would be so for the whole of the brief "spring" season on Europa; he even felt the sun on the back of his head.

He stayed at the outskirts of the gathering, stood behind the tall column of a pruned cypress tree. He scanned the crowd, searching every face. Up near the center of it, at the foot of the Academy staircase, he caught sight of Walt. But where was *she*? He had to see her first, had to see it for himself, and every second that passed without seeing it was agony. Then he would go to them and wish them the best, and he would mean it.

Walt was a better man for her, so long as he could keep her from some of her worst impulses. He had not thought this of Walt before, even when he'd realized that Walt cared for her. Back then, he had thought, *You? She runs roughshod over you.* I'm *the one who can handle Sydell.* And then he'd run roughshod over Sydell, and here they all were. He'd been wrong, and he'd be the first to admit it and give his blessing, which they probably didn't even want.

His jaw ached from clenching it, and he would be glad when it was all over.

He spotted her the second she rushed out onto the stairs from one of the Academy doors. She wore a lemon-yellow, floor-length dress. She pulled the large door open behind herself and another woman appeared, her blonde hair coiffed high, her dress white and spreading. His vision darkened, perhaps the sun was brighter? He let out a breath as a shameful wave of relief passed over him. He closed his eyes and put a hand to his temples. Then he looked at her once again, without the terrible certainty that she was marrying someone else.

Her hair had been cut short, a little longer than her jaw in length and she'd had bangs cut just above her eyebrows, an unusual but sweet contrast with the long, elegant dress. For her, the haircut was perfect. Her eyes stood out against the fringe, as large and expressive as a cat's. His heart stabbed in his ribs, and he wished he had not come but was also so glad he had.

The ceremony flew by; he paid it no attention but watched Sydell from where he stood at the tree. The crowd was large enough that he did not think he was noticed. Sydell stood up with Walt; Walt was giddy with happiness and kept mixing up the words of his vows. His bride smiled warmly, watching him. He dropped the ring, and Sydell bent down to scoop it up, artlessly, and Rhys grinned. He couldn't help it.

Then the service was over, and everyone applauded and headed to the garden for cake and champagne. Rhys stayed behind. The guard said, "Hey, we're at least having a drink, after sitting through that." No, he wouldn't be able to just exit. He needed to see her anyway, at least once more. He made his way toward the garden but could not catch sight of her again.

"Rhys?" Walt came over beside him, then held out his hand. Rhys shook it.

"Congratulations, Walt," he said a little stiffly. Everything felt so open here, after being in Io City rooms for so long. And he hadn't been around this many people in… well, the air certainly felt thinner, the atmosphere hotter. Sweat broke out on his brow.

"Thank you," said Walt. "She's a sales rep for Nav computers. Came here with a recruiting agent. She's off talking to someone right now or I'd introduce you."

Rhys nodded, smiled, tried to say something appropriate.

"I'm graduating next year," Walt went on. "Should I let them recruit me, or pilot for Europa Council? I hear you know more about that life than I do."

Rhys actually felt himself blush at this. But Walt was not taunting him; the words were sincere. He earnestly wanted advice.

"I think you'd be happier with Europa. There's going to be…" he glanced around, to be sure his guard wasn't in earshot, "there are going to be a lot of interesting changes in how we fly, over the next few years. A lot of new ships. And the Council will have them first." Well, he hoped so anyway.

"New tech, eh? Sounds great. Thanks, Rhys. And thanks for coming out."

"Yes. You're welcome. Thank you for having me." He grew warm, with a sudden awkwardness, and hated it.

"I think I saw Sy off near the fountain," Walt said, gesturing vaguely. "She said she thought she spotted you behind a tree and went looking for you."

Walt patted him heartily on the shoulder and turned back to an older woman, who was trying to get his attention. Rhys trailed in the direction Walt had pointed, holding his breath. The stone fountain rose in the distance, the figure of the god Mercury a mere shadow as the sun hung in the sky behind it, almost blinding him. He could see no one out there.

Then, as he drew closer, she jumped up onto the ledge of it, next to the stream of water. He caught a glimpse of combat boots under her dress. When he reached the hedge about twenty feet away, she spotted him and froze. The edges of her mouth contracted. She held her billowy yellow skirt tightly in her clenched hands, as though it could anchor her.

"*Rhys*," he heard her say, though it could only have been a whisper. There had been a sick, protracted space in which he could not feel his heart beating, as if it had stopped. She smiled, her cheeks dimpling. He exhaled, and his heart seemed to start again, slamming in his chest.

Not sure how to get around the hedge to her, he simply moved through it, clambering foolishly over the tight weave of branches as they caught at his trousers. He stumbled out about an arm's length from where she stood on the fountain wall, not three feet up. He swallowed and found his voice. "So," he said, "I hear you're going to become a pilot." It came out gruff, strange, and so he smiled at the end of it, trying to be friendly and casual. Was that possible? Or was it just worse?

"I'm trying to," she said. "I don't get lessons very often. I'm bad with the mechanical stuff. But my instructor says I might pull through." She laughed when she said it. A thoughtless smile sprang to his face when he heard her laugh.

Then he said, "I'm sorry if I… just seemed to drop you, after the letter. I thought it best that you have some space from me."

"That's what I guessed," she said. She cleared her throat. "I read your letter every day, for a while. I kept thinking you'd show up at the outpost." She laughed, shaking her head. "Well, not really. But that's how I made it through all of the days."

She paced a little along the wall, nearly treading on her skirt. She was going to trip on it, doing that. He readied himself to catch her if she did. "I'm sorry," he said plainly. "I'm not free to move about as I please."

"I know. I was only telling you. Anyway, I got tired of that, of being at the outpost, so I came here. But I still read the letter, sometimes." She turned pink. The last of her emerald streak had been chopped into green flecks around her cheek. She looked down at him, the brown of her eyes luminous.

"I thought I had destroyed you," he said, without any intention of saying it. Now that he had, it sounded absurd.

She chuckled softly. Her pale yellow dress was as light as her laugh, as light as the sun. Not this sun, but the sun as he remembered it back on Earth as a kid. A boundless and unfettered brilliance in an endless blue. "You're arrogant, Rhys," she said a little smugly. She seemed profoundly young for a moment. Maybe it was her haircut. "But I knew you'd come back to me," she concluded.

The blood rushed to his ears, deafening him. He waited a moment and then said in a rush, "I'm not free. I belong to the Council now; they *literally* own me." He cleared his throat. "I guess you'd think it's fitting, probably." That last, with a bitterness he could not help.

She shook her head. "No. It's just the way it has to be, for now. I wish it wasn't. I still want to go home."

He bent his head, for a moment unable to look at her. Nor did he trust his voice. Then he said, "I don't know when I'll even have a home."

"I have nothing to do but wait. I don't think they're in a rush to make me a pilot. That is, if you still want…" She trailed off, stringing her fingers together in a nervous motion.

He'd come here with the intention of seeing her for the last time, of seeing her wed even. Of saying goodbye. But now, having seen her and spoken to her? Well, having just seen her, he'd known. How could he have made himself believe that he could be happy seeing her with Walt? He would have tried, had she been content. But he could not lie to himself as to what he wanted now. Wanted more than anything he ever had. The choice, of course, had to be hers.

"Sydell," he said, "I'm the same man as I always was. I will try to never make the mistakes I did, but I haven't changed. You're going to trip, stop that," he scolded, at the end, as though to prove the point he was making. The hem of her skirt tore noisily beneath her boot.

"You're still the same overbearing Rhys who pulled me through hell," she said lightly, almost laughing, her eyes half closed. He gazed up at her glowing face, illuminated now with a certainty that he had never had, a tranquil certainty that he'd not seen in her before. "And brought me back again," she finished.

He made a gesture with his arms, opening them instinctively. She leaped down from the ledge, landing steady on her feet in front of him.

Epilogue

There would not be much time.

But having kissed her, and then fallen into kissing her, long and deep, over and over, until she whimpered sweetly in his arms, he sure as hell was going to make the time for it.

He scooped her up over his shoulder, and she giggled madly, grasping at the tails of his tuxedo to keep herself steady. He ran his hand up under her dress and squeezed her thigh. Where could he take her that would be out of sight? He did not want to set her down in the gravel, not now. He rushed around the labyrinth until he was assured that some of the larger shrubbery blocked them from view. He moved his hand higher up under her dress and tickled at the split of her with his thumb. She stiffened and wiggled her body from her perch on his shoulder. He lifted her down from him and doubled her neatly over one of the lower hedges.

"Rhys, what?" She laughed, squirming in the thick, woven leaves.

"Just relax, sweetheart," he said and lifted the skirt of

her dress up, while she gasped with shocked delight. She wore a pair of pink underpants, with lace at the thighs.

"Fuck, right out here?" she cried.

"Not fuck, exactly." No, that would be difficult. "But you're going to come hard for me, all right?"

"Oh!"

He tucked her dress around her middle, running his hands up and down her bare thighs. He pressed his fingers to her mound, over her panties, and rubbed gently, letting her pleasure build slowly. She was damp already, of course; a little dark spot showed beneath his fingers on the cotton.

"God, I missed you." It tore out of him, and he did not regret it. Her response came as a little cry, telling him more than words ever could. He wanted to have forever with her, here, to hold her on the edge for hours until she begged, pleaded… but he likely had less than fifteen minutes. He whisked her panties down.

She yelped. "Someone might see, Rhys, oh god…" She panted heavily. The thought of it didn't seem to be making her any less excited, that much was certain.

"They'd be lucky to catch a glimpse of your sexy ass," he said, and she squeaked delightedly. He pinched her bottom, pulling her cheeks apart. She kicked her legs, wriggling her hips. She sunk a little into the bushes. He leant down, nuzzling his face into her, gripping her downed panties like reins and pulling her pussy closer into his face. She smelled sexier than ever; he'd dreamt of her scent, he knew that now, just as he'd dreamt of her face, the way it waxed raw with sweet passion as she reached orgasm. He could not see it this way, but he knew it eternally, in his memory.

He crowded his tongue onto her sensitive little bundle of nerves and circled it eagerly, licking over and over her quivering lips. Her legs shook, and he kept her still with his hold on her panties, until all at once she was shrieking and squalling and he laughed happily into her soaked fur, while her pussy spasmed against his cheek. He backed away, his eyes not leaving her shiny cunt, swollen and ready. She'd come much faster than he'd expected.

"Oh, God, Rhys, I'm sure someone heard me."

"They might wonder who let a parrot out on the Academy grounds," he said absently, massaging her cunt with his hand. She moaned and shuddered. He leaned over her, squashing her into the bushes. "I might just have time to fuck you," he said in her ear.

She pushed her bare ass into him, saying in a hasty whisper, "Hurry up and do it then!"

He laughed, with a sudden stab of joy at the boon. He'd not planned for it; he'd only wanted to make her come, make her happy, but having done so, and seen her sexy, irresistible pussy, heard her lusty screams… well, it was too much. He undid the button of his trousers and pulled down the fly; his cock stormed out, and with no hesitation at all, he buried it deep into her.

She cried out, the tail end of it melting into a gasp. He seized hold again of her underpants and without further ado, rode her as hard as he could without losing her to the shrubbery beneath. Leaves fluttered around her and twigs snapped as she wailed with abandon, no longer caring, it would seem, whether anyone heard her cries. Her legs jerked against his and her pussy clenched at him urgently; she bucked herself farther into the bush in her frenzy until, at last, she howled as he drove her to yet another peak.

Sydell and the hedge had become one, somewhat, as he thrust into the disheveled mass of green and yellow. She clung to the branches, moaning, exhausted, but not insensate. She even howled for him as he came, as every memory he had of her tight cunt milking the source of him dissipated under the reality of this climax right now. Bright, hot, rocketing into her, an explosion of joy that obliterated nearly all of it, the whole gruesome year before, it dwarfed under the intensity of the pleasure.

He panted, briefly laying out his weight over her limp body. Wiped clean, at least for the moment, of all the weight he'd carried. He kissed her neck, passionate with gratitude. He stood, then, as he began to remember time. Time and obligation. She had not moved from the bushes; she whimpered slightly from her position, half-buried within them.

"Someone saw me, they must have," she whispered. He took her panties at the waistband and pulled them back up over her cheeks, even as his own thick, white cum started to stream out of her. He tugged them, even, up into her ass playfully and laughed softly when she whined. He gave her a sharp spank on the behind.

God, he felt so much better. He lifted her up out of the hedge, tucking her dress back down around her. She squirmed a bit, trying to fix her underwear. He brushed a few leaves out of her hair.

"I'm a mess. No way they aren't going to guess what I was doing."

"Who cares," he said, and meant it. For the moment, not caring came as an indulgence, one he'd not had in a long time. She huffed and started back quickly along the path. He caught her skirt, pulled her back, spun her and kissed her rough on the mouth, rough and just a little carelessly. He felt like himself again.

She sighed. "When are you coming back, Rhys?"

"Soon," he said. "Actually, the truth is it could be a while, but…"

She gazed up at him. Some of the lightness had gone

from her; she looked worried, hopeful. Her cheeks were still red with heat; in ecstasy and in love, she was beautiful.

"Nothing can keep me away for long," he finished with a smile.

He parted from her first, in the end; the pilot had already returned to the transport ship, and he had no more time to dally. He did peek back at her once as she returned to the crowd, still trying to adjust her underpants through the skirt of her dress, to no avail. He loved her completely, and it was time to go, and he had what he needed now to return, to get through the next stretch of it. He would see her again. The doubt he had come here with had gone; he was strong again.

He ignored the pilot mostly, as the man chattered on, apparently having gotten several women's social links. So, not a bad day. As the Academy grew small beneath them, Rhys had the flash of an idea, for what might be interfering with the rotation particles in the blink engine. That was all still theory, of course, it hadn't been built yet, but maybe this would lead to the breakthrough…

"That cake, huh?" the pilot called back loudly, "I think I ate three pieces. You try some?"

Rhys smiled. "Yes," he said, "delicious."

Avery Stern

Avery lives in the Great Pacific Northwest, but she still dreams in the hues of the American Southwest where she was born. Her stories are often inspired by both. She reads science fiction, loves vintage movies, and spends a satisfactory amount of time daydreaming out of windows with her cat. She works in a kitchen and curses like a sailor. Avery has been writing stories since she was nine years old.

Visit her Facebook page here:
https://www.facebook.com/TheAveryStern

Don't miss these exciting titles by Avery Stern and Blushing Books!

The Bad Rancher
Dark Star's Captive

Blushing Books

Blushing Books is the oldest eBook publisher on the web. We've been running websites that publish steamy romance and erotica since 1999, and we have been selling eBooks since 2003. We have free and promotional offerings that change weekly, so please do visit us at http://www.blushingbooks.com/free.

Blushing Books Newsletter

Please join the Blushing Books newsletter
to receive updates & special promotional offers.
You can also join by using your mobile phone:
Just text BLUSHING to 22828.

Every month, one new sign up via text messaging will
receive a $25.00 Amazon gift card, so sign up today!